Killer Deal
Sofie Sarenbrant

KILLER DEAL

SOFIE SARENBRANT

Translated by Paul Norlén

First Published in the United States in 2016 by

Stockholm Text

Stockholm, Sweden

stockholm@stockholmtext.com
www.stockholmtext.com

Translation by Paul Norlén
Cover design by Maria Sundberg

Printed in the United States of America

1 3 5 7 9 8 6 4 2

ISBN 978-91-7547-197-6

For Tommy

1.

SUNDAY, MARCH 30

She is lying completely still under the bed canopy. In the reddish glow of the night-light, I see her closed eyes and a face that radiates harmony. The covers have slipped to the side a little, but in her long-sleeved nightgown decorated with small flowers she's probably not cold. Her dark curls rest against the pillow, and her stuffed animals sit lined up next to it, almost like a protective wall. It's hard for me not to get nostalgic and think back to my own childhood, to how simple and carefree everything was. That was before I understood how many heartless people there are in this world, the kind who will walk over dead bodies to get what they want.

I really shouldn't disturb her when she is sleeping so peacefully, but I can't restrain an impulse to approach the bed. I tiptoe over quietly, sensing the wood floor under my stocking feet. I can't risk stumbling on a toy. I pull my hand from my pants pocket, past the opening of the canopy, and I let my fingertips graze her silken-smooth skin. Her cheek feels a little cold, but she doesn't move a muscle. She is so still you might think she was dead. I withdraw my hand and back away.

Now I just want to get out of here.

On the way out, I pass the master bedroom. And there lies her mother, alone in the double bed, with her back turned toward the door. She has the same color of hair as the girl, but it's cut in a short, boyish style. Unfeminine, if you ask me. I observe her at a distance before I head downstairs.

A step creaks when I'm halfway there. I freeze to assure myself that no one woke up. After a few minutes of silence, I continue without stopping all the way to the basement. There I put on my shoes and leave the house through the same door I came in.

I'll just have to come back tomorrow.

2.

MONDAY, MARCH 31

Only forty-five minutes left until the open house that will determine her future. Years of pain, grief, and denial may soon be over. Just one more day in the house remains, then Cornelia Göransson and her daughter, Astrid, may finally have peace and quiet. But Cornelia doesn't dare assume anything ahead of time. Experience tells her not to start relaxing too soon. That's when things can go wrong.

Her thoughts race as she crosses the newly repaired parquet floor, which should have been fixed long ago. It would have been smart to also repaint the walls and sand the floors before putting it on the market, but she didn't have the time or energy for that. Not when the focus has been on survival. Now she can only hope the rented props will meet her expectations. The idea is that exclusive armchairs, rugs, and lamps will draw attention from the defects, like the worn and loose wall sockets from 1926.

She adjusts the carefully selected cut flowers, smooths

out the bedspreads in both bedrooms, places the pillows on edge in a neat row, and refolds a rumpled blanket and hangs it on the armrest of the couch. *Ugh,* she thinks. *It looks staged. That could make people suspicious that something isn't the way it should be.* She tosses the blanket over the back of the couch instead, trying to make it look like it landed naturally.

Then she looks around the room again to assure herself that she hasn't missed any details. She wonders whether she has succeeded in concealing all traces of the misery deeply ingrained in the walls.

Suddenly, she becomes unsure about everything. The lilies. The bowl with the shiny, almost plastic Granny Smith apples and the lemons on top. They give a borderline-desperate impression. Experienced buyers won't fall for such simple tricks—certainly not die-hard home junkies who dream of villas like this one in the attractive Stockholm suburb of Bromma. Potential is what they're looking for, not something that reminds them of a booth at the Formex home show. There is a risk that people will laugh at her amateurish styling, a glimpse of which they've already seen on Hemnet and other real estate websites. What if that's why there were so few visitors at yesterday's open house? Or maybe the rumor is that there's something strange about the house, something unhealthy. Perhaps people perceive more than you think.

In the end, they can speculate all they want, as long as the secrets concealed behind the whitewashed facade don't come out. True, the neighbors may have heard something and put two and two together, but it would be unlikely, because the yard is spacious and the houses aren't that close to each other. An "open setting." That's what it says in the listing. Although the next-door neighbors, Mr. and Mrs. Svärd, have a view that may be a little *too* open. Is that why they avert their eyes as soon as she steps outside?

Cornelia shakes off her sense of unease and decides to make yet another round of the house to inspect. She sends a grateful thought to Josefin for offering to take Astrid home after school again today. What would she do without her friend? Josefin is an absolute necessity. With a six-year-old at her heels, Cornelia would never have been able to get the house ready on her own.

The next few days will decide what assets she'll have at her disposal. The money she makes from designing jewelry part-time doesn't go far in this city, especially not with a child to support. It was mostly a hobby to start with, and it's certainly not enough to live on.

She casts another quick glance toward the bedroom and forces herself to go in. Once again, she smooths out the lovely silk bedspread and tries to avoid looking at her side of the bed, where a depression in the white-painted wood floor remains. To an untrained eye, it is barely noticeable, but she knows exactly how and when the damage occurred, and how hard a pine floor feels against the back of your head. It wasn't easy to clean the walls afterward. White paint is hard to handle; the slightest fingerprint leaves an ugly smudge. To be on the safe side, she inspects the wall close-up, assuring herself that there is no discoloration left.

The bedroom with bay window and balcony will soon be only a memory, but she couldn't care less. Even in the beginning, she had difficulty breathing in this room.

Last night she was wakened by something, and at first she didn't know what it was. Then she felt his gaze from the hall, and she knew: Hans was standing there watching her. The hair on her arms rises when she recalls how she closed her eyes and thought that maybe this was it, that he would no longer spare her. But miraculously enough, he went away. Her first thought was that he was going to get something to kill her with, but he never came back. Instead, he must have gone back to bed in the guest room, where he'd promised to sleep for the time being, and then left for work early in the morning. Cornelia shudders as she remembers her first reaction when the alarm clock rang: surprise. She hadn't counted on waking up at all.

She goes downstairs and looks around again. The real estate agents ought to be here soon.

The rug under the coffee table had to be moved a little to the right to conceal the biggest scratch in the floor, the one that was caused by her sharp stiletto heels. Her scalp aches when she thinks about his hard grip on New Year's Eve. Strangely enough, her hair didn't come out, but after that, she chose to cut it short anyway, so that he could never drag her by the hair again.

Cornelia straightens the rug and nods to herself. There, now she can't do anything else to influence the result. She has used every means possible to show the house from its best side.

A knock at the door startles her.

The clock on the wall shows quarter to six. Cornelia curses herself for being frightened so easily, but she collects herself and goes to answer the door. Helena, the real estate agent, is standing outside, dressed in a classic navy-blue pantsuit with a carefully tied scarf around her neck. At first glance it would be easy to confuse her with an employee at SAS, minus the white pants. Her flight-attendant look, with her blue eyes, blonde hair, and fashion-model height, causes Cornelia to swallow enviously. Helena has everything Cornelia dreamed of but didn't get. She herself is small and slender, sinewy, almost boyish in appearance. Dark eyes, brown hair. Not a hint of Nordic origin.

In her arms, Helena is holding a box of blue shoe covers and a bundle of flyers. The exterior shot on the front looks stunning, but Cornelia can no longer see the beauty of the house.

"Hi. How's it going?" Helena asks politely, shaking Cornelia's hand.

"Outstanding, thanks," Cornelia replies, immediately hearing how false that sounds. "Are you fired up for tonight?"

"Absolutely," Helena answers in a professional voice.

"Are you working alone?"

"No, I just thought I would get here ahead of time to get everything ready," she replies, but she doesn't look Cornelia in the eye.

Cornelia hands over the house keys. "Fingers crossed that a good crowd shows up."

The real estate agent smiles with her unnaturally even teeth. "This is going to work out fine. It's a big house with an attractive address, just a stone's throw from the Ålsten pier. We believe in this property."

If Helena is the least bit nervous about the outcome, she doesn't show it in any way. But she's not convincing enough for her confidence to be contagious.

"No offers yet, I guess?" Cornelia can't help asking the question before she leaves.

"We're going to start calling everyone who came by first thing tomorrow," the agent says. "Most people want to see a home at least twice before they put in an offer, especially when there might be multiple bids. And when the asking price is so high. It serves no purpose to call too soon. In fact, pressing the decision can have the opposite effect."

"I understand," Cornelia says. "Can I come back at seven thirty?" She doesn't know if Astrid can stay up much longer than that without getting overly tired and impossible to put to bed.

The agent looks at her watch and nods. "They should all be gone by then."

3.

As soon as there is a knock at the door, Anton drops his markers and rushes to the hall. Astrid stays seated, unmoved. She is completely engrossed in her drawing. Anton throws himself against the door like an eager dog, and Josefin gets up to help him turn the stubborn lock. When he sees that it's Cornelia, not his dad, he forces out a faint "Hi" and sullenly makes his way back into the living room.

"Your mom is here," he says to Astrid, but she still doesn't raise her eyes from her drawing, not even when her mother's voice can be heard in the hall.

Cornelia goes into the living room and praises her daughter for the fine meadow she has drawn, with seven small fairies flitting around in the air.

Josefin can't help smiling. It's almost impossible to see what her son's drawing is; Anton might be trying to depict a car or a boat—or maybe a house.

Suddenly, Astrid turns around and looks at her mother

with a loving gaze. Then she extends her arms, and they embrace a long time. Josefin finds herself standing and watching them, perhaps with some envy. Her children—Sofia, Julia, and Anton—are affectionate, but Cornelia and Astrid have a special bond that is beyond the ordinary. Personally, Josefin appreciates that her children aren't so attached to just one adult, instead connecting with many people around them. But where Astrid is concerned, there aren't that many others, because Cornelia has hardly any contact with her parents or siblings and it doesn't seem as if the relationship with her in-laws is good.

When Anton and Astrid started at the same school three years ago, it didn't take long before they became best friends, even though Anton is a year younger. Astrid's development is delayed, especially her speech, and she relates best to younger children. Josefin has never heard any explanation for why Astrid is different, and now, after such a long time, it would feel silly to ask. But she has a special place in her heart for that little girl, who seems to need all the support she can get. The other children avoid her, so she is often by herself, humming in solitude when Anton isn't there. She is seldom invited to parties or playdates. Cornelia does everything she can, but it's obvious that it's hard. It's lucky that Anton is fine with having a playmate who isn't like everyone else.

While the kids continue drawing, Josefin and Cornelia go into the kitchen to prepare dinner. It strikes Josefin how thin Cornelia has become. The divorce seems to be eating away at her.

"It wasn't all that easy to get them to leave school today," Josefin says, bringing up a blurry picture on her cell phone. "When I got there, they had just dressed up as clowns, and they were dancing around. Astrid had a curly red wig on. Check it out. They're so cute you could die!"

When she sees Astrid's mischievous expression, Cornelia smiles so that her laugh lines stand out.

"Little darling. So sweet," Cornelia says, in a way that reveals that she's from southeast Sweden. Josefin thinks the accent is charming, but she keeps it to herself. She made the mistake of commenting on it once, when they'd first met, and Cornelia told her that it was just as rude to suggest that someone has an accent as to point out that someone has a cold sore.

"Would you like something to drink before dinner?" Josefin says.

"Some water would be nice, but I can get that myself." Cornelia gets a glass from the hutch. It's not strange that she feels at home, as she often comes over. Josefin wishes they lived even closer, so that they wouldn't have to drive back and forth when the kids want to play.

"I thought we could have cold cuts, olives, salad, and bread—if that's okay," Josefin says. "It's not a real dinner, but my imagination gave out when I was shopping."

"That sounds fantastic," Cornelia replies, but her face doesn't match her words.

Josefin can't figure out why her friend always resorts to a positive adjective, instead of toning down her word choice so that it more or less tallies with her anxious appearance.

Perhaps it's a built-in defense mechanism. Or Cornelia could be trying to keep her friend from seeing that she's miserable. But Josefin isn't that blind.

"Are you worried about the house?" she asks, in case Cornelia wants to get something off her chest.

Cornelia nods in response and runs her hand through her short hair, which frames her face in a beautiful way. As usual, she is sparingly made-up and casually dressed. Josefin seldom sees her in anything other than jeans and a comfortable sweater or a baggy blouse.

"I have a feeling it's not going to work out."

A howl from the living room interrupts them, and Cornelia gets there first. Astrid is beside herself with rage. She points at Anton, who crawls under the table. "He ruined my drawing!"

The crying gets more intense, and Josefin, who comes one step after, seeks Anton's gaze in vain. Sure enough, Astrid's beautiful fairies have black lines over them. Cornelia tries to console her daughter, but Astrid pushes her away. She doesn't want anyone to hold her when she is angry, and it usually takes a while before she settles down. Josefin has seen it happen before, so she doesn't try to talk with her. She knows there's no point until she's receptive again. But it looks awful when she gets so agitated that she can hardly get air.

Anton, still under the table, squirms self-consciously with an unhappy expression.

"You have to say sorry," Josefin says as calmly as she can manage.

"But—"

"No 'buts,'" she says. "You don't draw on other people's drawings without asking for permission."

Josefin places her hand on Cornelia's shoulder to apologize on her son's behalf. Cornelia pulls away, as if she'd gotten an electric shock, and her eyes are filled with anxiety. Josefin always forgets that she loathes touch.

"Sorry," she whispers.

"You don't need to apologize. Kids are kids," Cornelia replies, sitting down at the table with Astrid. "We can make some new fairies. What do you say about a big castle too, where they can live?"

Anton crawls out and seeks Astrid's eyes, but she refuses to look at him. Without a word, she goes and gets a new piece of paper from the pile. Then she sits down beside her mother as if nothing has happened. Anton sits down on the other side of Cornelia, and Josefin withdraws to the kitchen.

At a distance she listens to their lively discussion about what colors they should use and who should do what. Cornelia delegates tasks to the children and once again shows a unique capacity to deal with conflicts—or, rather, to divert them. Josefin herself struggles daily at not sinking to a five-year-old's level and howling back when the children provoke her the most. As the mother of three children, patience is in constant short supply.

The older children are up in their rooms doing homework—or maybe something else altogether, since neither of them is calling for help. There's a good chance they've been sucked into a computer game, but tonight Josefin doesn't have the energy to nag about that, especially not when Cornelia and Astrid are there.

While she places the food on a plate and rinses the lettuce, she can't keep from thinking that the open house is going on at just that moment. She knows how important it is for Cornelia that the deal closes so she can afford to be single. It was sheer luck that she found an apartment to sublet until she finds one of her own. However nice Hans seems to be outwardly, Josefin knows what Cornelia has been through. In the strictest confidence, she told her about the abuse. Half of it would be bad enough.

Personally, Josefin can't imagine being under constant threat. Her husband, Andreas, is the nicest man in the world; he would never raise a hand against her. Never ever.

Still, when Cornelia mentions how happy she is at being able to start over, Josefin lets her thoughts wander. She often imagines what it would be like to be Emma, her sister. Being able to decide for yourself and focus on your career, not serving as a slave in your own home, not always having to put yourself in second place. Not having to please others.

But now, of course, it's only a matter of time before Emma will have a completely different understanding of life, and it's not a day too soon.

4.

Emma Sköld reads the same sentence for the third time before she realizes she's looking at the words without taking in their meaning. The only thing to do is take another break. She sets aside the 2,400-page report. She's been working on an unsolved homicide case for over a week without making any progress. She ought to feel the proverbial barrel of the gun against the back of her neck, but she can't seem to summon sufficient energy to concentrate fully on reading. The letters have a tendency to squish together all the time, and the lack of fresh air in her cramped office at the police station doesn't help. But above all, something else is occupying her thoughts.

Emma sighs when she realizes she's already exceeded the government recommendations for daily caffeine intake. She had her fourth cup of coffee half an hour ago, just so she could keep her eyes open. It's only in the past few days that she has been able to tolerate the smell of coffee beans again enough to drink the police department sludge. She needs the kick, even though it leaves a bitter taste.

Emma's thoughts about everything and nothing are interrupted by a knock at the door. Lars Lindberg looks in with his worried-boss look.

"Are you still here?" he asks with surprise. "It's past six."

Emma points at the pile of papers. "I still have a lot of progress to make."

"Yes, but the idea isn't for you to spend your time on that after work hours," Lindberg says. "May I sit down a moment?"

"Sure, come in." Emma has no idea what he wants to bring up. The first thought is that she's done something wrong. Stepped on someone's toes perhaps, which can happen in the heat of the moment.

"You look pale. How are you doing, really?" He sits in the visitor's chair next to her cluttered desk.

"Just fine, thanks."

Lindberg doesn't look at all convinced. "I'm your boss, and I need to know if something is wrong. Especially if it affects your ability to do your job."

Emma knows he's right. So she gives up and tells the truth.

"I'm pregnant."

Lindberg's pursed lips break into a smile, and he beams, a departure from his usual heavy expression. Congratulations. That's great!"

Emma exhales; she didn't even realize she'd been holding her breath. Although she hadn't expected a negative reaction from him, you never know what someone's first reaction will be. She had thought there might at least be insinuations about her maternity leave causing personnel problems in the future.

"Thanks," she says, but she can't relax until she knows he doesn't intend to treat her differently. She wants nothing other than to work as usual.

"I thought you didn't seem to be feeling too well," Lindberg says hesitantly. "That much I picked up on. I just couldn't figure out why."

Emma smiles. "Actually, I was planning to wait until next week to say anything, because then I'll be in week twelve."

She can still see no signs that she is creating problems for him. But she knows he'll have to start thinking about a temporary replacement soon, someone who can live up to the high demands placed on a detective in the violent crimes section.

"I'm happy for you," Lindberg says, and he leaves the room.

Emma leans back in her chair. She spent a lot of energy thinking about how she should break the news to her boss and convince him to let her keep working as usual during the pregnancy. It turns out she didn't need to worry about any of that. Yet she feels guilty—partly because she withheld important information, and partly because she gave first priority to being a mother. She knows that way of thinking is absurd, but she can't help wondering about the obvious fact that for once she is valuing something higher than her job.

It won't be as dramatic for her male colleagues when they become parents. They can be fathers a hundred times over without losing important work time during pregnancy and the first weeks afterward. But for her, parenthood will mean a major sacrifice—and her absence for months. And as excited as she is about having a baby, Emma doesn't want to miss anything at work. Her occupation is her identity. Her life. She hardly knows anything else.

Before packing up for the day, she goes to the restroom. When she loosens the rubber band around the top button of her jeans, she is surprised that she doesn't see any difference in her belly even though her pants now feel too tight.

She looks in the mirror and adjusts her light hair. She's letting it grow out; soon it will brush against her shoulders. Short hair has its advantages, but she's tired of it. When she observes herself more closely, it strikes her that there's a luster in her face that she's never seen before and her cheeks are somewhat rounder, which is surprisingly becoming. She wonders what it will be like to have a protruding stomach.

Back in her office, she wonders how she got so lucky, what she did to deserve finally getting pregnant. She only wishes that Kristoffer weren't so occupied with his job. She'd had the idea that real estate agents mostly worked on weekends, but that turned out not to be true. Showings are just one of his many tasks. He's always on call, no matter what time it is. It doesn't matter if she and Kristoffer are doing something important. Whoever's calling has precedence, always, whether it's about something as minor as the placement of a flowerpot or when a prospective buyer suddenly demands to write a contract *now* and not tomorrow. A deal is a deal, and it has priority, whether it's a weekend or weekday, morning or evening. Emma is all too aware of how easy it is to be absorbed by your job, but it seems to her that lately, Kristoffer's been working more than ever.

Still, it's probably just as well that he has an open house in Bromma this evening. That way he can't distract her, and she'll get further in the unsolved case report, which is climbing like a high-rise on the desk in front of her.

5.

I t is a pleasure to waltz around the magnificent yellow
villa while snorting at basically everything it's possible to
snort at. Hugo Franzén cannot recall the last time he felt
as exhilarated—although possibly at the last open house.
The time in between hasn't offered very many satisfying
moments, even though his job as a photographer at least
made the days pass.

"I detect a faint odor of mold," Hugo says softly, but
clearly enough so that others around him will hear.

The effect is not long in coming. At once, a woman
starts sniffing the air in the fancy bathroom with expensive
mosaics, radiant floor heating, and a towel warmer that
goes all the way to the ceiling. She whispers something to
the man next to her.

Hugo gets down on his knees by the drain and raises the
lid to coax out the trap. A musty odor makes him wrinkle
his nose. With an ominous grimace, he shakes his head

and deliberately seeks the attention of the prospective buyers nearby.

"Sorry to have to say it, but a locking ring seems to be missing here. The inspector should have noticed that. I wonder if there's anything else they're trying to hide?"

"There hasn't been an inspection," the sniffing woman points out.

"Are you joking?" Hugo exclaims, pretending to be upset, almost as upset as if he'd just been told that the house's foundation was going to collapse within the space of a few minutes. "And here I intended to make an offer. But you don't want to buy a pig in a poke."

Hugo maintains his furrowed brow all the way out of the bathroom and into a meticulously furnished bedroom with a sloping ceiling. His adrenaline is flowing.

When he discovers that he's alone, he sits down on the bed, intentionally knocking the pillows out of their ridiculously perfect row. He thinks about Emma's lovely smile. The joy of life in those beautiful almond-shaped hazel eyes. The two of them in bed, skin against skin. The tingle in his belly when they touch. It's easy to start daydreaming that everything is like before, but actually Hugo feels like he's falling into a bottomless pit.

Every day without Emma is torment.

The sad fact is, she no longer wants to have any contact with him at all. He fires off a text message or two from time to time, usually after a few beers too many, and sometimes she answers, but seldom with anything encouraging. Usually he is totally ignored. After all the years they shared together, now he is worthless. And for one simple reason: he couldn't get her pregnant.

Eager voices approach the room, and Hugo quickly gets to his feet, but he doesn't bother to straighten the bedspread. He positions himself by the window and looks out.

"The neighbors can see right in," he says loud enough for others to hear. "Too bad the houses are so close to each other. Hmm . . . The sun doesn't seem to make it to this balcony." He turns around. "Too bad with such a nice balcony, but there must be good shade plants you can put there, I assume."

With feigned disappointment, he leaves the bedroom and makes a show of crumpling up the flyer as best he can. It's mostly a symbolic act, since in reality the flyer is made of thick card stock. Apparently, it takes special paper to highlight all the photos and hyped-up real-estate lingo that will entice a sale.

Hugo is in no hurry to leave, but hunger suddenly strikes, so he grabs a fistful of hard candies from the selling agent's bowl. He is on the verge of asking whether they intend to change to a softer kind, something that is possible to chew on without risking a subsequent dental visit. But that sort of comment might make people raise their eyebrows. It may seem strange for someone to seem so invested in an agent's offering of candy. If he doesn't want anyone to guess that he's not a serious prospective buyer, he has to constantly be on his guard. The plan is to seem just doubtful enough. Otherwise, it would be obvious that he's there only to create a disturbance. He smiles.

His smile dies when he sees Kristoffer's gaze cutting through him like a knife from the kitchen. There he stands, dressed to the nines—the man who stole Hugo's fiancée right in front of his eyes. And who got a fat fee besides, because he was the listing agent for their condominium and managed to trick his way into an unreasonably high commission. Now, in retrospect, Hugo feels like an idiot for going along with a 10 percent increase on the commission for any offer over three million kronor. But Kristoffer will have to pay him back a hundred times over, and he'll regret it bitterly too.

Hugo glares back until Kristoffer turns away and whispers something to his colleague. Both understand why Hugo is there, but they can hardly throw him out. Creating a scene in front of potential buyers would only backfire.

Just the basement remains. Time to fish the screwdriver out of his pocket.

In the curved stairway, he has to move to make way for a very pregnant woman. His gaze falls on her protruding belly button peeking out under a tight-fitting sweater. He swallows enviously and imagines an expecting Emma. She would look so amazing, the most beautiful pregnant woman on earth. They would lie there in the evenings caressing her belly and talking about their unborn child.

His grip on the screwdriver tightens. When did it go so wrong that she made up her mind to leave him? However he twists and turns his thoughts, he can't figure out when everything was decided. Hugo forces away the sorrow and concentrates on his mission. He goes around knocking on the walls with the screwdriver and hopes the couple crowded into the furnace room with him will ask what he's up to.

His wish is granted.

"Excuse me, but what are you doing with that screwdriver?" The woman looks at him with a curious expression.

"Listen," he says theatrically, knocking in two places. "Did you hear the difference?"

She looks uncertain. She probably doesn't want to offend him by answering no. "I think so."

"The farther down on the wall, the more obvious the moisture damage is." Hugo opens a hatch in the lower part of the furnace and sees that condensation from the pipe is dripping right onto the floor. "And here we have the explanation. There's no floor drain installed."

"What does that mean?"

"That you'd have to tear it all out and install a drain. And do what you can to save the walls."

Hugo could have just as easily responded that it was probably enough to put a drainage receptacle there. But he isn't there as an inspector or a seller.

"Thanks for warning us," the man says. "It's rotten of the real estate agent to withhold such important information."

Hugo smiles wryly. "'Rotten' is just the right word."

The woman and the man back out, and Hugo catches his breath. Damn, maybe he should be an actor when all is said and done.

Once he had come up with the brilliant idea of working in the wings at Kristoffer's open houses, he could hardly contain himself. It quickly turned into a sport. He has learned to stay as far from him as possible, so that Kristoffer won't be able to hear his comments. The point is to make prospective buyers wary enough to reject Kristoffer's properties.

Creating a bad reputation for Kristoffer hasn't taken much exertion. Social media has been an amazing asset there. Under a false identity, Hugo is on all conceivable websites, spreading his opinion about the agency Kristoffer works for, and primarily about Kristoffer himself. Hugo had no idea he was so good at expressing himself. A whole new world opened with this knowledge, and he would be lying if he said he doesn't enjoy having such power.

His newly discovered gift of writing means he has now expanded the services he offers as a photographer. A fair amount of extra revenue flows in for the advertising copy he supplies, but he has no intention of thanking Kristoffer for that, not on your life.

When Hugo comes up the stairs, that bastard is standing with a self-righteous expression, adjusting his hair. Hugo can't bear to think that Emma's fingers have tousled it. He has to put an end to it. Before Hugo can stop himself, he sends off yet another text to her.

6.

Even though she shouldn't feel guilty about Hugo, Emma can't help feeling responsible for his decline. At least partly responsible. At some point, he has to accept that the relationship is over, but judging by his most recent text, that's not going to happen anytime soon. Emma deletes it without reading the whole thing. It doesn't matter what he writes. It's over.

When she settles into her living room with part of the unsolved case report, she feels discontented. Alone and abandoned. It seems like Kristoffer has started taking her for granted, especially after the positive pregnancy test. Say what you will about Hugo, but there was never any doubt who was number one in his life. He worshipped her from the start, which Emma underrated when they were together. If anything, it was annoying that he was so over-the-top in love, wanting to be with her constantly. Now she knows what it's like to not always be noticed, to sometimes have to beg for someone's attention. To be the one who nags and looks for confirmation instead of having it served up. But she doesn't doubt Kristoffer's love, or that he's going to be an amazing dad.

Since the unexpected happy news five weeks ago, Emma's body has been playing a trick on her. The change seemed to happen overnight. The mere sight of her favorite foods gives her sour belches. Not to mention what happens when she eats anything with garlic in it—she made that mistake only once. Punishment came with immediate consequences: the most disgusting burps ever, three days in a row. Nausea took over her body, and she had a hard time getting out of bed in the morning without vomiting.

But no matter how tough it is to go around feeling carsick almost all the time, it hasn't dampened her joy over getting to be a mother. With every day that passes, her hope is strengthened that her dream of having children will finally become a reality. Still, she doesn't dare be really happy yet. The risk of miscarriage hangs over her like a threat. Almost every night, she wakes up panic-stricken, wondering whether the pregnancy is only imaginary. Sometimes she dreams she's giving birth to a guinea pig. But after all the failed attempts with Hugo, it's no wonder she's having nightmares.

Every time her period came, she was equally crushed. But she tried to be sensible, tried to accept that she might not ever be a biological mother. So every time, after a full day of crying inconsolably, she pushed her longing aside and looked ahead. She tried to see the advantages of a childless existence: She would escape poopy diapers, car-pools, and constant worry. She could focus completely on her job guilt-free, without a little one demanding her atten-tion night and day, which Josefin often complains about. She could devote herself to a time-consuming hobby, such as training for a triathlon, or get her own horse instead of just riding at Frasse once or twice a week. It was all about letting go of her image of a family, saying good-bye to that possibility and choosing a different path.

Leaving Hugo was a necessary step. She decided to enjoy single life and not rush into a new relationship. But things don't always turn out as planned. Emma blushes when she thinks that she fell in love before the condo was even sold. Suddenly, the agent, Kristoffer, was standing there with his broad smile, which she was attracted to immediately. So much for single life.

Only a few months after they got together, the thought of a child started sneaking up again. Maybe there was still a chance. Thirty-six wasn't disastrously old, but she knew she couldn't wait too long. The problem was, she didn't know whether children were part of Kristoffer's plans. She chose to interpret their active sex life as a sign that the thought had crossed his mind. Otherwise, he should have shown greater interest in using protection.

The day the pregnancy test showed double lines she had to restrain herself to keep from cheering out loud. The idea was to leave the bathroom and act as if nothing had hap-pened until she thought of a good way to present the news to Kristoffer. But he saw at once that something major was going on. To her great relief, he was happy, but he admitted that it was joy mixed with terror.

Now they plan to move in together, preferably soon. It would be great if they could be neighbors with Josefin in Smedslätten, but they'd need to win the lottery first. Emma thinks about what an idyllic world her big sister lives in.

The perfect life—something to strive for.

7.

The dirty dishes pile up, and toys clutter the living room. Andreas keeps saying they should get cleaning help, but what good would that really do? Who cares about a few dust bunnies, anyway?

Josefin can't keep from thinking about what she has achieved in her almost forty-two years on earth. Sure, it's amazing to have three children, but it's only a matter of time before they're big enough to manage on their own. When they move out, it will be just her and Andreas left. They'll have unlimited time for themselves and large gaps to fill to get the days to pass. It's almost as frightening as feeling insufficient. What will they do together that feels meaningful and life-affirming?

Her thoughts are interrupted by Andreas coming home and sticking his head into the kitchen. The wrinkles on his face get more and more prominent every day, but no signs of age can change her love for him. While many in their circle of acquaintances have gone their separate ways, their marriage continues to be stable.

As usual, he hugs her, but there is something awkward in the embrace, as if there's some reluctance.

"How's your day been?" he asks. "Stressful?"

"Why do you think that?"

"Your sweater's inside out."

Josefin notes with a smile that he is right. It must mean she picked up the kids from school with the seams showing. And shopped for groceries at Ica. Hopefully, people thought it was a new trend; that kind of thing can start quickly in Bromma. Maybe that's why Cornelia didn't react.

Josefin takes a deep breath, chooses not to bother turning the sweater right side out, and continues cleaning up the kitchen. Andreas remains standing instead of helping out.

"I've had a hectic day myself," he says.

She turns around and observes the man in her life leaning against the gas stove. The incipient gray hair at his temples has spread. His hairline is creeping higher and higher, and his teeth are not so white anymore. After forty, people say, things quickly go downhill, and her reflection in the door of the microwave proves that this applies to her too.

"I'll go give the kids a hug," Andreas says, setting his cell phone on the kitchen counter to charge.

Josefin nods in response while filling the dishwasher. Right away, she is back in her existential musings.

There were some setbacks at the event agency where she

worked for several years, but life had been on an upswing since she changed careers, becoming a personal trainer. Now, however, she is starting to waver about her job once again. The doubt is perhaps due to her clients; they live in a bubble. Their biggest worries revolve around issues like how they will manage to balance the pH in the pool when the technician is on vacation, or what color Lexus they should choose. It would be a real catastrophe if it were *too* colorful—that is, the wrong shade of gray. Not to mention the client who was so upset she needed grief counseling, not because a family member died but because a deer feasted on the expensive roses in her flower bed.

Josefin can't bear to hear another word about the first-world dilemmas that these Bromma residents are grappling with. Mostly because she herself is afraid she's becoming like them, someone who has to search for something to get upset about. Someone who should be grateful for what she has. You only have to look around to see that she has it so good she ought to be ashamed she doesn't appreciate it more. But she is a seeker, constantly searching for something she can't grasp. A feeling perhaps. A feeling of well-being that has nothing to do with money. Josefin can't recall the last time she was 100 percent satisfied.

The kitchen is almost clean. She dries the colander and puts it in the cupboard. Just then, Andreas's phone blinks. It wasn't her intention to read the message, but she sees it anyway.

She freezes in midmotion, her eyes on the display until it turns off. Tries to understand what it was she just saw.

A few seconds later, Andreas comes back into the kitchen. Something about him suddenly seems foreign.

"You got a text," she says. "Unfortunately, I happened to see what it said."

Josefin points at the phone, and her husband's face shows that he doesn't even need to read it to know what it's about. He takes a quick look at his phone anyway.

"So you've started reading my messages?" he hisses.

"That's not fair. Just tell me what's going on."

Josefin holds her breath when she can tell from Andreas's expression that he has something tough to say. Something she probably doesn't want to hear. Not now, not later. Never. Yet she has had time to guess what is lurking behind his tense expression, why he stumbles and the words get stuck along the way.

"I've fallen in love," he finally gets out.

The sentence stings like a whiplash on her face. Andreas remains standing in the same position, two arms' length from her, but the gap between them seems to grow. Then everything becomes crystal clear. All the late evenings and guilt-ridden looks have an explanation. When all she's done is complained that his boss asks too much of Andreas. Felt sorry for him. Encouraged him to talk with his boss and demand a change, put his foot down, or find a new job. Meanwhile, it was about something else altogether. He's been lying to her the whole time.

"How long has this been going on?" she asks in a sharp tone. She wonders how her voice can sound so steady when her life just collapsed like a carelessly built house of cards.

Will they have to sell the house? If so, what real estate agent should they use? Will the neighbors run around at the open house spouting opinions about their decor? How will the children take the divorce? Will she and Andreas take turns with them every other week, or does he think he'll be a weekend dad, who does only fun things with the kids? He can forget that. Josefin tries to breathe instead of falling apart.

Andreas swallows. "It's not what you think. I haven't gone behind your back. But I do have feelings for another woman, which is bad enough."

"Requited ones," Josefin says. At the same time, she tries to understand what he's rambling about. Either he's been unfaithful or he hasn't. Why pretend there's something in between?

"I assume so."

It seems to her more like an established relationship, judging by the message she saw: *Sweetest one, longing for you.*

"And you met at work, of course? The classic scenario."

Andreas fixes his gaze on the espresso machine, which is still in the kitchen even though it's been broken for over a year.

"We work together, which creates problems. I would prefer not to see her, but it's impossible to avoid her."

So evidently, Josefin thinks, *there are women at IT companies who are attractive.* She knows there are, of course, but she remembers only Irma, with the computer glasses and the mustache.

"Her text didn't make it sound like you've been trying to avoid her."

"I can't very well help what she writes."

"Can't you?"

Andreas looks away.

"So what have you decided?" Josefin doesn't really know why she's asking what he wants. She probably should have told him to go to hell. That's still incredibly tempting.

"I don't know, Josefin. Do you know what you want?"

"What *I* want? I'm not the one who's been unfaithful."

Andreas shakes his head. "Not me either. Not yet."

"*Not yet?* What do you mean by that?"

Josefin fixes her gaze on him.

"That I want this life—with a family and house, to be there for the kids' activities, to stand together and cheer at soccer games and ice-skating recitals. It's just that—"

Josefin senses what is coming, and she wants to rush out of the kitchen to before the final buzzer sounds. Preferably slamming the door hard. But she remains in place.

"—as things are right now, I don't feel that happy."

Who the hell does? she thinks.

"Life is too short to waste time pretending," he says. "Most likely, it's because we're not doing so well together that I've fallen in love with someone else."

Tears are burning in her eyes. "So it's my fault—is that what you're trying to say?"

"It's nobody's fault, is it?" says Andreas, sounding irritated.

Josefin can't bear to stand there a moment longer listening

to any more expositions on their marriage, which has clearly passed the best-by date.

She has to get out, away. She doesn't want to hear one more word from him.

The brand-new shoes she bought a few days ago are in the hall. The neon colors glisten in the light as she presses her feet in and leaves the house without saying good-bye. Andreas doesn't try to stop her, and she sinks down on the steps outside and waits for the tears.

8.

The "Showing in Progress" sign has ended up crooked on the sidewalk outside. Cornelia tries to keep her courage up, but the steam goes out of her when she sees the agent's somber expression. Astrid's whining doesn't make it any easier. The whole way home from Josefin's, she complained that she was hungry, but Cornelia knows that really means she's dead tired. It's always intense at Josefin's house, and this particular evening Astrid had been there later than usual.

"Can you hang on a few minutes? I just have to get Astrid set up with the TV," Cornelia says to Helena.

"I'm in kind of a hurry," she gets in response.

"Just one moment, okay? I'm curious about how it went."

Astrid jumps up on the couch and grabs the remote control. Her daughter might be somewhat developmentally delayed in certain areas, but not when it comes to technology.

In no time, she has managed to start her favorite show, *Winx Club*, on Netflix. *Good,* Cornelia thinks. She has secured twenty-three minutes of calm, then it'll be straight to bed. Before she goes back to the entryway, she moves the bowl of green apples to the coffee table so that Astrid can help herself.

Helena is tapping intently on her cell phone.

"Do I want to know how it went?" Cornelia asks.

A shoulder shrug says it all. "Not that many came tonight, unfortunately."

"How many people came for a second look?"

"Three. And four new prospects."

Cornelia tries to remain calm, but panic is creeping closer and closer.

"Only three returned? How many signed up as still interested?"

"The number isn't set in stone. When we start calling around tomorrow, we'll get a better sense."

"I'd really like to look at the current list, if that's okay."

"There's not much to see yet." Reluctantly, Helena hands over a list with a single name on it. A name Cornelia recognizes all too well.

"Don't get hung up on it," the agent says. "You can count on my expertise. I've sold shacks in Bromma for eight million. Your house is special—and so close to the water. A dream house for many people. You just need to have patience."

Easy for you to say, Cornelia thinks. *You have no idea how important this is.*

Without further ado, Helena turns on her heels, leaving Cornelia alone with her anxiety.

Are the fixtures too out of date? Should she have bet on trendier flowers? Did the house's bad karma shine through? Maybe the wide-angle pictures in the advertisement didn't live up to reality. The asking price of eleven million could make anyone choke; why didn't they go with ten and a half? Or maybe they're using the wrong agent. That could be it. She forgot to ask if Benjamin Weber had been there, the owner of the real estate agency. That so-called "good friend" who Hans thought would get them a good deal. Why wouldn't he be at the open house if they know each other so awfully well?

Cornelia has foreseen all possible pitfalls, except that the sale doesn't go through. Until now, that hadn't struck her as an option. *No,* she tells herself. *That can't happen. The house has to be sold, no matter what the offer is. Good Lord— this is a 220-square-meter house in one of the nicest parts of Bromma. A place most people can only dream of.*

Yet doubt is growing stronger. The thought that she will have to deal with Hans even a little longer is hard to accept. When she's been counting the days now. This can't go on. She can't take it anymore.

What if Hans has sabotaged the sale, making sure it doesn't go through, just so that she'd be forced to stay with him for financial reasons? Cornelia shudders when she realizes they have to live under the same roof for yet another night. She gasps for air and sinks down to the floor, trying not to hyperventilate. When panic strikes with full force, she doesn't have much to counter with; her extra resources are used up. Unfortunately, that includes her anxiety medication, and she hasn't had time for a doctor's appointment. She simply has to let the worst thoughts pass so she can get up again. For Astrid's sake.

No one can understand what she's been through. How horrible it is to be physically and mentally abused by your husband, in your own home—where a sense of security should be a given. She didn't even think it was possible, the way he treated her. The reality has been worse than the most disgusting novels she's read. The fear and powerlessness she has felt over the years have numbed her, practically turning her into a passive robot. It's only thanks to Astrid that Cornelia woke up and realized the situation was life-threatening, that she had to get out. Sooner or later Hans would have killed her, and that couldn't happen. Not now that Astrid was in the world.

It may seem unbelievable that Cornelia let it go this far, but she was naive. She thought marrying Hans was the best way to get away from Valdemarsvik and create a new existence in Stockholm. That's why she didn't react immediately when his spiteful remarks started coming. Or when he shoved her into the wall the first time. That was a mistake, he said, and besides, she'd provoked him.

So here she was, a smart, talented, quite ordinary twenty-eight-year-old. How could things have gotten so bad?

A dull thud somewhere in the house makes Cornelia freeze. "Astrid?"

She calls again, but there is no response. In a matter of

seconds, Cornelia is in the living room, where she finds Astrid staring listlessly at the TV screen. Each of the nine apples has a child-size bite taken out of it. Cornelia doesn't know if she should laugh or cry, but she curses herself for setting out the bowl instead of simply giving her daughter *one* apple.

"Honey?"

Astrid doesn't take her eyes off the screen when she answers. "You're bothering me."

"Did you drop something on the floor?" Cornelia asks.

"Uh-uh."

Cornelia looks around. What a relief it will be to escape this big house with all of its mysterious sounds. Either there's clicking from the attic or else there's rattling or squeaking somewhere in the basement.

She walks around the first floor and sees that the door to the basement is ajar. There is light coming from the laundry room; the real estate agent must have forgotten to turn it off. Cornelia goes down to see whether she at least locked up. The downside of such a big house is that burglars can get in on several floors. Thank goodness that hasn't happened to them, despite the growing wave of break-ins in the area.

Still, with every step she takes, a sense of discomfort is growing. She really must do something about her fear of the dark, which has been escalating ever since she met Hans. Being scared to go down in your own basement is silly, she knows. She passes the darkened hall, by way of the sauna, and goes through the furnace room toward the laundry room. A fluorescent light blinks, then dies as she steps in. *Why right now?*

She lights up the room with her cell phone and forces a smile to convince herself that the dark isn't as awful as it actually is. Her heart is thumping so loudly that it ought to echo in the room. Her whole body is ready for flight. But she makes herself walk through the spa area with the sauna in the corner, and past the hall with the wardrobes, Hans's gun cabinet, and the recycling bin. She checks that the basement door to the backyard is secured. Then she heads back upstairs calmer, her shoulders lowering and her breath returning slowly but surely to normal.

She pauses when she has almost reached the top of the stairs. That's when she hears the front door open and close.

9.

Agitated voices, sobbing, and a door slamming. Quick steps on the stairs. Even from here, I can hear that he's drunk. It sounds like a movie scene, but quarrels never turn out as well in reality as on the silver screen.

It figures that the light in the laundry room would fail just this evening. It was the only source of light I had. I try to understand why she was going around smiling to herself before. Her face was ghostlike, lit up by her cell phone with sharp shadows. Now I can no longer see the boxes in the basement, although I know they're there, carefully marked with clear labels: "Children's Clothes," "Christmas," "Easter," "Skates," "Helmets." The same steady handwriting on every carton.

But even neat storage can't camouflage the smell of misery in the walls. The place is vibrating with divorce, and when even strong-smelling cleansers can't cover up the odor of alcohol in the garage, you know someone has a serious problem. Worse than I thought.

The housecleaning in general seems done with care, apart from the floor under the bench here in the sauna. The floor mop has apparently never reached this far.

My legs are starting to get numb from my uncomfortable position. If they hadn't been so stingy with space when the sauna was built, there'd be room to sit up straight. And if other circumstances were different, I could have had the bad luck to be staring right up into Hans Göransson's anus. I try to push away the thought.

It has been quiet upstairs for a while now. Maybe it's time to start moving.

My legs don't go along with that at first. But once I wriggle out between the sauna benches and stretch, the blood starts flowing. There is tingling and pricking all over, but I enjoy the freedom. It's no problem to find my way to the stairs, because I've been on them before, plus I've reviewed the floor plan carefully. I know every nook and cranny in the house.

In the guest room on the first floor, he is lying spread out on the extra bed, snoring like a pig. He can do that a while longer, but not as long as he thinks. His open mouth and the saliva that has run out make me feel nauseated. And while I'm still afraid of him, I know I have the upper hand now. The power is with me for the first time.

I go into the kitchen in the hope of finding leftovers from dinner, but before I touch the refrigerator, I put on protective gloves. Even with lots of fingerprints left behind from two open houses, I'm taking no chances. I don't want to risk being associated with this place and ending up in the police blotter. My eyes are drawn to the vodka in the refrigerator door. That will be handy. I drink right from the bottle, without touching it to my lips. Immediately, I feel the alcohol go to my head.

Footsteps upstairs make me pause. I quickly plan where I should hide if someone comes down. I hear a toilet lid open, and I feel relief for the moment. Most likely whoever's up will go back to bed as soon as their needs are taken care of. I wait, all out of breath; I don't feel a trace of hunger anymore. Only when it's dead silent do I go toward the stairs. On the way, I stick my feet into a pair of slippers, to dampen the sound of my steps.

If it weren't for the missing slip of paper, I wouldn't have to go up. But I think I dropped it in the girl's room yesterday when I took my hand out of my pocket, so I have to look. A single silly notation is jotted down, but it would be enough to reveal me.

She is enchanting, lying there surrounded by her stuffed animals, arranged exactly the same as last night. The covers are at her feet, so I tuck her in, and once again I graze her soft cheek. I try not to think about who she reminds me of. Someone who never got the chance to be her age. I lean down and see the yellow slip of paper lying under the bed toward the wall, and I reach for it. The girl doesn't move a muscle, even when I stand up and back away.

But as I pull the door closed behind me, I see that she is awake and staring at me with big eyes. I try to remain calm. Instead of showing my dismay, I smile at her and put a finger in front of my mouth, hushing her soundlessly. After a few seconds, the girl's eyelids flutter and close.

10.

The sound of shuffling footsteps makes Cornelia open her eyes and peer out into the darkness. She is wide-awake at once, listening for more signs that Hans is outside the bedroom. The fear is there in no time. Considering how intoxicated he was when he got home, it's a mystery how he has managed to make his way up here. It's more frightening when he doesn't say anything, because then it's hard to figure out what he has in mind. Silence for too long is never good. Eventually he resorts to other means to get his point across, and if she tries to fight back or shows that she's afraid, that only eggs him on and things can easily get out of control. Besides, when he's been drinking, it's impossible to know if there's anything she can do to lessen the damage.

An hour or so ago, when he staggered into the guest room and collapsed on the bed, Cornelia considered leaving the house with Astrid immediately, even though they had no place to go. She thought about locking him in. But soon she heard deep snoring, and she ventured up to his door to double-check that he was out. Once he's asleep, he's usually stays that way for hours, so Cornelia was convinced she and Astrid would be out the door long before he woke up.

Now she is no longer as certain. She can't have imagined those footsteps coming from Astrid's room just now. Just as Cornelia is thinking about rolling over onto her back to get a better view, there is an ominous creak from the wood floor in the hall.

A chilling sensation makes her stiffen, and she tries to hear past the pounding pulse in her temples. It can't be Astrid. She would have just come right in, crawling in with her mother and lying down without a word.

Cornelia swallows as the muffled footsteps approach the bedroom door. There is no doubt that it's the sound of Hans's slippers; at any moment he'll come in, and she can't bear to think about what will happen next. Tomorrow she'll get the keys to her new apartment, and then he won't be able to get at her anymore. Could he have gotten wind of that?

She has to make it through just one more night, but the fear that initially made her freeze has now started to express itself in other ways. She can't stop trembling, and she prays to God that Hans will spare her. A scream has stuck in her throat, but she knows it could slip out of her at any time if she doesn't pull herself together.

The darkness in the room reinforces her discomfort,

and a shiver goes through her body. She knows he must be standing there observing her, and she has to struggle not to reveal that she is awake, to hold her body still. Perhaps he is simply hungry for sex. He doesn't want a divorce, and he won't be able to fill the void she is leaving behind until he finds a new woman to rule over.

Or perhaps he wants to end their relationship for good.

The desire to kill her is probably nothing new, but Hans cares too much about his reputation. Ending up in prison is not an option for him, because he would lose his social standing. Yet he's come close to completely losing control at times.

Cornelia's heart is pounding so loudly she can't believe he doesn't hear it. She squeezes her eyes tighter and prays to God again.

11.

TUESDAY, APRIL 1

As soon as she wakes up, Cornelia senses that something isn't right. It takes her a minute to realize that the alarm on Hans's cell phone is ringing nonstop from down in the guest room, and she figures he must still be completely plastered. Astrid has crawled into bed with her and is lying like a little ball in her arms. Gently, Cornelia strokes her head and hopes that she'll be in a good mood when she wakes up. That she won't be noisy. That she won't disturb Hans.

After a while, Astrid stirs, and mumbles something about an old man who patted her on the cheek during the night. Cornelia kisses her daughter on the forehead.

"An old man patted me," Astrid repeats, wide-awake now.

"Are you calling Daddy an old man?"

Cornelia smiles at her child, this amazing gift she has received. The light of her life. She can't keep from kissing her again, even if she knows her daughter will protest.

Astrid pulls back. "No, it wasn't Daddy."

Cornelia makes eye contact and sees that Astrid believes what she's saying. There is nothing wrong with the girl's ability to make up stories; she has difficulty distinguishing between dreams and reality. If Cornelia had half as good an imagination, she would be a writer.

Finally, the alarm stops ringing, but there are no other sounds downstairs. Cornelia breathes out. With a little luck, they will have left before Hans wakes up.

Their new life begins as of today. The bags are packed. The final terrifying night is over. And this afternoon Cornelia will get the keys to the apartment in Abrahamsberg, only seven minutes from Astrid's school. The three-room apartment is furnished—admittedly not with their own things, but it will suit them fine. Cornelia doesn't want anything from the house anyway, except her grandfather's old sideboard, and she can pick that up later. It's important that nothing associated with Hans be at the new place, so that she can start to heal. Obviously, Astrid is going to have pictures of her dad, but Cornelia doesn't want anything else that could trigger traumatic memories.

Now it's just a matter of slipping away. The smartest thing is simply to get dressed and leave. They can get breakfast at Gateau or another bakery on the way. Cornelia hurries into Astrid's room to pick up yesterday's clothes, which are lying in a heap beside the bed. She steps on a Lego piece but manages to keep her balance. In their new apartment, she will teach Astrid to organize her things better.

She looks around at all the My Little Pony toys, Barbie dolls, and stuffed animals, and considers bringing something else, even though she knows they'll come back later to get everything. The house is going to be here, and she should have plenty of time to pick up what is needed before the sale closes. For now, Astrid has packed her own backpack to go "away," as she puts it. Astrid has no idea that "away" will become "home," but she'll learn soon enough. Thank God children have a capacity to adapt to change faster than adults.

Cornelia picks up the backpack from the floor and grabs most of the stuffed animals. Without them, bedtime can be a catastrophe. She tries to remember whether there's anything else important in this room, but she has a hard time thinking clearly with her pulse ticking so fast.

The night-light maybe.

Hans's alarm starts up again, and Cornelia completely loses her train of thought. Her breathing stops abruptly, and her shoulders reflexively hunch up toward her ears. Why didn't she go down and turn off the alarm before? She feels the energy draining out of her.

It takes a few seconds before she gathers her wits and realizes there's no time to waste. Without explaining, she dresses Astrid, who resists the whole time. When her pants are halfway on, she kicks them off and screams, "No!"

"Shut up," Cornelia says in a threatening voice, but she is crying inside. She doesn't want to be a mean mother, but panic is breathing down her neck. Stumbling at the finish line is simply not in the plan. Hans can't be given the chance to obstruct her, which he most likely would if he saw her dragging several suitcases out of the house.

Everything takes twice as long when Cornelia is stressed. Her fingers get clumsy, and her own sweater gets stuck in the collar of Astrid's shirt. She carelessly buttons her daughter's jeans and belt, and grabs the socks closest at hand. *Don't let him wake up now,* she thinks. *Please, please.*

It feels as if Astrid has started to realize the seriousness of the situation. She's not completely cooperative, but she isn't protesting as wildly as she often does.

"If you're quiet and calm, we'll stop by Gateau for a snack," Cornelia says. "Before school."

"Can I have whatever I want?"

"Yes." Cornelia can already imagine Astrid pointing decisively at a big slice of princess cake.

It will be worth it, a hundred times over. What is a sugar buzz compared with a hard fist to the face and loose teeth in the jaw? The mere thought of the time Hans threw a vodka bottle at her head makes her stagger. Her body remembers, and suddenly the pain is back.

Focus now. Look ahead. Soon life will start over, very soon. Hang on. Cornelia gives herself a pep talk the whole way down the stairs. She quickly puts on her coat. Her knees are trembling, and she is starting to feel dizzy.

The cell phone alarm is pure torture. Not a sound is heard from Hans, however, not even his snoring, which usually penetrates through the thickest walls.

"Astrid?" she whispers.

Where did she go? She was just here a second ago.

Cornelia turns around and sees her daughter's curly hair moving away toward the guest room, where the door is ajar.

Her pulse is racing. Cornelia wants to yell at her to stop, but she hurries after her instead. Just as Astrid reaches the room, Cornelia gets hold of an arm and yanks her daughter away. Her grip is much too hard, and Astrid shrieks—whether from pain or fury, it's impossible to know. There is nothing Cornelia can do other than put a hand over the girl's mouth, forcing her into silence.

Suddenly, Astrid stops struggling. Cornelia raises her eyes toward the guest bed and stifles a scream of terror. She moves her hand to cover Astrid's eyes and shakily backs out of the room. She gasps for breath.

Then she looks at Astrid, who oddly enough seems unmoved.

"Are we going for a snack now?" she simply asks.

12.

If she needed a ride, she really should have called sooner,
Josefin thinks when she sees the image of Cornelia flash
on her cell phone. She puts the phone in her handbag and
lets it finish vibrating.

Once again, Josefin observes that she doesn't have the
bandwidth for everyone who needs her. She can almost see
the stress hormones cascading in free fall from her brain
and spreading in her body. Her heart beats faster, and she
gets tangled up in the seat belt as she tries to get out of the
car.

"We're going to be late, Mom," Julia says, in a voice
that's more pleading than accusatory.

Josefin gets out of the car and decides that if Cornelia
really needs something, she'll call again. She loathes walking into Anton's school with her phone squeezed between
her ear and shoulder, and anyway, how urgent could it
be?

Anton is running toward the gate to be sure of beating her there. He's very competitive, and she usually lets him win by a margin. He throws his hands in the air in victory and continues at full speed up the stairs and to his friends.

"Have a nice day," Josefin calls to Anton's back, but just as she is about to hurry back to the car she runs into one of the teachers, who is blocking the way with one arm. Either Josefin will have to do the limbo to escape, or politely stop and talk. Josefin chooses the latter alternative. The teacher must have something important to bring up.

"I'm so sorry about this," the teacher mutters, taking hold of her pilled fleece jacket, which looks like it's been through a war.

Josefin doesn't understand the problem; can't she just buy a new jacket? Just as Josefin's handbag starts vibrating again, the teacher fixes her eyes on her and clarifies.

"It's this damned weight," she says. "I don't know how to get rid of it. I can't afford a personal trainer, but I was hoping maybe you could give me a few tips—since you're here anyway."

Not now, Josefin has a desire to respond. *Can't you see I'm in a hurry?* But she restrains herself. She can at least take a few seconds to offer some brief advice. After all, the teacher sees to it that Anton is happy during the day. It would be small-minded not to share some knowledge, however stressed she may feel.

"Strength training in combination with quick walks," Josefin says. "Less sugar and no alcohol." Then she demonstrates a simple ab exercise, which involves placing your back and heels against a wall while you try to press the curve of the back in as much as possible.

While she talks, the phone never stops shaking in her bag. She finally fishes it out, starting to sense that Cornelia's desperate attempts to get hold of her are perhaps about something other than a simple drop-off.

"It's Cornelia. I have to answer," Josefin says to the teacher while hurrying toward the gate. "It's me," she says to Cornelia.

Sobbing and snuffling are all she can make out.

"Hello?" Josefin says.

"He's dead."

"What did you say?" She heard perfectly well, but she still has to have it repeated for her.

Josefin nods at another mother, who is on her way in through the gate, and then walks toward the car, which she now sees is parked a few feet into the street and in the wrong direction. She's turning into a real suburbanite.

"Hans is dead," Cornelia whispers, barely audible.

Josefin stops. "What do you mean?"

"Murdered. I think he was murdered."

It's April 1 today, but this doesn't seem like a joke. Besides, no one would joke about such a terrible thing.

"How do you know that?"

"It . . . shows."

"Where are you now?"

"At home in the house."

"Is Astrid with you?"

"She was the one who found him."

Josefin takes a deep breath. "Have you called the police—or an ambulance?"

"Should I?"

"I'll do it. Try to stay calm. I'm coming right away."

Josefin hangs up and calls the police. She provides the Göransson family's address and explains that there's a mother and child at the scene. She sees Julia and Sofia waving impatiently at her from the car. By the time she sits down in the driver's seat, she is about to start hyperventilating.

"Mom," Julia says from the backseat. "There's no way we'll get there on time now."

Sofia sighs, looking dejected.

"Yes, we will," Josefin says, casting a glance at the clock, starting the car, and flooring the gas pedal. In four minutes, the school bell will ring, but it wouldn't be the first time they'd arrived at the last second.

As they drive past Cornelia's neighborhood at full speed, she glimpses the white villa on the hill, behind a few pine trees. Everything looks exactly as usual, but Josefin shudders when she thinks that Hans is lying dead inside. Even if he was hardly one of the best people on earth, she wouldn't wish being murdered on anyone.

She doesn't understand why Cornelia stuck with the marriage so long when it was clearly a nightmare. But Josefin doesn't judge. She knows that Astrid is everything to Cornelia, which gave Hans a hold on her. Josefin never understood him. He was always polite and pleasant to her; nothing ugly ever shone through. Although perhaps it's the worst nutcases who seem most normal outwardly.

According to Cornelia, he was so awful to her that he didn't deserve to live.

And now he's dead.

Just as the bell rings shrilly, Josefin puts the brakes on. The girls hurry out of the car, and she rolls down the window to blow kisses after them.

"Have a nice day, Mom," Julia calls.

Sweet of her to say it, but the chance for a nice day is already gone. When Josefin sees the girls' bobbing backpacks disappear through the school entry, she heads reluctantly toward Cornelia's villa. She also tries to call her sister, but Emma doesn't answer.

13.

Emma is prepared to give the midwife one more minute at most before she interrupts her monologue. It shouldn't take five minutes to introduce yourself. Besides, shouldn't interest in the patient surpass the midwife's ego? Not in this case, apparently.

Emma has fantasized about her first visit to the maternity clinic for a long time, and she'd assumed she would be the focus of attention. But even as they shook hands, Emma sensed a lack of connection. The limp and uncertain grip made her lose all confidence. A real greeting should be solid and definite, never awkward.

It soon turned out that the handshake was the least of the midwife's problems. Yet Kristoffer sits nodding politely at her the whole time. Unfortunately, she seems to take that as encouragement to continue talking about all the babies she's delivered, offering detailed descriptions about things Emma isn't prepared to hear about yet.

She sees that Josefin is calling, but she has put the phone on "Silent"; her sister will have to wait a bit. Then Emma sneaks a glance at the blank patient record form, which prompts her into action. If the entire form has to be filled out, the visit might take a hundred years. She was granted an hour off from work, and not one minute more.

"Will we get started soon?" Emma asks, pointing at the paperwork on the desk.

"Sorry. I have a tendency to ramble," the midwife says, adjusting her glasses, which have ended up far out on the tip of her nose.

Once they get going, they make quick progress. They check off blood pressure, blood test, and weight at a furious pace.

When Emma sits down again, she sees that Josefin has called more than ten times and sent a text telling Emma to drop everything and call immediately.

Her first thought is that something has happened to their parents. In desperation, she starts thinking about everything she wants to say to them before they die—especially to her father. She has never dared to confront him with sensitive subjects, such as why he didn't want her to follow in his footsteps and become a police officer.

The midwife unfolds a chart full of dietary recommendations when Josefin's number appears on the screen again.

"Excuse me, but I have to take this," Emma says, getting up to leave the room.

The midwife looks annoyed. "Is there a fire somewhere?"

"I'm sorry," Emma says. "Are we done with all the tests?"

"Yes, but the food list is also important. Listeria—"

"Food just happens to be my responsibility," Kristoffer says. "We can go over the list without Emma."

"Okay then," the midwife says and starts reading out loud to Kristoffer the kinds of fish that may contain mercury, dioxins, and PCBs.

Good Lord, thinks Emma. *Can't we just go to the National Food Administration website? How hard can it be?* She steps into the waiting room and takes the call.

"Oh, thank God you finally answered." Josefin's voice is barely recognizable. "I'm with my friend Cornelia Göransson. Her husband died last night."

"How terrible," Emma says, relaxing now that she knows her mom and dad don't have anything to do with it.

"I don't know what to do. Cornelia says he was murdered."

"Have you called the police?"

"Yes, they're on their way."

Emma lowers her voice when she realizes she's not alone in the waiting room. "Are you sure it's a homicide?"

"I haven't wanted to go into the room, but according to Cornelia it's obvious he didn't die a natural death."

"Cornelia—is she the one you've told me about before?"

"Yes."

Josefin had asked Emma how you help someone who has been assaulted to file a report when the victim doesn't want to.

"How is she doing? How does she seem?"

"Jittery, but collected. She and Hans were in the process of divorcing, and the house is up for sale."

"She has a daughter too, doesn't she?"

"Astrid, yes. Anton's best friend." Josefin takes a deep breath. "She's often at our house. You've probably seen her, now that I think about it."

A small girl with curly dark hair appears in Emma's mind. "I think I know who she is."

"She was the one who found her dad."

"Oh no," Emma says with a sigh. "Poor child."

"She doesn't seem upset, strangely enough. Perhaps a delayed reaction?"

"Could be. But listen, is there anything I can do?"

"I don't really know, but it would be nice if you'd stay by the phone. Oh—someone's knocking at the door. I have to go," Josefin says, hanging up before Emma has time to say anything else.

14.

"I'll get it," Josefin says, turning toward Cornelia.

"Okay" is the only thing Cornelia gets out. She is sitting as if petrified on the couch.

Her head is itching infernally. She prays they don't have lice now too. Astrid may have dragged the vermin home from school, and Cornelia knows what a pain it is to get rid of them. The more she thinks about it, the worse she itches.

She can't get the image of Hans out of her mind. It's unfathomable that he's lying dead just a short distance away. Cornelia knows she's going to have nightmares about how she last saw him, with his intestines hanging out, his chest a bloody mess. She can only imagine how awful it was for Astrid to see her father like that. How traumatic for a six-year-old to see such a thing. It's lucky Josefin came like a rescuing angel so that she doesn't have to be alone with Astrid right now.

Cornelia hears unfamiliar voices in the hall now—probably the police. Soon they'll start asking her all sorts of things, and she doesn't know how she'll answer. She ought to be sad, but in reality Hans's death is the best thing that could have ever happened. Now her life can only improve.

It sounds like Josefin is showing the visitors where the guest room is. Cornelia closes her eyes and tries not to think about the blood sprayed on the walls and sheets. The voices feel far away, even though they're practically right next to her now. It takes all of her strength to open her eyes and force herself to sit upright.

"How are you feeling? You don't look so good," Josefin says as she approaches with two police officers at her side.

"A little dizzy."

"I'll get a glass of water." Josefin disappears into the kitchen.

The officers introduce themselves and ask if Cornelia can tell them what happened. The dizziness strikes in earnest, and she has to lean back on the couch so as not to faint. She closes her eyes and hopes it settles down.

"Is it okay if we sit down a moment?" one of the officers asks, and they settle into the armchairs opposite her before she has time to answer.

"We're sorry about what happened," the other officer says.

Josefin comes back and hands Cornelia a glass. She takes a few gulps. The cold water perks her up and clears her head a bit, and she wonders where she should start.

"I'm okay. I'm more worried about my daughter, Astrid."

Her voice cracks when she starts to talk. "You see, she's the one who discovered him."

"Can we take it from the beginning, please?" one of the officers asks. "From when you woke up until when Astrid found her dad."

"The first thing that happened," Cornelia said, "was that the alarm on Hans's cell phone started going off down in the guest room. Astrid had crawled into bed with me during the night, so we were lying together in the master bedroom upstairs."

"And you didn't go down and turn it off?"

Cornelia shook her head. "No, we were planning to slip away before he woke up."

"Slip away? Why is that?"

"I . . . well . . ." Cornelia turns toward Josefin, who helps get her back on track.

"They were getting a divorce."

Cornelia nods. *Just as well that they find that out right away.* "Today, Astrid and I are supposed to move into an apartment. So I wanted to get away from here as quickly as possible."

"Okay. Obviously, we're going to do a thorough investigation and in-depth questioning of many people, but do you have any theories yourself about how someone may have gotten into the house? Do you usually leave a door or window unlocked? Perhaps a patio door?"

"No, never. I'm careful about locking up. But there was an open house here yesterday . . ." Cornelia remembers that there was a light on in the basement. What if the murderer was somewhere down there waiting—only centimeters from her?

"What are you thinking about?" asks one of the officers.

"There was a light on in the basement when I came home, and I remember thinking it was strange that the real estate agent had forgotten to turn it off," she says, getting up on shaky legs. "You'll have to excuse me. I have to go to the bathroom."

Gasping for air, she is led to the bathroom by Josefin. She is ashamed that she can't hold herself together. What will they think of her? In her mind, she sees herself going down to the basement last night to turn off the fluorescent light, then watching it flicker and die.

"What . . . what if something had happened to Astrid?" she forces out.

She meets Josefin's serious gaze before she goes into the bathroom, closes the door, and sinks down on the toilet seat. Then she sits quite still and concentrates on breathing while listening to the conversation outside. The door isn't thick enough to keep the officers' voices out.

"We'll need to get crime scene investigators and detectives on the scene as soon as possible . . . From the county detective unit, yes."

15.

I t is drizzling outside Danderyd Hospital, and Emma and Kristoffer jog through the parking lot as if it were vital not to get too many raindrops on them, even though their clothes will probably dry quickly. Emma slows down the pace, trying to practice not hurrying unnecessarily, now that she has someone other than herself to think about.

The phone rings, and she answers breathlessly.

"Emma Sköld, Stockholm County Detective Unit."

"Lindberg here," her boss says in an urgent tone of voice.

Kristoffer makes it to the car first and gets into the driver's seat.

"I know you're occupied with other important things," Lindberg says. "But I need to know when you'll be free."

"I'm done with my appointment now and on my way back to the station."

"That's good, because you're needed here. A man has been found dead in a villa in Bromma. Probably murdered. I want you to go there as soon as you can."

"Does this concern the Göransson family?" she asks.

"How did you know that?" Lindberg says, sounding perplexed.

"My sister just called. She's a friend of the family, and apparently she went over to help the new widow." Emma didn't want the connection between her sister and the victim to come as a surprise down the line.

"Could this be a problem?" Lindberg asks.

Emma hasn't thought that far. She glances at the backseat, where the pile of papers from the old investigation sits in a box. She wants nothing more than to escape looking at that case for a while.

"Actually, I think my sister will be an asset. With her help, I can probably get information faster. And if it turns out to be a problem, can't we deal with that later?

Lindberg sighs and gives her the address. "I don't know much, except that the man was found lifeless in the guest room just this morning. Crime scene investigators are already on their way. When can you be there?"

"Within half an hour, if the traffic isn't too bad. Oh, one more thing. Josefin told me that the Göranssons were getting a divorce."

"Okay, we'll go over everything when we meet at the scene," he says. "Drive carefully."

Emma hangs up and tries to see the big picture. An abused woman who requests a divorce and is planning to move out. In all probability, *she* should have been found murdered—not the other way around.

"What was that all about?" Kristoffer asks without taking his eyes off the road.

"A suspected homicide in Bromma. Do you have time to drive me there? If not, I can take a cab."

"It's no problem. My meeting doesn't start for an hour."

"Thanks. That's nice of you," she says.

She thinks about Lindberg's question. Even though she was quick to dismiss a potential conflict of interest, she still wonders what it will be like to have her sister at the crime scene. Sure, Emma is good at compartmentalizing her emotions once she's focused, but that capacity may be put to the test now.

"So Josefin knows the victim?" Kristoffer asks.

She shouldn't tell him anything, but since he heard the call anyway, she can't very well deny it. "Yes. They have kids at the same school."

Emma has to roll down the window to get oxygen. It's stuffy in the car, which is something she's usually not sensitive to.

Without advance warning, Kristoffer slams on the brakes. Emma flies toward the dashboard, her seat belt pulling so hard she worries that the baby may be injured. Her heart rate goes from resting to maximum in a few hundredths of a second. Kristoffer dodges a car veering off to the side of the road. Fortunately, another lane was open. Otherwise, they would have crashed.

"Damn it! There are some crazy drivers on the road," Kristoffer says.

"Take it easy," she says, placing her hand on his. It is completely tense.

"Some people shouldn't be allowed to drive," he mutters.

Or maybe you *should keep better track of the traffic,* Emma thinks. She doesn't say anything about the hard pressure over her stomach. Good thing the child is well protected by the fat she's built up during the pregnancy. But it really hurts where the seat belt dug in. At the very least, there's sure to be an ugly bruise.

After an awkward silence, Kristoffer asks for the address. He looks startled when she gives it.

"That sounds familiar. Is the house for sale?"

Emma sighs. "I can't talk to you about this. You know that."

"Seriously?" he says, clearly offended. "The fact that it's up for sale can hardly be a secret."

"You've already heard too much," she says, hoping they'd be there soon. Josefin sounded shell-shocked when they talked, and Emma wants to exchange a few words with her before her colleagues get to the crime scene, not sit in the car and discuss the case with Kristoffer.

16.

Josefin is surprised to see her sister getting out of a car in front of Cornelia's house as the rain picks up. She glimpses Kristoffer behind the wheel as he turns his car around at the dead end. Their eyes meet briefly and he raises his hand in greeting, but Josefin doesn't have time to respond before he has passed. At the same moment, Emma bends under the barricade tape and starts talking with a police officer whose task seems to be to check that no one unauthorized enters the area.

Josefin goes to the door to meet Emma.

"I didn't expect to see you here so soon," Josefin says, giving her a hug.

"I'm here to investigate. The case ended up with my unit. The rest of the team will be here any moment," Emma says and lowers her voice. "How are you doing?"

"I guess I'm okay." The truth is, Josefin hasn't even had time to think about how she feels about Andreas's betrayal or Hans Göransson's death, and now she has yet another thing to digest. So Emma has been assigned to the case. She doesn't know if she likes that, but Emma doesn't seem to notice her quandary. At least she doesn't let on that she does.

"How are Cornelia and Astrid doing?" asks Emma, wiping the raindrops from her face with one hand.

"Astrid seems to be fine so far, but Cornelia is shaken up, of course."

"Where are they?"

"They're sitting on the couch in the living room." Josefin nods to the right.

"Is there anyone else on their way here we should know about? Relatives or friends?"

Josefin lowers her voice. "Cornelia has no contact with her family."

"What about Hans's side?"

"I don't know if they've been told yet. You'll have to ask her yourself."

Josefin has barely shown Emma in before she hears another knock at the door. Hard and definite. Outside, another six police officers are standing, and Josefin greets them, one at a time. She shows them into the living room, which looks unnaturally tidy right now, due to yesterday's open house. All the decorative objects are perfectly lined up on the shelves, dust-free, just like the books, which are arranged by color. The flowers are so fresh you might think they were made of plastic. It looks like an ad in *House Beautiful*. No one would ever guess that a murder victim was lying just a few meters away.

The newly arrived officers introduce themselves to Cornelia, who gives a calm, collected impression. Astrid looks indifferent about the commotion; her gaze is somewhere else. But when Emma explains to her that she's a police detective, Astrid brightens up and starts telling a story about robbers and police cars. The story gushes out of her, but because she has a hard time pronouncing some of the words, it's not easy to understand. Still, Emma plays along, and Astrid ends by asking whether Emma can braid her hair.

"Sure. I can do that once we've talked with your mom."

Cornelia hands her cell phone to Astrid, who opens an app and becomes absorbed in the world of Minecraft. A police officer asks Cornelia how she's feeling, while Emma takes Josefin aside.

"A lot of people are going to be running around here for a while," Emma says. "The medical examiner and forensics have to secure all the evidence, and they'll want everybody out of the way. So my suggestion is that we go to your house, where we can talk undisturbed."

Josefin envisions the piles of laundry left on the hallway floor and the breakfast plates on the kitchen table, all the things she was going to take care of after dropping off the kids. Obviously, it's not important that it's messy, but she doesn't want Emma's colleagues to think she's a slob.

"I guess that's okay," she answers, taking out her calendar to see whether she needs to reschedule any clients. She has a feeling that this is going to take some time.

17.

Very little is required to destroy another person's life. It's just a matter of being ice-cold enough.

I see a car stop in front of the big house. A gangly man in a worn leather jacket gets out. Around his neck he has a camera with a zoom lens, and he starts snapping pictures near the barricade. The police guarding the crime scene pay no attention to him. What a shit job to stand like a vulture outside a house where a family tragedy has just played out.

So far I haven't seen a trace of any relatives. I don't know if I even want to see them, but I stay where I am.

Lucky for me, I've chosen a profession that lets me devote time to side projects without being questioned. I'm the only one who knows my schedule, so it's easy to make small detours whenever I want. As long as I deliver, it's cool.

The restlessness is still tearing at me in a disturbing way. Maybe I'm naive, but I had expected to feel something else. Not exhilaration, but at least relief. Then again, the project isn't finished yet, so it's impossible to relax.

Doubt strikes me: *What if all this doesn't make a difference? What if it serves no purpose for me to take matters into my own hands?* I dismiss those thoughts quickly, because I know I have to carry out the plan anyway.

I owe her that.

Then perhaps we can move on. Start living again, even if nothing will ever be like before.

Suddenly, the door is open and I get a glimpse of the little girl, standing next to her mother. I can't tell if she is sad. Someone else looks out, and I know I can't stay if I don't want to be noticed by the police.

It's high time to leave.

18.

Emma, standing by the door, lets them know the car has pulled up. Josefin helps Astrid with her shoes and coat, and then takes hold of one of the suitcases. Cornelia is moved by her friend's involvement and how kindly she treats Astrid. A tear seeps out when she realizes there actually is someone in this world who cares about her.

"Thanks, Josefin. Without you, I don't know what I would have done."

"Oh, you don't need to thank me. Of course I'll help you as best I can. After all the hell you've been through. And now this." Josefin bursts into tears, which turns out to be contagious. Cornelia doubts they're crying for the same reason, though.

"How am I going to sell the house now?" Cornelia says, looking around at the police officers, the blue-and-white barricade tape fluttering in the air. "Who would want to live here after this?"

"Don't think about that now," Josefin says. "We'll take one thing at a time. Do you want all of these bags?"

"Yes," Cornelia answers, and they carry them out.

Emma nods at them to follow her.

It strikes Cornelia that Emma looks like a better copy of her big sister. She is really beautiful—prettier than Josefin and with finer features. Cornelia has no idea why that thought popped into her head when she has so many more important things to think about.

A man in a worn leather jacket is raising his camera and aiming the lens at her and Astrid. Automatically, she looks away, ashamed. She feels like a failure, the kind that others point at in dismay.

"Show a little respect," Emma calls to the photographer, who must have hurried here after listening to the police scanner. If nothing else, he can brag about being first on the scene.

"Just doing my job," the photographer counters and defiantly continues snapping away.

Astrid hides under Cornelia's coat so that she is barely visible. They load the bags into an unmarked police car and then get in. Astrid, in the middle of the backseat, starts humming to herself.

The events of the morning catch up with Cornelia during the short ride. Hans's death means that her life will take a new, unexpected turn. Now he can't hurt her anymore. But that's not all that occupies Cornelia's thoughts as she looks out the window and sees the empty field and the beach at Ålstensängen to the right. Besides being able to live her life without threats from Hans, she won't have to worry about money ever again. On paper she and Hans are still married, so she will be his heir. In addition, she'll get the payout from his life insurance, which they decided to take out a few months ago.

It occurs to Cornelia that she is going to be a millionaire. The thought is dizzying, and she staggers as she gets out of the car at Josefin's house. Her friend is there in an instant with a helping hand. As usual, within reach, prepared to support her.

"Are you okay?"

Cornelia nods and looks Josefin in the eyes for the first time today. She hadn't noticed the dark circles under them before and wonders if they just appeared or if she's had them for a while.

"I'm just shaken up," Cornelia replies, helping Astrid out.

"That's understandable," Josefin says, looking positively gloomy.

"I want to play Legos with Anton," Astrid says.

"He's not home right now," Cornelia answers.

Her daughter gives her an inquisitive look. "What are we doing here then?"

"We're going to talk a little and have coffee," she replies, hoping Josefin is following along.

"Are you hungry for cookies or cinnamon rolls?" Josefin asks.

"Rolls," Astrid answers, disappearing off toward the door.

Cornelia feels a twinge every time Astrid is out of sight. She imagines that something awful will happen whenever she's not in control.

"You don't need to take off your shoes," Josefin says, moving aside a pile of laundry that is lying on the floor.

Emma turns toward them. "We'll need to talk with each of you separately."

Cornelia doesn't understand the point of that and tries to think of a convincing counterargument, but her stomach knots up and she can't come up with the right words. The sense that she's losing her grip on the situation is growing stronger. She doesn't like that a police officer has been assigned to take care of Astrid.

A short time later, she is sitting in a room with Emma and one of her colleagues, Thomas Nyhlén. They look so stern that she has a hard time staying calm.

"We need to get a few more details from you concerning your husband," Nyhlén says. "Can we take it from the start? Tell us about this morning."

Cornelia forces herself back to the sound of Hans's alarm cutting into her dreams. She tries to pretend that she's actually sad. Under no circumstances whatsoever must it come out that her husband's death actually makes her feel free.

19.

It doesn't take an expert to see that Cornelia is not particularly distressed. Her behavior is inconsistent. She's clearly affected by the incident, but she is far from crushed. More like nervous. While Nyhlén leads the interview, Emma focuses on reading between the lines of what is being said. Many people believe they can conceal their true feelings by acting a certain way, but body language reveals more than you might suspect. Cornelia's gestures look artificial, which makes Emma draw the conclusion that she's hiding something.

She wonders whether this might have something to do with the domestic violence Josefin told her about. Sooner or later, they'd have to broach that sensitive topic. Not because Cornelia is suspected of anything, but to see whether it reveals any new leads.

"What was your relationship with your husband like?" Nyhlén asks in a neutral voice.

Cornelia looks at him tensely. "Like I said before, we were in the process of getting a divorce."

"Was the desire to separate mutual?"

She shakes her head barely noticeably. "I was the one who requested it."

"Why?" asks Nyhlén.

Cornelia throws out her arms.

"I thought we were going to talk about Hans's death. What does our divorce have to do with it?" she asks. When she raises her voice, her accent clearly emerges. She seems about to lose control.

Now the key is for Nyhlén to back off a little, but not too much.

"We need to know everything about your husband and the people closest to him to move the investigation forward. However uncomfortable that may be, everything has to be brought to the surface, big and small. A murder has been committed, and our job is to find out who is guilty. So please answer my question: Why did you want to leave your husband?"

Cornelia sighs and whispers, "He assaulted me—many times."

"I'm sorry," Nyhlén replies. "How long did this go on?"

"Almost from the very start. It's a long story, which I'd prefer not to go into in detail. I don't know how much I can bear right now. I hope you can understand that."

"Have you ever reported him?" Nyhlén asks.

"I was afraid to."

"You're not alone when it comes to that," Nyhlén says

in an apologetic tone. "Do you know what he was doing yesterday?"

"He went to work. In the evening he came home reeking of alcohol. He was really drunk. After a while, he passed out in the guest room."

"Would you say he had an alcohol problem?"

"Yes," Cornelia answers. "Definitely."

"Do you know who he saw yesterday?"

Cornelia shrugs. "No idea. You'd have to check with his secretary."

"We'll do that," says Nyhlén. "We're going to work day and night to clarify the circumstances around your husband's death. We'll question everyone he's been in touch with lately, and we'll probably have to ask you more questions again soon. Is there anything we've missed that you think may be significant?"

"I don't know if it's important," Cornelia says, "but I woke up during the night and he was standing outside the bedroom watching me."

"Is that unusual?" Nyhlén asks.

"When he's drunk, he usually sleeps like a log. And there's something else—something Astrid said. She said an old man patted her on the cheek during the night. An old man who wasn't her dad. I assumed it was a dream or something she imagined, but now that I think about it, she sounded very certain," says Cornelia, stiffening. "Someone was standing outside my bedroom the night before last too. Maybe it wasn't Hans after all."

"You never saw him?"

Cornelia shakes her head. "No, I was scared to turn around."

Emma can't decide if Cornelia is trying an after-the-fact reconstruction to move the focus away from herself. But what if what she is maintaining is true? The mere thought of a stranger in her house at night subdues Emma.

"Did Astrid describe the man?" Nyhlén asks.

"I didn't ask her more about it. I let it go, because I thought she'd made it up. She told me this before she discovered her dad in the guest room. Then I forgot about it."

"May we have permission to talk with Astrid later?"

"It's okay by me, but it's probably best if I'm there—or Josefin is—so that she feels safe."

"Naturally," Nyhlén says.

20.

The police officers are accommodating, but they ask so many questions that Josefin is starting to feel uncertain about whether she is relating the day's events correctly. It's hard to remember exactly what Cornelia said when she called, but in any case Josefin is positive about the time.

She is distracted by the fact that they are sitting in Andreas's study, his private sphere, which now includes an exposed affair. *I wonder what she looks like, this irresistible creature he has fallen for.*

When Josefin looks around among his binders and objects, everything suddenly seems foreign. There are small piles of invoices, a half-full wastebasket, and unopened mail. Some thumbtacks on the floor and streaks of dirt on the windowpanes. Just like usual, actually, but after yesterday's disclosure, nothing is ever going to be the same again. Josefin simply cannot understand how Andreas could let himself be swept away without thinking about the consequences. *He has a wife and three kids, for heaven's sake.*

"How long have you and Cornelia Göransson known each other?"

Josefin blinks and tries to focus on the question. "Since Anton started at the same school as Astrid three years ago."

"How would you describe your relationship?"

"We're close. We got to know each other well because we carpool. Then the kids became best friends. So we see each other quite a bit in our free time."

"And Hans Göransson—how well would you say you know him?"

As soon as Josefin hears his name, she shudders. It's unbelievable that someone has taken his life.

"Not well at all," she says. "He worked a lot, so he was seldom around."

"But Astrid you've gotten to know well?"

Josefin nods. "She comes home with us in the afternoon to play with Anton fairly often."

There is a knock at the door, and Nyhlén sticks his head in. "Excuse me, but can I have a quick word with you, Lindberg?"

Josefin is happy to get a break. She needs to send a message to Andreas so he knows to pick up the kids today. She stares at his filing cabinet, then can't resist an impulse to open the drawers with the key, which is in the usual place. She rummages around without finding any signs that Andreas is having an affair. Maybe he's telling the truth after all, that it hasn't gone as far as she thought. But before she has time to really calm down, her heart starts beating faster. In the bottom compartment, under a pile of folders, she finds some receipts. Large sums have been spent on dinners at fancy restaurants, but worst of all is the invoice from Hotel Reisen. Double room. Champagne. When she sees the date, the fourth of January, fury erupts with full force. How long has this been going on?

When the detectives come back, Josefin feels like she's been caught red-handed, with the receipts in her hand. She sets them aside and sits down again, and tells herself that it could have been worse. At least Andreas, unlike Hans, is still alive.

"We will continue the interview with Josefin Eriksson," Lindberg says. He goes on to say the current time, the reason for the questioning, and who is present in the room.

Josefin does her utmost to concentrate, but her anger at Andreas will not go away and her energy is running out. Too much is going on at once.

"We were just talking about Astrid," Lindberg says. "Since you see her a lot, how would you assess her imagination?"

Josefin laughs involuntarily. "It's extremely good. She's creative, and she's very good at drawing, singing, and dancing."

"Does she ever confide in you and tell you if something has happened?"

"Not directly. She lives more in the present. She isn't like a lot of other kids, who often have a need to get everything out of them and a little more."

"Do you mean that she's more in a world of her own than other children?"

"Yes, I think so. Sometimes she mixes up days and events, but for the most part she has pretty good command."

"Can you give an example?"

"If she says it was really fun when they dressed up at school yesterday, it may actually be that two days ago they had a costume party. She has a hard time keeping the days straight and finding the right words. It probably has to do with the fact that her speech is delayed."

The officers look so disappointed Josefin wonders what went wrong.

"Did Astrid say something?"

"Unfortunately, we can't go into that. Let's move to another matter—the Göranssons' divorce."

A shiver sweeps along her spine when Josefin hears the dreaded word. Could this be how it will end for Andreas and her too? What wasn't even a remote possibility two days ago is now a conceivable scenario. She tries not to lose focus, but the room feels cramped and stuffy.

"What do you want to know?" Josefin asks.

"Everything you know about."

"He hit and threatened her during their entire marriage. I've tried to get her to file a police report, but every time she changed her mind. She simply didn't dare. So I was pretty surprised when she made the difficult decision to separate."

"How did he react then?"

"I don't know exactly what happened when she told

him, but he clearly wasn't happy about it." Josefin remembers Cornelia's harrowed gaze when she told her how Hans had taken it. Her frightened eyes held so much darkness that it hurts just to think about it.

"Was the abuse physical or mental?"

"Both," says Josefin, looking at the family photo on the wall. Andreas's nice smile, his kind eyes. And the lie that has been lurking behind them.

21.

Cornelia pats Astrid on the head and fixes some curls that have gotten tangled. "Honey, can you tell me about that old man you saw last night?"

From the corner of her eye, she notices the door to Andreas's study opening and police officers leaving the room, closely followed by Josefin. They all look like they're carrying a heavy weight on their shoulders, and Cornelia is afraid to think about what that might mean. Josefin couldn't have said anything against her. She can't even imagine what that might be.

"You didn't want to listen," Astrid says, still coloring with a felt-tip pen.

"What is that you're drawing?"

"A fairy." Always these fairies wandering around in the little girl's world.

"How nice. But listen. Mommy would really like to hear about that old man now. What was he doing in your room?" Cornelia shivers simply listening to herself.

"He patted me, I already said that," says Astrid, looking at Cornelia with big eyes. "He was staring at me."

"What did he look like?"

"Not like Daddy."

"So you're sure it wasn't Daddy?"

Astrid picks up a black pen and draws lines right over the fairy. "It turned out ugly."

"Oh," Emma says. "That's too bad."

Cornelia turns around in surprise and wonders how long Emma has stood there eavesdropping.

"Shall we do braids now?" says Emma, holding out two hair bands.

Cornelia wants to protest. *Let her be,* she thinks.

"Yes," Astrid exclaims enthusiastically.

"What were you talking about?" Emma says as she parts the girl's hair in the middle and starts to braid.

"That old man."

"Who?" asks Emma.

Cornelia sits silently alongside and listens, prepared to intervene if Emma goes too far. The other police officers keep their distance so as not to interfere. But the whole situation feels deliberately rigged, because everyone's eyes are on them.

"First braid done. Now there's only the other one left. Is this someone who usually pats you at night?"

Astrid laughs. "Course not."

"I didn't think so. What did the old man look like?"

"Taller than Daddy, but not as heavy. He didn't look dangerous."

"So you didn't get scared?"

"Will you be done with the braid soon?" Astrid asks impatiently. She twists her head to try to see.

"Very soon," says Emma, but she has slowed down the pace. "Would you be able to draw that old man, do you think?"

"I don't want to."

"If you wanted to."

"But I don't want to."

"Okay. Do you want to draw your room instead?"

"I guess so," says Astrid, making a square on the paper. "Here is my room, and there in the corner is my bed."

"How nice. Do you have any stuffed animals?"

"Lots and lots."

"Where do they live?"

"In the bed, around my pillow. They protect me."

"From what?"

Astrid draws something that looks like a rug on the floor. "Monsters, ghosts, and pelicans."

"Pelicans? Oh my! Are your stuffed animals able to protect you then?"

Astrid's hand stops in midmotion. "They can transform the monsters. Make them nice."

"Have they done that?"

"Mm-hmm."

"What monsters have they transformed?"

"The ones I see at night. Like that old man."

"Can you draw him?"

"No, I don't want to ruin my drawing."

"I could get you a new piece of paper."

"I don't want to. I said that."

Cornelia is about to protest, but Emma looks so sternly at her that she stops short.

"Could the stuffed animals transform him?"

"I think so. At first he looked mad, but then he smiled. He just patted me on the cheek, then he left."

Emma nods. "Your braids are done."

Eagerly, Astrid jumps down from the chair and runs to the mirror in the hall. Then she bursts out in a cheer.

Cornelia looks at Emma and shakes her head. "It's not possible to force her."

"We won't try to, but we may bring in our specialist in child interviews, if you don't mind."

Cornelia hesitates. She would prefer that Astrid not be subjected to more unpleasant questions, but she doesn't want to hinder the police investigation either.

"Only if you think it's absolutely necessary," she says.

22.

The police have just left the house when Andreas and the children come home.

"Are you okay?" Andreas asks, but Josefin doesn't know what he means. Is he referring to the murder, the subsequent police interrogation, or the fact that he's sleeping with another woman?

"I've had better days."

Josefin is ashamed when she realizes that she didn't give Hans a thought at all until now, instead wallowing in self-pity.

"It's unreal," he says. "Did you see him?"

Josefin shakes her head. "Thank God, no."

Andreas reaches for her hand, but she pulls back.

"So the police have been here?"

"They wanted to question us somewhere other than the scene of the crime."

"How did it go?"

"Good, I think. It was Emma and her team."

Andreas looks surprised. "Didn't that feel strange?"

"Actually, no. I feel more secure with her than with strangers."

"But she wasn't the one who questioned you, was she?"

Josefin gets irritated. "What do you think? We're talking about an experienced homicide investigation team at the county detective unit. They know what they're doing."

"Sorry, I didn't know it was such a sensitive subject," says Andreas, offended. "Shall I drive Cornelia home?"

"Ask her."

Josefin glares at Andreas as he goes into the living room and greets Cornelia. Then she follows to hear what they say.

"You're welcome to stay here, of course. That's totally fine," Andreas offers.

He gets a shake of the head in reply. "I can get the keys to the new apartment today. Astrid and I could use some time alone. She needs peace and quiet."

"Can I at least get you something to eat before you go?" Josefin interjects.

"Thanks," Cornelia answers. "But I think we should go now. I can grab something on the way to pick up the keys."

"I'm happy to drive you," says Andreas.

"It's not necessary. We can walk."

Andreas points out the window. "But it's pouring."

"Well, okay. That's very kind of you. I'll just get Astrid. Did she go up to Anton's room?"

"I'll check," says Josefin, heading for the stairs. "Did you pack any toys?"

Cornelia stares at her bags out in the hall and shakes her head. "Just the stuffed animals."

Josefin thinks about what they can let Astrid borrow so she doesn't end up empty-handed in the new apartment. Their house is almost bursting with toys. She brings the picnic basket into the hall and throws a few toys in.

When she makes it upstairs, she sees that the children have built a fort under Anton's desk and she has to coax to get them to come out. At last she succeeds, by enticing them with the basket, which leads to Astrid cheering and Anton howling with rage. He doesn't want to lend out anything. Josefin can see she's going to spend half the evening trying to get him to understand why she's doing this.

Cornelia looks grateful when Josefin comes down with Astrid and the basket of toys.

"You don't need to," she says.

Josefin smiles weakly. "I know."

The rain is pouring down when Andreas opens the front door with bags in hand and starts walking to the car.

23.

After three minutes in the car, Emma starts to feel nauseated again. Nyhlén is talking on the phone with Lindberg as he drives back to the station, where they will try to get a preliminary report from the crime scene investigators. She concentrates on looking out the window. The problem is she hasn't eaten in hours.

"Emma, hello?" Nyhlén asks, slowing down. "Are you feeling okay? Should I stop?"

Emma clears her throat. "No, keep going. Sorry, I was thinking about something else."

"You don't look like yourself," he persists. "Are you sure you're okay?"

On the one hand, she wants to tell him what's going on so he'll understand why she isn't the same as usual. On the other hand, she wants to wait. If anything were to go wrong, it would be best that as few as possible know.

"Everything's fine. I think the situation was just starting to get to me."

"Anything in particular?" Nyhlén asks. "Lindberg was grateful that we could do the interviews at your sister's place. So you don't have to worry about that."

"Thanks," Emma says. "Do you know what they've got on Hans Göransson?" Emma wants to change the subject to anything but her condition.

"Age forty-nine, high income. No police record. Had three board positions but mainly spent time on his own commercial real estate company. They've contacted the secretary who handles his calendar."

"Nothing else of a personal nature?"

"Well, he was married before. But it's been fifteen years since they split."

"That's not much to go on," says Emma. "What do you think so far?"

"That she looked extremely pale," says Nyhlén. "Cornelia, that is."

"That's to be expected."

"Yeah, but I still get the feeling she's holding something back. She seemed so high-strung."

Emma looks at Nyhlén. "Don't beat around the bush."

"There are nothing but advantages for her that her husband is dead."

"So you think it might be Cornelia?"

"I never said she actually did it."

"You mean she hired someone? A hit man?"

"I don't know. That's just one theory. What does she have to lose?"

"Her child. If she went to prison."

"But what if it was part of the plan that Astrid should see the perpetrator?"

Emma tries to follow Nyhlén's reasoning. "So she can exonerate her mother, you mean?"

"Exactly," he says, stopping at the white villa for the second time that day. "What did the girl say?"

"That the man was taller and thinner than her dad."

"She has a night-light and he was by her bed, so she ought to have a pretty clear picture of him, right?"

"I see what you mean, but I don't see how a six-year-old could precisely describe a person's appearance."

Nyhlén sighs and gets out of the car. "It's not easy. That's for sure."

They are hardly in the door before one of the technicians looks at them triumphantly. "We've found the murder weapon."

Emma studies the Global carving knife he is holding out, similar to one she herself has at home. Sharp and effective. The difference is that this one is bloody and has been placed in a transparent plastic bag as evidence.

"Where did you find it?" she asks, taking an apple from the bowl on the table, too hungry to care that she isn't at home. But she puts it back when she sees that someone has already chewed on it. Then she glances at the other apples and sees bite marks on all of them. Strange.

"It was in the laundry room."

On the tiled kitchen wall a few meters from the couch, Emma sees several Global knives on a magnetic strip. A gap is seen, big enough for a knife. She points to it. "The murder weapon has been taken at the scene, it appears. Could that mean the crime wasn't planned?"

"It could," the technician says.

"Have you found anything else?" asks Nyhlén.

"An empty bottle of rum, a cell phone, and a wallet with credit cards and cash in the guest room. A piece of a necklace too, under the victim's right shoulder. That's basically everything besides an awful lot of fingerprints, which are probably from the open house. We'll have to see what the lab comes up with."

"No signs of a break-in?"

"Nada," the technician replies.

Emma hadn't thought so. "Then we can rule out a robbery attempt or a burglary that went wrong," she says.

"I think that's a safe bet. I'd also venture to say the killing was personal—it was unusually violent—but the medical examiner will have to state an opinion on that when he's done."

Nyhlén looked thoughtful. "You think the victim and the perp knew each other?"

"It wouldn't surprise me."

"Can you show us exactly where you found the knife?" Emma asks.

"Sure."

The technician heads for the basement stairs, and Emma and Nyhlén follow along, down to a lavish spa area. The decor is tasteful, with many subtleties. The tile on the walls and ceiling is in shades of gray, with sea stone on the floor, a whirlpool tub, and a glassed-in sauna with two benches and spotlights in the ceiling. They haven't scrimped on anything. There's even a TV with surround sound and an adjustable screen facing the sauna.

As they pass the laundry room, the technician points at a half-full basket of dirty clothes.

"Here. It was completely visible at the top of the pile."

Emma sees traces of blood. "So the perp didn't seem worried that the murder weapon would be found."

"Not a bit," the technician says, scratching his forehead. "More likely, he wanted it to be found."

24.

So this is what the ceiling of the new apartment looks like when you study it closely, Cornelia thinks as she stands in the living room. Completely flat, with no niceties like stucco or beveled edges. No stylish cornices either. Ordinary, nondescript, just like the rest of the apartment. None of this really comes as a surprise to her, because she was here before. It was to be her and Astrid's free zone, a divine place where Hans would never gain entry.

Now Cornelia knows for sure that he will never set foot here. But even as her anxiety is starting to recede, Hans still shows up as a figment of her imagination, and she knows it will take time to be rid of him in her nightmares. It won't be easy. Not after an eleven-year relationship.

The main thing is that they'll get to sleep undisturbed at night. Cornelia looks at her daughter, who is sitting on the floor beside her playing with Anton's plastic fire-breathing dragon. It flies back and forth and hisses angrily. Astrid is completely involved in her play and shows no signs of trauma. For her part, Cornelia is staring up at the ceiling light. Is that a crack or a shadow beside it? Either way, it's not going to be her problem; they won't be here long-term. Soon they will have the means to buy something better, maybe even a house in tony Ålsten.

There is a house on Storskogsvägen for sale, with a view of the well-known row of town houses on Ålstensgatan— the so-called Per Albin houses, which cost as much per square meter as an apartment in the inner city. Cornelia would have claustrophobia in one of the town houses. But the place on Storskogsvägen is bigger, with afternoon sun on the balcony. It's roomy enough but not too big for two people.

If she estimates on the low end, she will have seven million kronor after all the loans are paid off. So Hans would contribute something positive at last, even if she would have preferred being destitute and married to a nice man. Someone who didn't hit and humiliate her. Someone who loved her for who she was. Who was a good father for their child.

But those kinds of men never seem to cross her path. She grew up with a domineering, unsympathetic father. Then Hans came into her life. The man who would make her dream of life in Stockholm a reality. The man she thought would turn her dismal existence upside down.

In the beginning, being with Hans was exciting. He was an experienced man with unlimited resources and a broad network. She was seventeen years old, and he was thirty-eight. Everyone in his circle of acquaintances was successful, with interesting occupations and the right contacts. She hadn't even taken the university placement exam yet. Instead of going on dates at the pizzeria, she got to hang out at high-end restaurants like Gondolen, where he knew half the clientele. He showered her with accessories and expensive clothes, spoiled her without rhyme or reason. It wasn't hard to be drawn in without engaging in any deeper analysis. She never realized she had become his puppet, someone he manipulated as he wished. And she had no idea she was behaving exactly like the bottle-fed lamb she had cared for as a child, the one that followed her wherever she went.

Now that her greatest threat is gone, she finally feels peace in her soul, even though she knows better than to count on anything. Still, her muscles are starting to relax, and something reminiscent of soreness after exercise is aching in her body. Perhaps it is because the tension is letting go. Only now is she starting to realize how bad she has been feeling.

Not a word about Daddy has come out of Astrid's mouth since she discovered him. She has neither asked about him nor wondered about what she saw. It will take time for both of them to process. Everything happened so fast. Suddenly the house was full of police officers, who took over and decided what to do.

Josefin's sister, Emma, was good to have around, but she kept a certain distance, gave her a suspicious look or two, and almost looked nauseated at times. Cornelia doesn't have the energy to think about what that might mean. Emma's partner seemed more relaxed, or maybe he was better at concealing what he was really thinking. They said they would probably contact her for further questioning. That's not something Cornelia is looking forward to. The only thing she wants is to move on: to sell the house and be left in peace.

A new idea is starting to take form: to move from Bromma, to avoid being reminded of Hans. But fleeing the area now might raise suspicions that in some way she was involved in his death. The police already have some suspicions; she understands that. That was probably why Emma looked uncomfortable. Perhaps one of their theories is that the abused wife got revenge—and gets rich, to boot.

She needs to remember to schedule a meeting with the insurance company, then to sell the house as fast as possible and buy a house of her own. It strikes her that she hasn't even called the real estate company to tell them what happened, so she dials Benjamin Weber's number. The phone rings, but no one answers.

25.

The sign that says "Real Estate" in a designer typeface makes Emma wonder what Kristoffer is doing right now, and whether he's thinking about her. Most likely not. He probably has his hands full. There are new properties on the market all the time, more or less depending on the season. During school breaks it's calmer, but Kristoffer is never going to have nothing to do. He's not the type who wants to take it easy—more like the opposite. It probably works that way for most people who get paid on commission. They know that little extra bit counts. Even the arrival of their child won't slow Kristoffer down.

Nyhlén squeezes between two cars outside the real estate agency, and Emma takes a deep breath when she feels fresh air. True, on the busy Karlavägen esplanade the air is far from pristine, but it's still better than sitting enclosed in a stuffy car.

They make it to the agency entrance five minutes before

closing. With a little luck, someone responsible for the sale of the Göransson house will still be there. A well-dressed man meets them at the door. Emma introduces herself and explains that they are from the police.

"What can I do for you?" says Benjamin Weber, showing them into the tastefully furnished office.

"We need to speak with the person who held an open house last night, for a property your agency is listing." Emma gives the address in Bromma, and Benjamin stiffens. She already knew that he was the one selling the Göransson house, but she wanted to see his reaction. Although it's unlikely he knows yet what happened, he looks worried.

"Helena Sjöblom and I are in charge of the sale. Is there a problem?"

"Can we talk somewhere more private?" Emma asks, looking out over the open-office floor plan, where a few employees are still sitting at their computers. "If Helena is here, she's welcome to join us."

"I just saw her," he says, going off and coming back almost immediately with a beautiful blonde woman by his side. He shows them into a glassed-in room with an oval conference table, and they sit down on black Fritz Hansen chairs.

"We're from the county detective unit, and I'm afraid we have some bad news," says Nyhlén before telling them that Hans Göransson died at his home last night. "Everything indicates that he was murdered. Naturally, we're investigating."

Both agents turn pale.

"Dreadful," Benjamin says after a while.

"We would like to know how you run your open houses and see a list of names of the prospective buyers who were at the open house in question."

Nyhlén leads the discussion this time, and he gets names for both of them and notes the time of day and place. Then Helena describes the two open houses and who showed up, and which people came to both.

"There were three return visits and four new ones at the second open house, but only one who signed the list indicating that they were seriously interested."

Not likely the murderer.

"Should I go and copy the list of everyone who was present?" Helena asks.

"We can deal with that when we're done here," Nyhlén answers. "We'd like to have a copy of the brokerage agreement too."

Benjamin and Helena exchange glances.

"I was also wondering," Emma says, "is there any other way to get in during an open house besides through the front door?"

"What?" Helena looks dismayed. "Do you think the murderer came during the open house?"

"We can't rule that out."

"The garage door was open," Helen said. "Also the terrace door and the entry through the garden. It has to be that way at an open house. The prospective buyers have to be able to walk around everywhere and look at everything." Helena looks for support from Benjamin, whose expression doesn't change.

"Do you recall whether you locked the doors behind you?" Nyhlén doesn't sound accusatory, but Helena looks like a reprimanded child.

"Yes," she answers, but she sounds uncertain. "I'm always very careful, considering the responsibility I have for the property."

Emma can't help jumping in when she sees how nervous Helena is. "We're not criticizing you for anything. Not even if you did forget to lock up. No one could know what was going to happen."

"I know I locked up." Helena's voice is tense. "I always make several rounds to be sure."

"But you forgot to turn off the lights in the basement?"

Helena looks disconcerted. "Who said that? Konrad?"

"Who is Konrad?"

"Konrad Kowalski," Benjamin says.

"The inspector," says Helena. "He was there to answer any questions about his report."

"Where can we get hold of him?" Emma asks.

Benjamin glances at his Breitling, which it was unlikely he bought on a charter trip to Phuket. "Right now, he's inspecting another house in Bromma for us—on Klövervägen."

Emma makes note of the address.

"I know I turned the lights off," Helena says, still with a guilty expression.

"How can you be so sure of that?"

"Because I went down to the basement two times. I started there and then went through the house, room by room. When I got back to the first floor, I saw that there was still a light on in the basement. So I went down again and turned the light off, and then Cornelia and her daughter came home. We talked a little while, and then I left."

"It never struck you that someone could still be in the house then, considering the light that was on?"

Helena is unable to hold back her tears any longer. "No, not even in my wildest imagination."

26.

Helena has to rush to the restroom, but Benjamin stands by the window to assure himself that the police officers really get in their car and drive off. The chalk-stripe suit feels too small, and the white shirt is chafing against his chest. The cuff links are so tight it feels like they're cutting off the blood supply to his hands. He loosens the cuff links and draws a hand through his water-combed hair with becoming streaks of silver. Since he took over the agency from his father three years ago, he has managed to hang on to a relatively distinguished reputation, which isn't easy in this tarnished industry. Sooner or later, you run into a rotten egg of a seller—or buyer, for that matter—and in the end it is Benjamin who is held accountable and has to take care of the mess.

He doesn't maintain that he has nothing to hide. But who the hell does? If that were the case, he would have had to shut down the business long ago. This profession requires cunning—and faith that it's possible to sell anything, if you just present the offer convincingly enough and to the right people. The key is to project nothing but confidence to the client. It's also important not to attract attention and to eliminate the slightest hint of impropriety.

When the car with the zealous police officers pulls away, he should be able to relax, but something is gnawing at him. Where to begin? There is far too much to discover if anyone were to get the idea of nosing around in his business. It's bad enough that the authorities, in the form of the Estate Agents Inspectorate, are already hanging over him like a hawk. Now to have the police investigating a murder at one of his clients' houses is almost too much. Thank God the police forgot to get a copy of the agreement with Hans Göransson before they left, considering that it doesn't exist.

"What are you thinking about?" Helena's voice sounds pitiful.

He turns around and fastens the cuff links again. "Hans and Cornelia. Sad story."

Helena looks so downcast he has to restrain the desire to embrace her. The risk is that he'll want to go further than that, and with the open floor plan, there's a good chance they'd end up with an audience.

"What do we do now?" she asks. "About the sale, that is?"

"It's probably best to lie low for a while, then hold another weekend open house," he says to his own surprise. Normally, nothing can stop him from proceeding. "Even if another open house is worthless, I see no other alternative as long as the house is considered a crime scene. Provided no one makes an offer over the next few days."

"Isn't it smarter to sell as soon as possible? Showing the house again clearly signals that something is wrong."

Benjamin tries to see if Helena is serious. If so, she outdoes him, or is at least in the same class. "Everyone is going to find out what happened, and it could damage my reputation if we try to keep people in the dark about a murder committed there."

"Who said we were going to withhold anything? We have to tell the truth to everyone left at the end of the bidding. No one else needs to find out," she says, turning on her heels.

As she leaves, he can't tear his gaze from her sexy rear end as it sways under a tailored skirt. If they were alone, he would run after her, pull her down on the floor, and tear off her clothes before she had time to react. There's so much chemistry between them that he feels a swelling between his legs every time she's around. They are playing for high stakes, considering that anyone at all could expose them, but those are just the moments of excitement that keep him going. Benjamin loves living dangerously, eagerly pushing boundaries, as long as he's in control of the situation. Now with his wife, Monika, away at a conference in London, there are no obstacles. He sends a thought of gratitude to their sons, who had the good sense to move away from home as soon as they were old enough.

Benjamin observes two newly certified agents who appear to be working feverishly even though it's after hours.

A young woman looks up from her screen and smiles at him. She is one of those who chase new properties without great success, one of the superfluous ones who get to stay simply because it looks good to have a lot of employees. He answers her smile. Judging by her rosy cheeks and her desperate expression, she is prepared to go far for her career. Good to know. In his imagination, he decides she has black lace string panties on. Or perhaps none at all.

A tense look from Helena makes him grasp his genuine crocodile-skin briefcase and leave the office as quickly as possible before he suggests a spontaneous orgy out of sheer eagerness. Actually, all he has to do to make desire disappear is to think about Konrad. He just hopes the inspector doesn't start wagging his tongue.

27.

The rusty Saab parked outside the house on Klövervägen looks out of place, and Emma guesses that it belongs to Konrad Kowalski. Her curiosity is aroused, even though the fatigue after the long workday is starting to make itself known in the form of a headache and dizziness. She and Nyhlén walk swiftly toward the pillars that hold a grand wrought-iron fence in place. A stone lion's head adorns one pillar, which is also equipped with a "Beware of Dog" sign. At the sight of the warning, Nyhlén slows down and looks around.

"It's okay," Emma says. "If it were loose, it would already have attacked us."

"Thanks, I feel better already. You really know how to calm me down," Nyhlén says, giving her a friendly pat on the shoulder.

No barking is heard even when they knock on the door, and it takes a while before a young woman appears.

"Hi. Sorry to disturb you, but we're from the police. We're looking for the owners of the house," Emma says, realizing she has blanked on the name of the family.

"Ms. Heed," Nyhlén fills in.

"That's me," the woman answers. "What do you want?"

Emma explains that it's actually the home inspector Konrad Kowalski they're looking for.

"Has he done something?" she says, looking around nervously.

"We just need to ask him a few questions. It has nothing to do with you or your house. He just happens to be here right now, and our business is urgent."

Emma shows her police identification, and the woman shrugs. "I think he's in the basement. Feel free to go down and talk with him."

Then she leaves the door wide open and goes off to her laptop on the coffee table. "You'll have to excuse me. I have to answer an important e-mail. The stairs are to the right."

Emma takes the lead, with Nyhlén at her heels. An empty garage is straight ahead; the door to another room, on the right. Then they pass a long corridor with closets on both sides and finally come to a laundry room. Emma stops abruptly when she sees a man wearing only his underwear. He has his back to them. Thanks to the wall-to-wall carpeting, he must not have heard them coming. *But why is the inspector half-naked in the laundry room?* Automatically, Emma takes a step back, bumping into Nyhlén and stepping on his toes.

"Ouch," he exclaims, and quickly the inspector twirls around, with a tool in one hand.

"Who are you?" he asks with a frightened expression.

"We're from the police. We want to ask you a few questions concerning a house you inspected yesterday," Emma replies.

"You can get the report from the real estate agent," Konrad says, but he stops short when he seems to notice his bare legs. "I'll be done here in a moment. I need to change. If you'll excuse me?"

They wait for him in the adjacent room, and Emma feels some relief when he comes out with a shirt and jeans on. Now he almost looks like any normal fifty-year-old man. Apart from the toolbox with the handwritten label "Touch This and You Die."

"Jerry-built construction," he says, nodding toward the room he just left. "How hard can it be to install a floor drain with the right incline?"

He is noticeably irritated, or else he just wants to buy time by making small talk about something else.

"Do you have time to answer our questions now?" Emma tries to sound accommodating, but she is losing patience when Konrad stamps on a clinker tile with all his weight so that it lifts up at the joint.

"If they'd laid the tiles according to the rule book, it wouldn't have come loose."

So he's not just zealous but a total nut, Emma thinks. *If Ms. Heed knew about the inspector's work methods, she probably would have kept an eye on him.*

"I have to go through the results with the mademoiselle," he says, pointing toward the floor above, "and she's not going to like it. But I can fit you in if you get it over with quickly."

Nyhlén nods. "We promise to be efficient, but we prefer to talk in our car. We're parked on the street."

"Good. Then I can take the opportunity to put my tools away," he answers.

On the way out, Konrad babbles on and on about bungling tradesmen. He doesn't even stop once they've gotten into the car and closed the doors, so Nyhlén interrupts him abruptly to try to get to the point. But no matter how they ask their questions, they can't get a single valuable piece of information out of him. As soon as they stray from his agenda, it's as if he's transformed into a robot that can say nothing but yes, no, or maybe. Sometimes they get only a vacant stare in reply.

"What did you do last night?" Emma asks.

"Slept, what else?" Konrad replies. "At home with my old lady."

"And you don't remember anything out of the ordinary from the open house yesterday? A prospective buyer who behaved oddly? Maybe someone who asked strange questions?"

Konrad finally makes an effort. "There is something shady about that place, the sort of thing you feel after years in the industry. I've inspected hundreds of houses and learned to look behind the facade, find the cracks even if they aren't visible on the surface. Do you know what I mean?"

"You should probably clarify," Emma replies, waiting for further explanation.

"The roof . . ."

Konrad, completely absorbed in his musings, forgets to finish the sentence.

"The roof?" Emma asks.

"I think there's a little moisture problem hiding under the shingles, but I can't get at it to inspect."

Emma sighs to herself and thanks Konrad for allowing them to interrupt his workday.

"No problem."

He leaves the car and goes back to the house. When he's out of sight, Emma and Nyhlén look at each other in mutual understanding. Even though they're in the middle of a serious investigation, they can't hold their laughter in.

28.

WEDNESDAY, APRIL 2

"Hugo's been at it again. You've got to have a talk with him so he stops disturbing my open houses" is the first thing Kristoffer says when Emma wakes up beside him. No hello or good morning. She can't even remember him coming to her place last night; it must have been after midnight, when she was sound asleep. A nice surprise, apart from the introductory comment.

"How about a 'good morning'?" Emma asks. "Shall we start over?"

Demonstratively, she closes her eyes and then opens them full of pretend expectation.

He smiles wryly and gives her a hug. "Sorry, I'm just so damned tired of him running around and bad-mouthing me. Yesterday it happened again. Doesn't he have anything better to do?"

"I wouldn't know. I avoid having contact with him."

"Good. Keep away from that lunatic." Then, as if Hugo

can hear their conversation, Kristoffer mutters, "Get yourself a life, damn it."

"Was it a late one last night?" she asks to change the subject.

"Later than usual. I hope I didn't wake you when I slipped in."

"Not at all. For once, I slept like a log. I didn't wake up once."

"Nice," he says, extending his hand toward her to massage her neck. "Do you have time for breakfast with me?"

Emma nods, but she knows she ought to get going as soon as possible, since the investigation is in the critical start-up phase. She pulls on the same sweater as yesterday and goes to the bathroom to wash and put on deodorant. One advantage of her job is that she doesn't need to pay much attention to her appearance. That suits her fine. She doesn't like to wear makeup, and she's completely uninterested in fashion. In barely a minute, she's done, and she puts together a breakfast tray and takes it into the living room. It takes the air right out of her when she sees Kristoffer sprawled out on the couch watching the news. Although he was the one who wanted to have breakfast together, he made no effort to help out.

"When are we going to actually move in together?" she asks. "It would be nice if it happened before our child goes to college."

Kristoffer laughs dryly. "It's a matter of finding the right place first."

"Seems like that could take an eternity." Emma reaches for the remote control and turns off the TV.

"I see everything that comes on the market. Don't worry." He gives her a fleeting glance.

"And until then we live separately and pay double rent? Or should we settle down in the cottage in your allotment garden? It has running water six months of the year, right?"

Kristoffer is rescued by his cell phone ringing, and he gets up and moves away. As usual, he manages to avoid the question. Emma doesn't understand what the problem is. He's living with her basically all the time anyway. True, it can be rather irritating when he comes home in the middle of the night, she tells herself. On the evenings he works late or sees clients or buddies, she almost prefers that he sleep at his place. The nights are unsettled enough that she doesn't want to risk being wakened when she's just managed to fall asleep. Especially if he's been drinking.

Perhaps having separate living arrangements until the baby arrives isn't such a bad idea after all. Emma decides to let it go for now; Kristoffer doesn't seem to be in the right frame of mind for major decisions. She turns the TV on again and follows the news broadcast sporadically while Kristoffer finishes his phone conversation. When there is a story about Hans Göransson, she turns up the volume. Nothing that could hurt the investigation has leaked out to the media. It occurs to Emma that she hasn't thanked Josefin properly yet for her help, but there will be plenty of opportunity to do that in the future.

"Sorry," Kristoffer whispers behind her back.

She jumps in surprise. "Stop sneaking up on me."

His big hands start massaging her shoulders. He squeezes hard, which she likes, even though it hurts a little too. It doesn't take long before his hands slip inside her bra. She tries to relax and enjoy it, not be so surly and cheerless. Then her mind wanders, and she thinks about Kristoffer's first words in bed this morning.

"Does he show up often?"

"Who's that?" Kristoffer says absently followed by a moan.

"Hugo."

"Do we have to talk about *him* right now when I have a morning hard-on?"

"You were the one who started it. Do you always have to put off all our discussions with either work or sex?"

Kristoffer pulls back his hand as if he burned himself. "Now you're being unfair."

"Sit down."

Still looking miffed, he sits down beside her, seizes the remote control, and changes channels. "Yes?"

"It was a tough day at work yesterday, and it's going to be more of the same today. Could we at least talk to each other?"

"How's it going with the open-house murder?" he asks.

"Is that what they're calling it?"

He shrugs. "There's talk among the real estate agents, as you can understand. How far have you gotten?"

Typical of Kristoffer to ask something she can't talk about.

"I can't tell you. You know that. But we haven't made any major progress yet—that much I guess I can reveal. Do you know Benjamin Weber?"

Kristoffer pretends to gag. "A swine."

"Him personally, or his whole agency?"

"Both. He's notorious for his affairs with women. Rumor is, he sleeps with his employees. But why are you asking about him in particular?"

"Because his agency is listing the house."

"That's right. We talked about that at the office yesterday," Kristoffer says, seeming puzzled. "We had an open house in the same area that evening, so I guess we were lucky our house wasn't hit."

Emma shakes her head. "I don't think so."

"How can you be so sure?"

"We'll have to change the subject now," Emma says, sighing to herself. "I've already said too much."

29.

I t's an ordinary building—far from Stockholm's most beautiful—in varied shades of brown. It's not the first time Hugo has stood outside Emma's place in the center city near Vanadisplan, stamping impatiently. If she knew he was there, she would presumably be furious and tell him to scram before she calls the police. As if he would be scared by that. Besides, why would she need to call anyone when she's a cop herself? The thing is, he can't stay away. He knows the two of them are meant for each other, and that is worth fighting for. Soon enough, she'll agree with him. Maybe even thank him for not giving up. But he hasn't gotten that far with her yet.

No matter how hard Hugo tries, he can't understand how someone else could have come between them. For over a year, he has tried to deaden his feelings by having consolation sex with fashion models, but it hasn't done any good. The more insecure the other women are, the greater his need is to be with Emma. The strong, tough woman he shared his life with for several years. It's not fair that it would simply come to an end just like that.

Right after they broke up, it was actually nice to be away from her. To escape the angst about having a child. It was all about that in the end; Emma didn't talk about anything else, ever. There was constant crying, anxiety, and fear of being childless, not getting to call herself a mother. He was swept along in her depression without really knowing how he felt. They were sad all the time.

When she broke the engagement, and his shock had settled down, if felt like stress relief. It was liberating to go out for a beer with the guys whenever he felt like it, without having to ask for permission first. If he was in the mood to go to the Hammarby soccer match, there was no one to stop him. If he came home late from the studio, no one protested. And he could simply say yes to all the fun business trips, just like that, regardless of which models were going along. Summer and sun, good-looking ladies, and generous open bars that never ran out. A whole new world opened up. Life was play.

Then autumn crept up, and as soon as the twenty-four hours of the day consisted mostly of darkness, an out-of-control panic at being alone, forgotten, and unnecessary arrived. The last straw was when Hugo read about a man who had been lying dead in his apartment for two years, discovered only when the building was going to have new pipes installed. That could just as well be him. The insight made him gloomy. Slowly but surely, he realized what he had lost. There was no one like Emma, and he hadn't nurtured the relationship or supported her in the right way when they were a couple. He hadn't been the man she needed. Hugo loathes the concept of hindsight, but this new knowledge led to sleepless nights and endless harping in solitude. The apartment was overflowing with dirty laundry, dishes, and pizza boxes. He couldn't even make the effort to open the blinds.

If he could just have an honest chance to explain to Emma what he feels, surely he could clarify everything. He'd tell her how much she means to him, that he's never going to find a woman as amazing as her, that they'll have a child eventually. It's important to never give up. The problem is, she refuses to listen to him. Her rejection of him is so painful that he lies in bed writhing at night.

A tall man steps out through the entry, and Hugo ducks instinctively, although he's on the other side of the street. Kristoffer, talking on his phone, doesn't even look in Hugo's direction. The man who has destroyed everything for him is heading for an extension of his penis, in the form of a pathetic sports car. Nothing that impresses Emma, Hugo knows that. Emma doesn't care about such worldly things.

Kristoffer guns the car and sweeps past Hugo without letting go of his phone. Must be an urgent call, because you're not allowed to use a cell phone while driving anymore. Now at least he knows that Kristoffer can't make problems for the moment. He looks around anyway as he walks toward the entry, trying to ignore the warning signal in his head, sounding stronger and stronger the closer he gets. He enters the building code that he committed to memory when he helped Emma move. With every step up the stairs to her door, his self-confidence flags. Should he have thought this out more? What will he say to her? He stops outside the door, hesitates a moment, and is about to ring the bell when he changes his mind and leaves.

30.

As Emma leaves the building, she imagines for a moment that she sees Hugo disappear around the corner. He doesn't live in the area and doesn't even do business here. It must just be her mind playing tricks on her, since Kristoffer was talking about him when they woke up. As she makes her way to the police station, she wonders if Hugo is becoming an obstacle for her and Kristoffer. Bad feelings are often in the air between them. But she's not sure she can blame it all on Hugo, or whether it might be about something else. Sooner or later, it will be evident. She gets a knot in her stomach. In her world, it's the nuclear family that counts, not parents who live in separate places.

In fifteen minutes, she is taking the elevator up to the sixth floor. The whole team is gathered in the conference room, and Lars Lindberg, the investigation commander, is starting to talk just as Emma sits down breathlessly beside

Nyhlén. She is usually the first one there; now she has to nod apologetically at Lindberg because she is a few minutes late. He nods in reply and then gets right to the point.

"Hans Göransson died from twelve stab wounds from a sharp object in the stomach and chest. The murder weapon is most likely a Global brand kitchen knife, probably the family's own. We have secured fingerprints from the knife, but the results may take a while even though the case has been prioritized. We'll have to see if the forensics lab can do any more to get us the results fast. At the time of death, the victim had a high blood alcohol content, according to the medical examiner's preliminary report. Emma, I thought you should read through everything we've brought in so far. Officers from the Västerort Police District have started going door-to-door in the area. So for the rest of us, it's a matter of continuing to chart the last hours of Göransson's life and who is in his circle of acquaintances. Twenty-four of the golden forty-eight hours have already passed, so get ready for a long workday."

What happens in the first two full days after a homicide can make or break a case. Witnesses still have everything fresh in their memories, suspects haven't yet managed to find out what the police know, and recordings from surveillance cameras are still intact.

"The nature of the wounds indicates a high degree of aggression, which in turn implies a personal connection. So we believe that the victim and perpetrator knew each other and that the perp was in Göransson's circle. Let's start with his wife, Cornelia, and work outward. What impression did you get of her?" Lindberg asks, looking at Emma and Nyhlén.

"The first thing that struck me was that she isn't particularly sad," Nyhlén says.

"And that she acted nervous and exaggerated," Emma adds.

There is silence in the room as everyone seems to be thinking about what that might mean.

"On the other hand, she is in shock, of course," Emma says. "My sister knows her, and she told me that Cornelia was subjected to severe abuse by her husband during their entire marriage."

"Are there any reports against him?" Lindberg asks.

"Unfortunately, no," says Emma. "But she was the one who wanted a divorce."

"Why did she wait so long?" one colleague asks.

"She was scared," says Emma. "She didn't want to do anything for fear of how her husband would react."

"So what changed her mind?"

There is silence, because no one has an answer to that.

One of the analysts clears his throat. "The couple took out life insurance in January. With her husband's death, Cornelia Göransson will immediately get just under four million kronor, right in her pocket. Plus the money for the house, which is assessed at twelve million. They had a prenup, but because they were still married, she'll inherit his 90 percent share, so that will be several million kronor she wouldn't have gotten otherwise. Her 10 percent share would have brought in a million at most. The house is mortgaged for a couple of million too."

Lindberg looks at Emma and Nyhlén. "What do you think? Is it time to bring her in for a longer interview to clarify certain things?"

"It sounds like it," Emma replies.

"Then see that she comes here immediately," Lindberg says, letting his gaze sweep around the table. "What other leads do we have?"

Emma's thoughts drift to Astrid. "The daughter asserts that she saw an old man in her bedroom the night of the murder."

Lindberg sighs. "Little kids with good imaginations are hopeless witnesses. Who knows, maybe she was just dreaming."

"I don't think so," Emma says. "She seemed very sure about it. Almost too sure. An idea that struck me is that maybe Cornelia asked her to say she saw someone, so that we'd keep our eyes off her."

"We'll have to talk with the girl again, in a more methodical interview. Make sure she comes here with her mother."

"Sure."

Lindberg gives Emma a look filled with what she interprets as doubt; he must be wondering whether she can manage everything. She intends to exert herself to the utmost to prove to him that she can. As long as she keeps her blood sugar in check, it should be fine. She just couldn't be careless about eating. She still has high hopes of arresting the guilty party, and she intends to dig in and perform at her best.

"What else do we know about Hans Göransson?" Lindberg says. "Who has he spent time with over the years? But above all, who did he see during his last twenty-four hours of life?"

Two of the detectives have gathered a long list of names. "We've already gone halfway through it and been in contact with several of his former associates, his friends, and his ex-wife, but we haven't managed to track down everybody yet. Of those we've talked with so far, we've hit nothing but dead ends. Everyone has an alibi for that night. But we're still in the process of figuring out exactly who he saw last Monday. He had a number of meetings, according to his secretary."

"Okay, continue going down the list," says Lindberg. "If we go back to who had access to the crime scene the day in question, it was Göransson, his wife, and the real estate agent. No housecleaner or contractors?"

"Yes, the inspector, Konrad Kowalski," says Nyhlén. "But he was at home with his wife the night of the murder."

"Have you double-checked his story?" Lindberg asks, getting a shake of the head in response. "Considering that he has a connection to the victim's house, we ought to at least make sure he really has a wife."

"Duly noted," Nyhlén replies.

"Okay then. Now we're getting to the open house itself. Have you done a search of the prospective buyers we know of?"

One of the analysts nods. "Nothing further to go on there."

"Have you contacted them?" Lindberg asks.

"Yes, most of them. There weren't that many."

"So what did the agent say who is selling the house?" Lindberg says. He reads the name from a report in front of him. "Benjamin Weber?"

"He has a reputation for being an asshole," says Emma.

Lindberg raises his eyebrows. "I prefer facts before rumors. Where did this information come from?"

"That's what lots of people say," Emma replies, to avoid exposing Kristoffer. "He reacted as soon as we mentioned which house we were talking about. Before we even said a word about what happened. I got a feeling that he knew something he didn't want to reveal. And his assistant, Helena Sjöblom, acted nervous in his presence."

"There could be something to that," says Nyhlén. "According to the crime scene report, no doors or windows were unlocked. So the real estate agent may have let the murderer in."

"Or *be* the murderer," Emma adds.

Lindberg clears his throat. "Let me remind you that we aren't brainstorming the plot for a mystery novel now."

"Good thing you pointed that out," Emma says, acting offended.

"Before we bring the wife in," Lindberg says, "it may be worth holding an interview with Weber again. Start at that end instead." Emma nods.

When the meeting is over, Emma goes straight to her

office and calls Cornelia to ask her to bring Astrid and come to the police station as soon as they have a chance. She explains that the specialist in child interviews prefers to meet here and that they'd like to ask Cornelia some supplementary questions anyway. Cornelia sounds reluctant, but she promises to come in about an hour. Emma thanks her and hangs up.

That means she and Nyhlén will have time to go to Weber's office first, exactly according to plan.

31.

When I step into the room, she doesn't react. She is humming a monotonous tune and staring out the window with her back to me. I notice a new hyacinth in a flowerpot on the counter; otherwise, everything is the same. The light-yellow walls are depressing and bare, except for a few drill holes. Maybe the last patient took all the pictures home.

"Hi. How are you?" I ask, sitting down on the bed at a slight distance from her.

The tune fades away, and she turns her head toward me without really seeing me. Her gaze is cloudy. She is too absent to take in what is around her, the doctor says. She is in another world, one that no longer exists, one she refuses to leave.

"Did you come alone again today?" she says, looking disappointed.

"Yes, I had an opening and thought I'd just drop by for a minute."

She shrugs. "I see."

"Did you sleep well?"

"So-so," she says, glancing at the gray clouds. "Looks like there'll be rain today. You didn't forget to take the rain pants to day care, did you?"

I shudder inside and answer with a quick shake of the head, not capable of saying anything.

Suddenly, she looks suspicious. "Why do you seem so uncertain then?"

"Trust me."

I lean forward, place my hand on her knee, and try to see something that reminds me of the woman she once was. But nothing is the same. I want to say something that will make her happy, but I find no words.

"By the way," she says, "was it today the chimney sweep was supposed to come?"

I just nod, exhausted.

"But who's going to meet him if I'm here?"

"I'm keeping track of the time. You can stop worrying about the house," I say, getting only a snort in reply.

But the last part is true. She doesn't need to worry about the house, because it no longer exists.

32.

They made the drive to Weber's real estate agency in Östermalm unnecessarily, it turns out.

"Benjamin's not here today," the woman in reception says.

"For the whole day?" Nyhlén asks. "Where is he? We can go to him if you give us the address."

"I'm afraid that's not possible, unfortunately. He's sick. It sounded like the flu from his description."

Benjamin Weber must have gotten sick in record time, because he didn't show any symptoms last night. If he thinks it's smart to stay away from the police right now, he's wrong. Any attempt at avoidance immediately raises suspicions. Emma is feeling irritated, but she also knows that she's let herself be influenced by Kristoffer's opinion. *A swine.* When she sees Helena Sjöblom go past, she follows her instinct.

"Then we'll be happy to talk with Helena for now," she says.

The receptionist looks uncertain and starts to stutter. "I should ask if she has time to see you."

"She does," says Emma, stepping in and pretending not to notice the woman's attempt to stop her.

Because they are in plainclothes, no one at the office raises an eyebrow, but Helena turns somewhat pale when she sees them approach. Then she forces a smile.

"How can I help you?" she asks tensely.

"We'd like to ask a few more questions."

"Now? I'm right in the middle of—"

"It will only take a few minutes." Emma looks around at the stylish minimalistic designer furniture, all in a narrow range of gray. "Do you prefer here or behind the glass door over there?"

Helena doesn't hesitate. "In the conference room."

Once they are seated in the same spots as yesterday and have gone through all the formalities, Emma leans toward Helena. "How long have you worked here?"

Nyhlén gets to be the assistant and observer this time. She hopes he keeps quiet, because Emma wants to do this her way.

"For a year. Why do you ask?"

"Are you content?"

"No complaints. Again, why do you ask?"

"What is Benjamin like as a boss?"

"Good, but I don't understand. How can that have any significance?"

Emma smiles flatly. "If I ask the questions and you stick to giving answers, it will make it easier for everyone and we all save time. Because you do have a few things to do?"

"But . . . am I suspected of anything?"

"No."

Helena breathes out and becomes more cooperative. Until they come to the sale of the affected property.

"Benjamin is the listing agent and you're the assistant?"

"That's correct," Helena says.

"Do you usually work closely?"

Emma sees a faint blush on Helena's cheeks, and she swears to herself. She can't believe she didn't see right away how things were between them. "How long have you been together?"

"I've worked here for a year, as I said," Helena answers as she starts to pick at her charm bracelet. The charms dangle back and forth on her wrist, and the bracelet rustles now and then in an annoying way.

"So you've been together all that time?"

Helena stares at her. "What are you implying? Benjamin's my boss. Besides, he's married."

"Do you know why he's staying away from the office?" Emma asks. It's better to wait in hopes that Helena will trip herself up.

"He's not staying away, he's sick."

"What do you mean, 'sick'?"

Helena appears to be searching for the right answer. "I don't really know."

"Why are you protecting him? What is he hiding?" Thank God Nyhlén does not interrupt. Emma doesn't intend to leave until she finds out what's going on.

Helena looks distressed. "I don't understand why you're digging into this."

"We're trying to solve a murder," Emma replies. "Everything that has to do with the victim is important."

"But I didn't do anything. Neither did Benjamin."

"How do you know that?"

"I just do."

Emma feels like she's forgetting something important, and then suddenly she remembers.

"According to Cornelia, you were the one who came to the house on Monday and you were there afterward. Where was Benjamin then?"

Helena's fiddling with the bracelet escalates, and the charms jingle continuously, then she looks right at Emma. "He must have already left then."

"Did you see him leave the house?"

"Well—" Helena stops short. "He called good-bye, but I didn't see him drive away, if that's what you're getting at."

"Where were you when he left?"

Helena stares at the table, looking uncomfortable. "In the bathroom."

"Don't you usually leave together?"

"He was in a hurry to go somewhere else."

"And the inspector, had he left yet?"

"Yes, I was the last one there."

Emma leaves her contact information with a request for Helena to call if she thinks of anything else. Or if Benjamin is in touch. They'll take any information they can get.

33.

Seventeen missed calls, the majority from Cornelia Göransson, but also a few from Monika. Benjamin stares at the phone but decides to continue ignoring all the calls, mainly because he can't bear to hear what they want. He can't handle any more hassle now. It's enough that those anal characters from the Estate Agents Inspectorate are after him again. As soon as he gets some wind in his sails, there they are, nosing around for a reason to stop his progress. As if he'd asked to take over his father's agency. Nothing could be further from the truth, and he's tired of the bullshit.

It's never been his thing to run a psychological game of strategy between two parties with diverging interests. Success in the real estate industry requires intuition. It's a difficult balancing act between regulations and those undefined gray areas. Special offers are more rule than exception—why make an issue out of that? But the Estate

Agents Inspectorate probably doesn't have anything better to do. It's damned impossible to follow all the guidelines if you're going to close a sale and earn yourself a buck. Commissions are undercut, and profit margin sinks to the bottom. And right now he has three idle good-for-nothings at the office, who hope that sellers will serve them properties on a silver tray. The country is crawling with real estate agents willing to work, but few succeed in making a career worth the name.

Helena's number blinks on the phone's display. She's one of the agents who actually has all the prerequisites for success, not least of which is the right appearance. He decides to take the call, mostly to hear her sexy voice.

"Where are you?" she almost shrieks when he answers after the fourth ring. It took a little while to get his fly unzipped.

It sounds like she's standing out on the street, because he can hear the sound of rush-hour traffic.

"At home. Are you in the mood?"

"Stop. It's not funny. The police were just here, asking a lot of tough questions. Why are you hiding out?"

That's all he needs. Why have the police turned their attention on him? All he wants to do is mind his own business.

"I'm not feeling well." He does his utmost to sound pitiful.

"Me neither. Don't you understand how sick it made me feel to lie to the police?"

"Lie? About what?" He stops playing with his dick and concentrates on what she has to say.

"The open house—you let me run it myself."

Benjamin changes position in bed, where he is lying, and tries not to let Helena's nervousness rub off on him. "But you didn't mention that, did you?"

"No, of course I didn't. I didn't want to arouse unnecessary suspicions."

Benjamin is thinking that perhaps it wasn't all that prudent to withhold information that's so easy to double-check. Simply by asking the prospective buyers who was there.

"Why didn't you just tell the truth? If I wasn't even at the scene of the crime, they won't think I'm involved in the murder."

"Who said you had anything to do with the murder?" Helena sounds hysterical, almost as if she can't breathe.

"The police aren't saying so flat out, but they're investigating every possible clue that can lead them to the perpetrator. Don't you watch thrillers?" Benjamin says, laughing disarmingly.

"No, I prefer romantic films. About unrequited love."

There is a pounding in his abdomen when she says that. He avoids looking at the photograph on the wall, where he is standing together with his wife in California, at Joshua Tree National Park. At that time, Monika was attractive and willing. They still sleep together regularly—at least twice a year.

"Come here. Then we'll figure everything out," he says, and his hand searches inside his pants again.

"I'm working," she protests.

"You can take time off," he counters, pulling back the foreskin.

"Benjamin, I don't know. It doesn't feel right anymore. I have to—"

"Not now. We'll discuss it when you get here."

As soon as they touch each other, he'll get her to think about other things. She can't resist him; both of them know that. The one talent he definitely has in this life is handling female bodies with precision.

"Just one thing first," he says. "Can you call up Cornelia Göransson and explain that you're taking over the sale? That way, you'll be sure to get a solid reward later," he says. He glances at the growing manhood between his legs, which has satisfied many fortunately favored women over the years. The occasional man too, because no one wants to die curious.

"Sure, boss," she says acidly. "Believe it or not, I got an offer today."

"Someone taking the opportunity to submit a low-ball bid?"

"Not exactly. It's fifty thousand over the asking price."

"I'll be damned."

He knew she was talented, but this still took the cake.

34.

Benjamin Weber seems to have gone underground. He doesn't call back, even though Cornelia has left several messages. Each try was somewhat sharper in tone but evidently not sharp enough for him to pick up the phone. He can't very well treat a customer like this, can he? She has to find out how the sale is going, especially since the only name on the list she saw was the person who was going to help her jack up the price. Cornelia won't go so far as to call him a front—more a kind of guarantee that she'll get an acceptable price. It would be just her luck if his involvement were discovered because of the ongoing police investigation.

Hand in hand, Cornelia and Astrid get off the subway at Rådhuset and take the endless escalator up from underground. She is never going to be friends with the blue line; it's frightening that it's so far belowground. What would happen if a fire started? She knows she needs to do something about her claustrophobia, but it's just one of the anxiety disorders she suffers from. As soon as she is up on the street, at Bergsgatan, she breathes out and her pulse returns to normal—until she remembers what she's doing here. Instantly, she feels pressure in her chest again.

Cornelia has no idea why the police want to see them for further questioning. They must have found something, and she shudders at the thought. Astrid, on the other hand, seems to be looking forward to the visit. She happily skips alongside, humming a song. Cornelia tries to smile but fails, although it's funny that, of all people, it's Josefin's little sister running the investigation. They are extremely different yet alike in some strange way, with the major difference that Emma makes Cornelia nervous. It would be easy to be fooled by her looks and think she doesn't know what she's doing, but it could turn out that she's as calculating as anything. There's no question that she's smart. That's the impression Cornelia has, anyway. And it clearly shows that Josefin has great respect for her sister. It doesn't take more than that for Cornelia to feel at a disadvantage.

They cross on the path through Rådhusparken and approach the entrance to the police station on Kungsholmsgatan. Just as Cornelia is about to open the door, her cell phone rings. She recognizes the Weber real estate agency's main number.

"Cornelia Göransson," she answers.

"Hi. This is Helena Sjöblom. How are you doing?"

"Okay" is the only thing she can get out.

"Is this a bad time to talk?"

Cornelia lets go of the sturdy door handle and backs up. "No, no. It's fine."

Astrid climbs on the railing and tries to do a somersault. Cornelia places herself closer, so that she can prevent a fall against the stone staircase in case her daughter loses hold.

"I'm very sorry for your loss, and I realize the house sale isn't at the top of your list of priorities right now."

Yes, it is, Cornelia thinks, but she answers, "You're right about that."

"Nonetheless, I needed to tell you that there has been a change. Benjamin is sick, so he's turned over the responsibility for the sale to me. I hope you don't have any objections."

"Of course not," Cornelia says without taking time to reflect properly. Actually, Benjamin should have called and told her this himself, and taken the opportunity to express his sympathy. He and Hans had made a special deal, which she hopes will still apply.

The tension in Helena's voice lets up a little. "Then I can tell you that we have an initial offer."

"Really?" Cornelia has to hold in her excitement. "Considering what happened, I wouldn't have expected that. How much is it for?"

"Eleven million fifty thousand."

Sell! she wants to yell, but she stops herself. *Just so it isn't . . . No, it can't be him.* "What's the name of the person who made the offer?"

"Wait. Let me look . . . Henrik J. Carlsson."

Cornelia has to support herself against the railing.

"Does he seem serious?" she manages to force out.

"Extremely."

"Okay, but I guess we should wait and see if any more offers come in during the week. It's silly to get excited and take the first one."

"Well, in your case anyway, you may want to consider—"

Cornelia interrupts Helena abruptly. "I have to run. We'll talk later."

Her heart is pounding as she ends the call, and she struggles not to scream. How could Henrik be so stupid? Now that Hans is dead, he should have waited. But maybe he doesn't know. Cornelia thinks it over and realizes she didn't call him. She swears to herself.

"Hi." Cornelia hears a familiar voice behind her back, and she turns around.

Emma and her associate, whatever his name is, come walking toward the stairs. Cornelia swallows and hopes they didn't hear anything. She had intended to call Henrik at once. Now that will have to wait until after the questioning.

"It's great that you found your way here," says Emma. She tries to greet Astrid, but the little girl doesn't give her so much as a glance. When she's in that mood, there's no point in coaxing. Emma seems to understand.

At the guard desk, Cornelia signs in. Then they follow the line through a rigorous screening checkpoint and into the elevator. The silence is about to suffocate Cornelia when the elevator door closes and they go up. She has nothing to say, and the police don't seem to have any desire to make small talk. Even though they are there in a few seconds, the short ride is a torment. Only when she gets out can she breathe again.

"The room we'll be using is straight ahead and to the right," Emma explains as they walk. "Do you want anything to drink, by the way?"

"Water would be great," Cornelia answers for both of them.

A few minutes later a woman comes and leads Astrid to another room. Cornelia had thought they would be together. Her pulse races and she wants to protest, but she doesn't dare. Then a man approaches. Detective Chief Inspector Lars Lindberg introduces himself, and his sheer authority makes her terrified. Cornelia's voice trembles when she returns the greeting, and she has to force herself not to turn her eyes away. She prays he isn't the one asking the follow-up questions.

35.

E mma can understand that the dark-haired woman sitting across from her isn't grieving her deceased spouse,
considering how he seems to have treated her; it's hard to
imagine being under constant threat from the man you
live with. What Emma doesn't get is why Cornelia gives off
such a nervous vibe. She can't quite figure her out. So the
strategy is to leap between topics to see whether Cornelia's
answers are consistent.

"How did you happen to choose Benjamin Weber as
the real estate agent?" asks Nyhlén, who is leading the
questioning this time. Emma will fill in what Nyhlén
misses.

Lindberg and two colleagues sit in the adjacent observation room, to study Cornelia's expressions and analyze her
responses. If there is anything they want to discuss, they
will knock on the door and interrupt the questioning.

"Benjamin is an old friend of Hans's."

Emma can tell that Nyhlén is sincerely surprised. "Why haven't you mentioned that before?"

"No one asked." Cornelia looks offended. "Is that important?"

"Anything could have significance in a homicide investigation."

"Do you have a suspect?"

"Not yet, but it's only a matter of time," Nyhlén answers to Emma's surprise.

What is he basing that statement on? So far they aren't anywhere near pointing the finger at anyone, even if Benjamin has done his utmost to stand out. Cornelia, too, is high up on the list.

"Were Benjamin and Hans close friends?" asks Nyhlén.

"I don't think they got together socially, but I know they've done business together before."

"Do you know any individuals who had a score to settle with Hans?"

Cornelia shakes her head. "Not that I can think of, but I didn't have anything to do with his professional life. You'd have to check with his work colleagues."

"Do they know about his dark side?" Nyhlén clears his throat. "That he assaulted you?"

"I doubt that. To everyone else, Hans was sociable and upbeat, a master at fooling the people around him. He always spoke well about me and Astrid to others. They must have thought he was a mother-in-law's dream. But as soon as we were alone, it was like he was transformed."

"And you, who have you told this to?"

"Only Josefin. No one else."

"Do you remember the last time he attacked you?"

"Yes, it was the night he died. He chased me up the stairs, took hold of my hair, and banged my head on the doorway to the bedroom." She brings her hand to the side of her head, and her gaze becomes vacant. "I cut my hair short so that he couldn't drag me by the hair again, but it didn't work."

Emma searches for bruises or other signs of injury, but she sees nothing. She is about to ask if she can feel the bump, to be sure it really exists, but that would be going too far.

"Did you and Hans have life insurance?" Nyhlén asks, as if it were a completely natural follow-up question and he didn't already know the answer.

Cornelia is slow to respond. Perhaps she's trying to decide which explanation is most credible. If she should pretend she has no knowledge of this or whether she should tell the truth.

"Doesn't everyone have that these days?" she says, with a shrug. "How else would you be able to stay in your house if your partner passed away?"

"Of course, you were in the process of moving," Nyhlén points out, leaning back. "How much was your policy for, all in all?"

"A few million kronor."

"You don't know more precisely than that?" Emma says. She is trying not to show how skeptical she is when she hears Cornelia's fuzzy figure. "There's a pretty big difference between two and three million."

Cornelia looks perplexed but answers after a brief hesitation.

"Four. I will get almost four million kronor from the insurance company." Her voice is on its way up into falsetto range. "But I would have gladly gone without it just to escape Hans. No money in the world can repair the damage he has caused me and Astrid."

"Why did you wait until January of this year to take out an insurance policy?" Nyhlén asks, showing his hand.

"I know we should have done it sooner, but we just didn't get around to it until then."

"How did you meet Hans anyway?"

Cornelia dries a tear on her cheek. "I was young and stupid. I'm embarrassed to say I was a bit of a gold digger. I saw Hans as a way out of the gloom at home in Östergötland."

"He's quite a bit older than you, right? How big is the age difference?"

"Twenty-one years. I know it seems like a lot, but I was probably looking for a father figure. My dad was never there for me. That is, he was there physically, but never paid any attention to me. And the few times he did, I was reprimanded. Browbeaten. Only got to hear what I had done wrong."

"Can you tell us a little more about that?" Nyhlén says.

"It's hard to explain, but Dad ruled over me, Mom, and my brother. He was extremely dominant and had no empathy at all. I think that explains my lack of self-confidence. The only way to pull through was to escape."

"And then Hans came to the rescue?"

Cornelia laughs, but it sounds more like a snort. "I met him on a trip to Mallorca. I moved to Stockholm as soon as I took the university entrance exam the following year. The worst thing is that my brother stayed behind with my parents. I feel very guilty about that."

Cornelia stops short, and Emma nods to encourage her to continue.

"These days, my brother sends a card on Astrid's birthday, and that's all the contact we have," Cornelia says mournfully. "I haven't had the energy to visit him, and I'm ashamed that I escaped Dad only to end up with an even worse man."

Emma can tell that Nyhlén is moved. He nods at Emma, and she knows to take over.

"How is the house sale going?" she asks.

"I don't really know. It's probably going to be hard now, after what happened. Benjamin Weber has turned over responsibility to Helena, who helped him at the open houses. She and I were talking just before I came here, but she didn't have much to report."

"Then we must have spoken with her at almost the same time as you," Emma says.

"Did she have any news?" Cornelia asks tensely.

"Nothing that we didn't already know," Emma replies. "So, how did your living arrangements look after the move? You were going to move into an apartment after the sale, right? But what about Hans?"

"We never talked about it. I figured that was his business."

"What about Astrid? Had you worked out custody?"

"He proposed shared custody, but I refused. It would be terrible to leave Astrid alone with him. So I asked for sole custody."

But he didn't consent, thinks Emma, sneaking a glance at Cornelia. *That could be the motive. But would Cornelia have had enough nerve to kill her husband for her daughter's sake? Would she even have had the nerve to hire someone?*

Emma wants to have a serious conversation with Josefin right after the interview. To make sure she didn't leave anything out.

36.

Anton is sitting on the seesaw at the playground when Josefin arrives at the school to pick him up. She waves happily in his direction, but he doesn't see her. He seems completely absorbed in his solitary play, which tells Josefin that Astrid is home today.

Her phone rings, and Josefin hesitates. It's lousy timing to take a call. But when she sees it's Emma, she answers anyway.

"Hi. How are you?" Josefin asks.

"We have to talk," says Emma.

"I gathered that, because you're calling." Josefin laughs at her own witticism but notices that she gets no response. "I'm at Anton's school now. Can I call you later?"

"Preferably not. Cornelia and Astrid are here at the police station, and I have to ask a few uncomfortable questions. Can I trust you to be completely honest?"

The mere question suggests that there is doubt. "Come on. I think you know me."

"Sorry. There's a lot going on with the investigation right now. I'm feeling really lousy and dizzy, besides. And I have to keep that to myself so that no one will tell me to go home."

"Maybe you should take a break," Josefin says.

"Not you too," says Emma. "It's not that bad."

"What do you want to know?" Josefin asks, moving to the side so that Anton won't catch sight of her.

"I have to ask a hypothetical question."

"Okay."

"Could Cornelia have been capable of killing her husband?"

As usual, Emma makes no attempt to cushion anything, leaving Josefin temporarily at a loss for words.

"I think she actually was afraid of him," Josefin says after thinking. "Otherwise, wouldn't it have happened sooner?"

"I've thought about that too. Why would she wait so long?"

"Could it have been in self-defense?" Josefin suggests.

"Could be, but there were no signs of a struggle," says Emma. She pauses for effect. "Did you know you're the only one Cornelia confided in about the abuse? Any idea why that would be?"

"Well, we've seen each other quite a bit, because our kids are more or less married to each other. I don't think Cornelia has that many people to talk with. She's a bit of a loner."

"She must have had some nasty injuries," Emma says. But at the same time, Anton shrieks and puts his hand to his cheek. A boy next to him looks guilty, averting his eyes when Josefin looks over.

"I have to hang up. There's a little conflict here on the playground," she says, glaring at the boy. "What was it you said?"

"That Cornelia's injuries must have looked horrible."

The assertion catches Josefin completely off guard. "Now that you mention it, I've never seen anything."

"What do you mean?" Emma exclaims in surprise. "There haven't been any physical signs that Cornelia was assaulted?"

"No, I can't really remember any. I assumed she was trying her best to conceal the injuries. She often wears a scarf. But don't draw any hasty conclusions from that, please. To me, it was obvious that she wasn't making it up."

"Thanks," Emma says, ending the call abruptly.

While walking over to the children, Josefin tries to digest the conversation. She feels like a traitor, but what could she have done differently? She couldn't lie and say she'd seen something, especially not to her sister.

"What's going on here?" Josefin asks the boys as she sees that one of the teachers is approaching.

"He hit me," says Anton.

"Did not," the boy replies.

The teacher makes the children say sorry to each other, but Anton is furious at the injustice. "But he started it." His cheeks are now bright red.

Josefin mumbles something in response as they leave—she hardly knows what. There is too much going on in her head, and the anxiety grows when she thinks about what she and Emma discussed. All she wants is to be a help, not a hindrance, to Cornelia.

37.

Emma missed the one-thirty coffee break but grabs a cup on her way to the conference room. Cornelia and Astrid have gone home, and Emma is curious about how the interview with the girl went. Her cell phone rings as she hurries along the corridor. When she tries to answer, the hot coffee splashes out and burns her hand. She makes a face but still manages to say hello.

"Hi. It's Helena Sjöblom, the real estate agent. You said I should call if I thought of anything else."

Emma goes to her office, sets the mug down on the desk, and wipes off the coffee with a shabby workout towel. "Of course. Let's hear it."

"I don't know if it's important, but I talked with Cornelia Göransson earlier."

"When approximately?"

"Over an hour ago, maybe two."

So before the questioning, exactly as Cornelia said.

Emma stops cleaning up the coffee and concentrates on listening. "What did she say?"

Helena lowers her voice. "I told her that I'm responsible for selling the property now and that an offer has come in at fifty thousand over the asking price."

Emma wonders whether the bidder knows there was a murder in the house. "How did she react to the news?"

"At first, she was all enthused and said that I should accept it."

"But?"

"Well, after I told her the bidder's name, she reversed herself. She said she wanted to wait, to see if any more offers came in. I thought it was strange that she changed her mind so abruptly, especially when we were lucky to get an offer at all right now."

"What's the name of the bidder?"

"Henrik J. Carlsson."

"Does he know about the murder?"

"Not yet. It wouldn't be very good for the sale to bring that up."

"You'll have to, sooner or later."

"Naturally, we'll tell him what happened, but not too soon in the process."

"By the way, have you heard anything more from Benjamin?"

"No," Helena answers, sounding ambivalent.

Emma would like to get more out of Helena, but that will have to wait. She ends the call and slinks into the meeting a few minutes late. "Sorry about that, but the real estate agent, Helena Sjöblom, just called."

"What did she have on her mind?" asks Lindberg.

Emma sits down and gives a summary.

"Wish we would've known about that before we sent Cornelia home," Nyhlén says with a sigh.

Lindberg nods. "But why in the world would Cornelia withhold that information from us?"

"I was thinking about asking this Henrik J. Carlsson that as soon as we're done here," Emma replies. "I just found out something else remarkable when I spoke with my sister. Josefin told me she can't recall ever seeing any bruises on Cornelia, or any other injuries. And Josefin is the only one who knew that Hans hit her."

"So that may mean there wasn't any abuse?" Lindberg asks.

Emma nods hesitantly in response.

"But why would she lie about that?" Nyhlén says.

"In any event," Emma says, "we have to take that possibility into consideration."

"A darn shame we didn't know *that* before she left," Nyhlén says.

The specialist in questioning children then gives her report. It took a lot of coaxing to get Astrid to talk, she says.

"She told me about a man who patted her on the cheek during the night and said she's quite sure it wasn't her dad. If it's true, she probably has a clearer picture of his appearance than she wants to remember, thanks to the glow from the night-light in her room. It may be worth bringing her in to make a composite sketch."

The detective unit's profiler wrinkles his nose. "But why

would a murderer pat her on the cheek? Were they acquainted? In that case, she should have recognized him."

"The little girl said she'd never seen him before."

"Any chance that Cornelia asked Astrid to make it up?" Lindberg asks.

The specialist shakes her head definitively. "That's been ruled out. I tested her story in several ways, so I would have seen through that."

Lindberg crosses his arms. "However, this is an imaginative six-year-old we're talking about."

"Who isn't your average kid," Emma adds. "Does she have a diagnosis?"

"She's been examined by a child psychiatrist," the specialist says, "which resulted in a number of recommendations, but she didn't meet the requirements for a diagnosis."

"For the moment, I think let's focus on Benjamin Weber and Cornelia Göransson," Lindberg says. "We need to know everything about them, and I mean everything." His gaze goes around the table, and everyone nods in response. "Is there anything else?"

A female detective raises her hand. "I got hold of a person who reports that Hans Göransson was with her on Sunday night. She described the evening thoroughly. I found out more than I wanted, to put it mildly."

"So Göransson had a mistress?" Lindberg asks. "In that case, the motive could be jealousy. Perhaps there was no abuse. Perhaps Cornelia found out her husband had been cheating on her, so she murdered him."

"It's conceivable," Emma says. "But there's still something

that doesn't add up. In the previous interview, Cornelia stated that Hans was standing by the bedroom door watching her on Sunday night—that is, the night before the murder. So if Hans wasn't at home that night, who was it?"

"The same man who patted Astrid on the cheek?" Nyhlén suggests.

Everyone in the room is silent until Lindberg says, "But why would the perpetrator be in their home the night before the murder?"

"Maybe the perp was waiting for Hans, but he never came home," Nyhlén says.

Emma looks at them. "Or else Cornelia is lying."

38.

Now, in hindsight, Cornelia frets over the fact that she just didn't tell the truth to the police; she should have mentioned something about the offer. At the same time, why would it matter to the investigation? If it comes up, she can always say she didn't understand that it was important.

Cornelia looks at her daughter, who is lying stretched out on the couch. Astrid whined the whole way home from the police station and refused to listen to anything Cornelia said. Once they were inside, she went straight to the couch. She didn't want a snack, not even a cinnamon roll. Maybe she's getting sick. Cornelia goes over and places a hand on her forehead. It seems a bit too warm, but she didn't think to bring a thermometer with her, so she can't check for a fever. She tucks Astrid in with a blanket and sits beside her.

All of a sudden, Astrid starts whining again, but Cornelia

ignores her and tries to concentrate on the news she's reading on her phone. There are several articles about the murder of Hans. The descriptions are graphic, without really saying anything at all. The house and the neighborhood are mentioned, but police are holding on tightly to the little else they know. No progress in the investigation is presented except on one site, where an anonymous source maintains that police are close to an arrest. *Surely, that's just a wild rumor,* Cornelia thinks, *even if that detective, Nyhlén, also insinuated that.* But if that were true, wouldn't she have been informed first, since she's the closest relative?

Cornelia looks again at Astrid, who is breathing heavily. She looks so little and innocent lying there with her favorite teddy bear in her arms. Cornelia feels bad that she's been so hard on her daughter. It's to be expected that Astrid would be upset and whiny after the police interrogation. The last few days have turned their existence upside down. Suddenly, they are living somewhere else, just the two of them. In an apartment with borrowed toys. It has to be confusing, especially for a child who needs structure and routines. Cornelia vows to bring the rest of Astrid's toys here as soon as she can, to make it nice for her sake, even if they won't be staying here long-term.

She can't bear to think that Astrid saw Hans after he was murdered. All the blood on the walls, the frightfully surreal sight. The image is so clear and detailed that Cornelia has to rush to the bathroom, but nothing comes up when she leans over the toilet. When she collects herself, she calls Henrik, who answers on the first ring.

"Why did you already make an offer?" she says after she identifies herself.

"I was just doing as I was told." His voice sounds almost scornful.

"But no one asked you to start the bidding, did they? Now that could make trouble for both of us."

Cornelia goes into the kitchen so as not to disturb Astrid.

"How's that?" he asks. "And by the way, why are you calling and not Hans?"

"Because he's no longer alive."

"What the hell are you talking about?" Henrik exclaims.

"He was murdered in our house on Monday night, the day after the second open house. Haven't you seen the news?"

"No. Why didn't you call me sooner?" The contemptuous tone was back.

"I've been a bit held up—being interrogated by the police."

"Then it probably won't be long before they're knocking on my door. Thanks so fucking much."

"Lay off with your self-pity," Cornelia says. She wonders where her cockiness is coming from, considering that she's actually afraid of Henrik. "You don't have anything to do with the murder, do you?"

"Of course not, but I did make an offer on the house. My whole operation could be discovered because of your misstep—do you get that?"

Cornelia couldn't care less.

"To make matters worse, I'm the only one who has made an offer. Shit!"

"What do we do now?"

"I have to withdraw it right away."

"Can't we wait a few days until things have calmed down? Keep a cool head until more offers come in."

"What do you mean, 'a cool head'?" Henrik mutters, and says something she can't make out, but she's pretty sure is "bitch."

Then he slams down the receiver.

Her legs are shaky as she goes back to Astrid asleep on the couch. It's not even four o'clock yet, but Cornelia also wants to fall asleep, to escape all the worries that are twirling around her head, to let the rest of this awful day disappear. She feels as if she could use a serious cry, but no tears come. All the worry is about to suffocate her, the anxiety about being alone with her anguish and all the decisions that have to be made. She tries calling Josefin, but after three rings there is suddenly a busy signal.

When she thinks about it, she decides that Henrik's anger is justified. She should have called him right away and called off his assignment, effective immediately. Now his side business could end up in the spotlight, gaining her nothing but a new enemy. As if she doesn't have enough as it is, with an entire police unit keeping their eyes on her.

The one time she met Henrik was enough to convince her that he'll stop at nothing to get what he wants. The man's contact network is enormous, and he can surely do whatever he thinks is required.

Cornelia nestles closer to Astrid and feels the dampness in her eyes leaking out.

39.

enrik J. Carlsson does not look a bit surprised at the unannounced visit when he opens the door to his apartment. Emma and Nyhlén introduce themselves and ask if they can come in. At first, Henrik doesn't reply, but then he backs up so they can squeeze in. A strong aroma of cologne hovers like a cloud in the hallway, but remnants of pungent underarm sweat penetrate through. In the tiny hall, there is unopened mail on the laminate floor, and there are shopping bags full of old newspapers and empty cans; Norrlands Guld is apparently the beer of choice. Judging by the shoes and coats lying around and the bare walls, Emma figures Henrik lives alone.

So she is surprised when she steps into the living room, which doesn't look bad at all. The expensive designer furniture is unexpected, and the room is tidy, which may explain the bags of trash in the hall.

"Have a seat," says Henrik, wiping the sweat from his forehead. "I'm just going to open a window."

Emma sits down on a black leather couch and decides not to point out that she feels cold. Henrik opens the window wide and then sits down in an armchair across from her.

"I have a lot to do today. How long do you think this will take?" he asks, fingering a piece of paper impatiently.

Emma sees that they are tickets with today's date on them.

"Well, we're here to gather information in a homicide investigation, and that's probably higher priority than a soccer match," she says matter-of-factly. Out of the corner of her eyes, she sees a quick smile from Nyhlén, who always praises her for her capacity to pick up on things.

"It's a derby, damn it," Henrik mutters.

Emma doesn't intend to give up any leads. She has laid out a strategy for the interview that will quickly reveal whether Henrik is going to be straight with them.

"Do you know this woman?" she asks, showing a picture of Cornelia.

Henrik looks like he's trying to remember.

"Göransson," Emma prompts. "Does that sound familiar?"

"I can't place her," Henrik says, pushing the picture away a little too quickly to look nonchalant.

Emma firmly moves the photo back, almost in front of his nose. "Are you quite sure of that? Take a good look. We have all the time in the world."

She can almost see how his thoughts are fluttering around and how hard it is for him to guide them where he wants. But at last, he chooses the altogether most complicated path.

"No, I don't think I've ever seen her before."

Emma suppresses an audible sigh. "You don't think? So you're not certain?"

Henrik looks concerned. "Has she done something illegal?"

"Maybe we should continue questioning you at the station," Emma says.

"Shouldn't it be the other way around?" he protests. "That I don't need to go in to the station because I don't know this Cornelia."

Emma looks at him in triumph. Waits for him to realize that he just gave himself away.

"What is it?" he asks. "Did I say something strange?"

"How did you know her name is Cornelia if you have no idea who she is?"

"You said her name just now."

"Göransson, yes. But not her first name." A trick that usually produces results.

Henrik collapses. "Okay, I give up. I admit it was stupid, but I thought you'd be done quickly if I pretended I didn't know her."

Emma can't sound anything other than acid. "But now you've decided that you do?"

"What does it matter? What's the deal?"

"So you do know who this is?"

When Henrik doesn't answer, Emma continues.

"You were at an open house at the Göransson family's house in Bromma on both Sunday and Monday. Was it nice?"

Henrik nods.

Emma looks around his two-room apartment and wonders if he can tell that her thoughts are spinning away. And what the natural follow-up question will be: How did he intend to finance an expensive house with only this apartment as a down payment? They've already checked whether he owns any other property, which is not the case.

"Can you describe the open houses?"

"Describe them? What do you mean? I walked around the house the way you usually do."

"Did you notice anything different? Anyone who behaved out of the ordinary?"

Henrik thinks for a moment, looking perplexed. "No, but I don't see why you're asking."

"Because a man was found dead in the house the day after the second open house."

Henrik immediately shows surprise, but Emma can tell that he already knew.

"Do you remember the real estate agents who were there?" Nyhlén asks.

"Benjamin Weber is well-known, of course, but I talked quite a bit with the woman who was there both days. I don't remember her name."

"How did Benjamin behave on Monday?"

"Benjamin? He was only there on Sunday."

Emma cannot keep from gasping. "So you're saying that only the female real estate agent was present on Monday? Are you sure of that?"

"A hundred percent. And there was an inspector who stood there babbling in a corner."

It only took a glance from Emma for Nyhlén to understand that the evening was far from over. Over the last two years, they've developed their own wordless way of communicating with each other. From the look she gave him, he'd know that Benjamin Weber has a few things to explain, and Emma doesn't intend to let that go until tomorrow.

Henrik drums his fingers impatiently on his soccer tickets. "Was there anything else?"

"Were you thinking about moving there alone?" Emma can't keep from asking.

"Is there something wrong with that?"

Emma ignores the counterquestion. "Well, I was just wondering how you planned to finance the house. We're talking about several million kronor."

"What the hell is this about? Why do you sound so accusatory? I'm just a simple prospective buyer."

"Because we're working on a homicide investigation, and you're giving us the impression that you're withholding important information."

Henrik's face turns bright red. "How can you maintain something like that? I let you into my home, just like that. I expected to be treated with respect. I don't intend to say another word without a lawyer."

"Take it easy," Nyhlén says. "We're just wondering why you didn't tell us that you've made an offer."

"What does that matter?" Henrik asks, unable to hide his panic.

"How do you explain that the seller wanted to accept the offer until she heard your name?"

Henrik shrugs. "No frigging idea. I'm no mind reader. Ask Cornelia."

40.

It's almost impossible to make out what Henrik is saying, because he's swearing like a sailor. Cornelia can picture the saliva spraying out of his mouth as the furious tirades pour out of him. What possessed her to answer the phone just now, when she knew it was him? At first, she had the idea that he would be calling with good news now. Perhaps that someone else had made a higher offer. But his fury can mean only one thing: that the police have been in contact with him and it didn't go very well. Just as she is about to click "Off," he roars, "Don't you even think about hanging up!"

Cornelia looks nervously around the apartment; he can't very well know what she's doing right now, right? She goes over to the window and peers at the cars parked on the street. Even if someone were spying from there, they wouldn't see far into the room. Astrid is still asleep, thank goodness, so she doesn't have to see her mother upset.

"What do you want me to do?" she asks, resigned.

"Call up the real estate agent and say that you were confused when you last spoke with her and that you have to digest what happened before you can make a decision about selling the house. Put the shit on pause."

"Why?" She did not want to wait a second longer than necessary to sell.

"You have to ask her to withdraw the listing. Say you can't bear to go through with it now. She'll understand that, because your husband just died."

Cornelia shakes her head. "I'm sorry, but it's not possible."

"You're going to have to make it possible. You sicced the police on me. Now you'd damn well better put everything right. Otherwise . . ."

"Otherwise, what?"

"How is Astrid doing?" Henrik says in a completely new, chilling tone of voice.

Cornelia turns completely cold and then looks at her sleeping daughter on the couch. The teddy bear has fallen to the floor, and she picks it up. "I'll talk with the real estate agent."

"Tonight."

"As soon as we hang up," Cornelia replies.

Henrik signs off with another swear word.

Cornelia pounds the phone against her head. First hard, then even harder. Everything is going wrong. She wants to pull on the emergency brake, but she doesn't know if there even is one.

"Why are you doing that?" Astrid suddenly asks.

Cornelia, startled, stops hitting herself with the phone.

"I don't know, honey. Grown-ups do strange things sometimes," she answers. Then she sees that it's already past six. "Do you want to lie down in bed instead?"

"Not really, 'cause I'm done sleeping," Astrid says, sounding as energetic as anything.

Cornelia sighs to herself. As if it weren't enough that she'll be up all night going over everything, now she'll have company.

41.

Benjamin strokes Helena's shoulders with his finger-tips and then rolls her over onto her back. Decides it's worth making another attempt before the candles in the silver candelabra go out.

"We can't keep on like this," she protests, but he can tell she doesn't mean it. What she's really trying to say is that he should take her again, but harder this time. Preferably with her face turned toward the bay window, which looks out onto the open setting of the lot.

But while he tries to seduce her, she is as compliant as a refrigerator with a childproof lock. The magic dies completely when a shrill ringing cuts through the air. It takes a while before he realizes what is making the sound. If it weren't for the bill that shows up quarterly, he would have forgotten the existence of the landline. Reluctantly, he gets out of the bed with built-in massage and adjustable head-board, slapping his feet across the whitewashed pine floor, and reaches for the receiver on the marble countertop. He is about to hang up when he hears a sharp voice on the other end.

"Hello? Benjamin?"

Dutifully, he puts the receiver to his ear and rolls his eyes at Helena.

"Finally. I was beginning to think I'd never get hold of you."

Monika's voice makes him wobbly.

"Hi there."

"How are you?" she asks without sounding the least bit interested in his reply.

"I'm just fine. Yourself?"

"I don't know. Should I have to read about a murder at one of your open houses on the news sites? You could have called. Didn't you know I'd be worried?"

"But you're busy at the conference. You don't have time to think about anything else, do you? I didn't want to disturb you when there was really no reason."

Monika laughs dryly. "Well, it would still be nice to hear from you every once in a while, so I know if my husband is alive."

"I am," he says, making a gesture to Helena to stay put when she looks like she's about to get up. She won't get away that easily.

"You sound different," Monika says. "Has anything happened that I ought to know about?"

Besides the fact that I'm having hot sex with one of my employees? Benjamin keeps that to himself.

"Everything is as it should be. Don't you worry. Was there anything in particular you wanted, other than checking in to make sure I'm alive?"

"I just wanted to let you know I'll be staying here over the weekend—if that's okay."

Benjamin doesn't even bother to ask why, for the simple reason that he doesn't care. "That suits me fine, actually. I still have a lot of business to take care of."

He almost shudders at the game they're playing. Why even make the effort to communicate with each other? She doesn't really care about him, as long as everything looks good to the outside world. The kids have moved out and wouldn't be noticeably affected by a divorce. But he doesn't have the energy to deal with that. And besides, Monika loves this house on Drottningholm. It's probably the main reason she stays.

"Okay then. Kiss."

"Hug." Benjamin hangs up, sets the receiver to the side, and then looks at Helena. "Where were we before we were interrupted?"

She shakes her head. "I was going to take a shower. That's where we were."

Disappointed, he watches as she gets up from the bed, but he decides it's pointless to try to coax forth an erotic atmosphere. Monika succeeded in destroying that.

A car brakes outside the house, and Benjamin goes over to the window to see if it's a tourist who got lost. Then he discovers two familiar figures getting out. He takes a deep breath and tries to locate his bathrobe.

"What the hell now?" he mutters to himself, going toward the stairs. "Will this never end?"

42.

The first thing Emma glimpses is a face in an upstairs window. The face pulls back as they approach the house. Benjamin Weber can't be that sick if he's on his feet. Of course, it might have been someone else. Emma couldn't tell if it was a woman or a man before the person disappeared. The top floor is dark apart from a faint, swaying glow of light somewhere. Candles, perhaps.

"So they hired a shill," Nyhlén notes, who still has Henrik J. Carlsson on his mind. "What do we do with him?"

"He's certainly not a sympathetic character, but he's not the one who murdered Hans."

"I don't think so either. He would never have made himself so visible by making an offer," Nyhlén says.

"I have a hard time believing he would have made an offer at all if he'd known the circumstances," Emma says, taking the opportunity to briefly answer the messages Kristoffer has sent. He wants her to meet him at an address she doesn't know, and she asks what's going on, but he answers that it's a surprise. Not inclined for any adventures tonight, she texts back that she has to work late. A new message from Hugo pops up. She erases it without reading it and tries not to let his insistence affect her mood.

"No one could be that dense," Nyhlén says, and Emma tries to remember what they were just talking about, her multitasking capacity failing her. "Let's just tell Lindberg about Carlsson," Nyhlén continues. "Then he can decide what to do about him. Ready for new challenges?"

"Sure thing." Emma has her sights set on Weber's fin de siècle villa.

Benjamin opens the door before they even reach it. He looks paler than last time, with red eyes and tousled hair.

"I'm sick," he says, coming out in his bathrobe and standing on the stone stairs so that the entry is blocked.

"We need to talk with you. May we come in for a moment?" Emma asks.

Benjamin sighs and backs up. "Sure, come on in."

"Is your wife at home?"

"Monika? No, she's out of town," he answers.

"I thought I saw someone standing by the top-floor window when we arrived," Emma says. "Was that you?"

"It was me." Helena appears. Her hair looks disheveled. Her clothes are wrinkled and somewhat crooked.

Benjamin glares at Helena but keeps quiet.

"It's just as well that we tell the truth before it goes too far." Helena's voice barely holds, and her gaze is fixed on the floor.

"Easy for you to say," Benjamin mutters, pulling on the belt around the bathrobe.

"What is it we ought to know?" Emma asks, hoping the investigation is about to get a shove in the right direction. Often it's hard to predict when that will happen. Maybe now, maybe never.

"We're a couple, just like you thought." The words come like a whisper from Helena's lips.

"Is that all?" Emma can barely conceal her disappointment.

Helena raises her eyebrows inquisitively. "For us, of course it's extremely important, because it means we both have an alibi for the night of the murder."

You've got to be kidding, thinks Emma. *How reliable is an unfaithful couple watching each other's backs?*

Despite the awkward circumstances, Benjamin's shoulders appear to lower a bit.

"Are the details of the investigation going to be available to the public?" Benjamin asks.

"Everything will be sealed as long as an indictment has not been made."

"But then . . . what happens then?" Benjamin looks like he's pleading with Emma.

"Then the preliminary report will be public."

The answer makes him shut his eyes and scratch himself on the back of the neck. Helena does not appear as dejected as her lover.

"So the two of you have an alibi, you say. Where were you that night?" Emma asks.

"We were at my place," Helena answers. Benjamin looks up and confirms by nodding curtly, but he still appears to be occupied by other thoughts.

"There's something else, though," says Nyhlén. "Why did you lie about Monday's open house?"

Helena and Benjamin exchange glances, but they look like they don't know what he's talking about.

"What do you mean?" Benjamin says.

"Why didn't you tell the police that you weren't at the open house?" Nyhlén says.

Benjamin shakes his head. "Sorry, that was stupid."

"It was my fault," Helena says. "I was afraid it wouldn't look good if the listing agent wasn't there. That's why I didn't mention it."

"But don't you realize it looks suspicious when it comes out after the fact?" Emma asks. "Did you know about this, Benjamin?"

He nods mutely.

"What were you doing that was so important that it was worth lying about?"

"A doctor's appointment. I can prove it if necessary."

Helena looks crestfallen. "I just wanted to help Benjamin. I didn't mean to create problems for you. Please forgive me."

Nyhlén and Emma sigh at the same time. Now it would be back to square one. They'd have to hope Benjamin and Helena understand the consequences of what they did—they've wasted valuable police time by keeping their infidelity secret. It wasn't the first time, however, that a sensitive extramarital affair stood in the way of the truth.

The listless atmosphere in the car is almost suffocating on the way back to the city. As they cross the Drottningholm Bridge and pass the turnoff toward the Nockeby neighborhood, Emma's thoughts turn to Josefin. She sounded depressed on the phone before, which isn't hard to understand. What a nightmare position to be in—to have to answer questions about something her friend told her, something that was shared in strictest confidence. Emma wonders how her sister would react if she found out that Cornelia is the only one the police haven't been able to remove from the possible suspect list yet.

43.

Josefin knows she should call Cornelia and ask how it went with the police, but she doesn't have the energy. Mostly she doesn't know what to say. The conversation with Emma still torments her, and she racks her brain, trying to remember a bruise or even a little redness on Cornelia's skin, without success.

"What are you thinking about?" Andreas asks when their paths cross in the first-floor hallway after a drawn-out bedtime procedure. The kids are having a hard time settling down lately, maybe because they sense the tension between their parents.

Tentatively, he places his hand on her shoulder, but she quickly pulls away and looks at him with distaste. She thinks about the receipts she found in his office and argues with herself about whether she should confront him. Last summer, Andreas told her he was starting to train for this year's Stockholm Marathon, but she hasn't seen a trace of him in running shoes. Now she knows why: he's been running after women instead.

"There's a lot going on in my head right now," she says. "I don't know which dilemma I should think about first."

"Same here," he says. "Have you thought any more about what we talked about?"

Josefin is dumbfounded by his gentle tone, as if they faced the difficult choice of whether to take a family vacation trip to Thailand or the Maldives.

"I think it's more like you're the one who ought to be thinking about what you want. And why you decided to hurt me by going behind my back."

Andreas sighs. "It wasn't my intention to hurt you. But I was hoping we could talk about it like two adult people."

"Talk about it like two adult people," she mimics and walks away. Even she has her limits.

She can't possibly bear to hear one more word about his midlife crisis, which is clearly getting the best of him. She feels a strong desire to tear down the black-and-white enlargement from their wedding, but she stops at the stairs and studies the photograph instead. Tries to understand that the man in the picture has lied to her, has been unfaithful, and hasn't had the courage to tell her the truth.

Exhausted, she sits down on the stairs with the messy hallway as a backdrop. Julia's roller skates and helmet are thrown in a pile on the floor. Three backpacks and Anton's dirty rubber boots sit alongside. Normally, such a sight would either make her cry or provoke her into action, putting everything in order and then throwing out a few bitter comments at the children the next morning. But she sits here as if petrified, just staring at the mess.

"Are you sitting here?" Andreas approaches with two cups of steaming tea in his hands. "Would you like one?"

It would be nice, but she says no anyway. "I'm not in the mood."

"Do you want to talk about Cornelia?"

The need to express the guilt she feels at what she and Emma discussed is enormous, but when she looks at him she can't make herself. "No, I'd rather not."

"I understand," he answers. "But I still want you to listen to what I have to say."

She gives a barely perceptible nod while he sets the mugs down on the bench in the hall, moves a fleece sweatshirt aside, and sits down on the edge. They have never sat here in the hall and talked before, and it feels unnatural. Josefin listens for a sound from upstairs so that she has an excuse to leave, but the children seem to have fallen asleep at last.

"I promised to live with you until death do us part," Andreas begins solemnly, glancing at the wedding photo, but Josefin is already starting to stand up. She doesn't want to hear this pathetic drivel.

"Let me finish." The angry tone in his voice makes her sink down on the hard step again. It's dusty too, with strands of hair everywhere. She pulls her finger along the edge and studies the dirt in detail. They shouldn't have chosen a white staircase.

"I have been loyal and faithful to you—you know that," he continues. "You've always been able to rely on me completely, but what has happened now I think is due to something greater than a promise. Life."

Josefin wonders what Andreas is really trying to say, as he continues his sermon.

"Life goes on in the here and now, and I don't know how long I can go on feeling the way I have recently. There's always this nagging worry about not being loved—and liked—for who I am. All I hear from you is what I do wrong. Sure, the criticism is justified sometimes, but I don't have the energy anymore to try to be the one I *believe* you want. I'm me. And I love you. But my perception of you is that you mostly think I'm in the way. So I guess what I'm trying to say is that I'm no longer able to try to live up to the dream image you have of a man."

Her eyes narrow when she looks at him. "You've already crushed that image completely. By lying to me right in my face."

"What do you mean?" Andreas asks, but he looks a shade paler.

"I found the receipts from a night at a hotel. Double room."

Andreas shakes his head. "So you've been rooting in my drawers now too?"

Instead of offering a reasonable explanation or asking for forgiveness, he gets up and stomps past her up the stairs. Then he closes the door to the bathroom with a slam, despite the fact that the children are asleep in the next room. The lock clicks. His untouched teacup is still on the bench.

Josefin tries to take in what Andreas just said, to

understand what made him cross the line and put their marriage at risk. Is there any way to repair the damage? She doesn't know. Right now she has a very hard time seeing how she could ever forgive him.

44.

Lindberg sounds just as gloomy as Emma feels when she calls him from the car to report on their latest interview. Dark clouds are visible through the windshield, matching the mood.

"How do you assess their credibility?" he asks.

The phone connection drops for a second, and Emma sees that she's the one who has poor coverage.

"I believe them," Emma says, "although it's clearly a drawback that Helena lied about Benjamin's presence at the open house. He maintains that it conflicted with a doctor's visit."

"I'd really like to see proof of that appointment before I let him off the hook completely," Lindberg says. "It must have been something serious if he was at the doctor at six o'clock in the evening."

"I know, but if he wasn't at the scene he's probably not the one we're looking for. Isn't it time to bring Cornelia in again?" Emma asks. "At the moment, most everything points to her."

"Yes, but it won't hold up. I've already discussed the case with the prosecutor. As long as we only have circumstantial evidence, it's not sufficient for an arrest."

"Circumstantial evidence?" Emma repeats in frustration. "No one broke into the house, she was the one who wanted a divorce, and the murder weapon is from their kitchen. Not to mention the new information about a mistress, and that no one can confirm that Hans abused her."

"But according to the daughter, another man was in their house during the night. We can't overlook that."

Emma snorts. "I still think Cornelia may have put that into the kid's head."

"Not according to the child specialist. We'll have to try a new tactic tomorrow."

Nyhlén shakes his head when the call is over. "I agree with you about Cornelia, but there isn't much we can do if the prosecutor is opposed."

"There must be something else we can do," she sighs, taking a sandwich out of her bag.

After work, Emma just wants to go home, put some old clothes on, and laze around, but Kristoffer has other plans. He'd better not have made a restaurant reservation and think she'll be happy about it. If he did, she'll just have to be honest and tell him that she can't handle it. The long workday with all the dashing back and forth has used up her energy. And she hasn't been in the best mood since the setback with Weber. Sure, Benjamin is a slimy character, but he seems too occupied with his lover to have carried out a murder.

"You can let me off here," says Emma when they get to Vasastan, thanking Nyhlén for the ride.

"See you tomorrow," he answers.

She double-checks that she's at the right address, because Kristoffer is nowhere to be seen. It turns out she's three blocks away. As if that weren't bad enough, it's starting to rain. Emma has no umbrella, and she quickens her pace. Her stomach tightens, and she slows down again when she remembers the midwife's advice about taking it easy: *If you're stressed, the child is stressed.* Even if the midwife was annoying, perhaps that advice at least is worth following. Emma is so absorbed in her thoughts she literally jumps when a car brakes abruptly right beside her, so close that she feels the heat from the hood. The window on the passenger side glides down, and she sees Kristoffer's broad grin.

"Hey, good-looking, want to get in?" he says.

Emma sees that there are only five meters left to her destination. "I think I'll walk the rest of the way," she says.

He double-parks and gets out, not a bit concerned that he's blocking half the street plus the car he's pulled up alongside. "You're looking incredible."

Right now she appreciates his talent for lying convincingly, because she knows she looks terrible. "What's the plan? I have to admit I'm longing to go to bed," she says, giving him a hug.

She sees hope ignited in his eyes. "Me too."

"To sleep. Don't get carried away."

"Who said you need to be awake? The main thing—"

"Quiet," she says. "You're off your rocker."

"Have I ever claimed otherwise?" Kristoffer laughs and then nonchalantly waves a bunch of keys. "Come with me. I have something to show."

What has he done? she thinks. Kristoffer's impulsiveness worries her.

"You haven't bought an apartment without checking with me first? Just so you know, I wouldn't be happy. It's important to me that we make a joint decision."

Kristoffer slows his pace and turns around with a grimace. "I'm not that crazy. We're just going to check out a place. Try to relax and trust me or you'll ruin the surprise. You don't always have to be in control."

"Sorry," she answers, embarrassed. "I'm going to blame the hormones. And a rough day at work."

"Are you making progress?" he asks, holding the door open for her.

"Everything fell apart right before I came here. I neither can nor want to talk about it."

"I see." Kristoffer looks sullen.

The elevator has room for only two people, and they have to squeeze together to fit. When the door closes, he embraces her and they kiss on the ride up. At first, she's not at all eager for intimacy, but slowly she gets in the right mood—almost to the point that she is disappointed when the elevator rocks to a stop. Kristoffer goes ahead toward an apartment door without a nameplate. He unlocks it and the white iron security grate hidden behind it. Then he disables the alarm and turns around.

"Welcome," he says triumphantly, stepping aside so that Emma can get past. "What do you think?"

Hesitantly, Emma goes into the entryway, wondering what has gotten into Kristoffer. From a display on the wall, he turns on the lights. Evidently, the gadget is connected to a speaker system too, because a ballad starts playing with a beautiful piano intro. But instead of being swept along by the romantic gesture and spontaneity, Emma feels ill at ease. And once her fault-finding capacity is activated, it's nearly impossible to stop.

Even from the hall, it's apparent that the apartment is expensive. It looks like a showroom for Svenskt Tenn or another upscale store, with all of the exclusive designer furnishings. Surely the owner doesn't want them running around here.

"Whose apartment is this?" she says. "And why do you have the keys?"

Kristoffer rolls his eyes. "It's for sale, but the seller doesn't want to advertise it publicly. I did private showings here all day, and then I started to get interested myself."

He embraces her, but she pulls away.

"What's bothering you?" he asks.

"The fact that we're here in the evening. Doesn't anyone live here?"

"No, they live abroad half the year. They're thinking about getting something smaller in Stockholm instead of this four-room."

Four rooms and a kitchen. Four beautiful rooms with a sizable kitchen. A penthouse apartment in Vasastan with exposed wood beams, a sloping roof, and whitewashed walls.

"If you don't like it, we can leave." Kristoffer doesn't even try to hide how offended he is.

Emma smiles. "If I don't like it? Are you joking?"

No one she knows has this nice a place. She walks around and notes that the bedrooms face a lovely inner courtyard with typical Stockholm facades, giving off *Karlsson-on-the-Roof* storybook vibes. When she looks out the window, the rain seems to have stopped. She allows herself to be swept up in the intoxication of the apartment for a while, getting lost in dreams of what it would be like to live here together with Kristoffer and the baby. It's too good to be true. She bumps into reality: there's no room in the elevator for a stroller.

"What are you thinking about?" Kristoffer asks.

"It doesn't matter. It's too expensive, in any case."

He pulls her next to him and kisses her again. "Don't think about that now. I knew you had good taste. You like me."

"I don't just *like* you," she says quietly. "I love you."

45.

The first article I find on the Internet is about a woman who had intended to move, but due to the murder of Hans Göransson no longer dares to sell her house. Talk about having a high opinion of yourself. Just because someone else was murdered after holding an open house doesn't mean everyone who is selling a house is going to be a victim. The probability that something would happen to her is so small she ought to be ashamed to show her mug in one of Sweden's most widely read newspapers. That, if anything, puts her at risk.

I scroll down to see what the police have to say.

A media spokesperson maintains that they have high hopes of quickly solving the case. A little farther down, I find an interesting tidbit: an interview with the man the police should have their eyes on. As usual, he only offers empty rhetoric.

It's repugnant to see his false face with his wide row of

teeth, yet I can't look away. I've heard that you should face your worst fears, something I've tried to remember. So I sit here glaring at him—true, only by way of a still photo on a cell phone, but even so.

Are you lying sleepless now, wondering what this means?

The man in the picture doesn't change his expression, but I choose to answer his smile.

Soon his expression's going to stiffen for good.

46.

THURSDAY, APRIL 3

Emma enters the police station just after seven in the morning. Lindberg runs into her in the corridor and reports that he just got off an important call with one of Hans Göransson's former colleagues, Bengt Roos.

"He seemed to have something to tell me, but I couldn't get him to talk about it on the phone under any circumstances," Lindberg says. "Can you and Nyhlén drive out to Täby right away?"

Emma nods and notes the man's address. Conveniently, Nyhlén steps out of the elevator just then, and she only needs to gesture for him to understand that it's time to get back on again. Because it's still before rush hour, the drive to Roos's house is smooth and takes less than half an hour.

The aroma of fresh-brewed coffee makes Emma perk up after a restless, almost sleepless night. A cup would be welcome now. But as they step into Bengt Roos's drably furnished entryway, her nose itches. It must be the incense sitting on a shelf by the coat rack. An odor she associates with unpleasantness.

"Sit down on the couch in the living room, and I'll be right out with coffee," Roos says with an American accent.

Despite the early hour, he is already dressed in a suit and tie, presumably on his way to a meeting. Emma takes off her shoes when she sees the Oriental rug that covers almost the entire floor. Not something for muddy April shoes with bits of sharp gravel stuck on the soles. As she passes the mirrored doors, it's like stepping into another world: African masks and dream catchers cover the walls, along with dried plants in frames and mounted animals.

"We travel a lot, my wife and I."

Emma turns around and nods at Roos. "I would have guessed that."

"She works for Doctors Without Borders, so she's away for long stretches, like right now. It's lonely, but nice in some ways. It keeps the relationship fresh."

"And you work in real estate?"

"I did. For the past few years I've been involved in an aid project in Bangladesh, where we're building new communities with better standards for the local population," Roos explains, setting a tray down on the oak table in front of the couch. "May I pour you some?"

"Yes, thanks," Nyhlén and Emma answer in chorus.

"How nice that you could come right away," Roos says. "I have an important meeting at quarter past eight, so I wanted to meet you before that."

There is something about Roos's way of emphasizing the

end of every word that irritates Emma. Perhaps because it sounds forced, as if he's trying to sound American. His origin is of no importance to them, so Emma sets questions about his accent aside so as not to make him self-conscious. But mainly so that he'll get to the point.

"We understand that you and Hans Göransson were good friends," she says. "I'm sorry about what happened."

Roos sinks back in a rustic leather armchair that creaks under his considerable body mass. "It's unreal that he's no longer here. I don't understand who would wish him harm."

"How did you find out?"

"I read about the murder in the newspaper and got worried when I realized it happened at a house that was for sale in Bromma. The description fit Hans's house exactly—something like a 'large white house at one of Bromma's best addresses, a stone's throw from the harbor.' So first I called Hans, and when I didn't get an answer, I tried Cornelia. I called the police as soon as I heard they were trying to reach me."

"We're contacting everyone in the Göranssons' circle of acquaintances," Emma explains. "Did your families socialize?"

Roos picks up his coffee mug but doesn't drink. It rests in his hands while he appears to be searching for the right wording. "Not exactly. It was mostly Hans and I who got together after work sometimes."

Emma senses that there's something else he wants to say.

"It seems like you're holding something back. Don't worry. Just say what you're thinking," Nyhlén says.

"Well, Cornelia and I have never gotten along. I keep asking myself if it's just me, but when it comes down to it, it's hard to overlook the fact that she has a difficult personality. And it's just not because she's young."

"In what way is she difficult?" Emma notices that Nyhlén's sleepy eyes are wide-open now.

"She has mood swings, and she always changes her mind at the last second. I thought Hans seemed really tied down, to be honest."

"Can you give any specific examples?"

"Most recently, when we were going to a hockey match, Hans canceled with no explanation an hour before. There I sat with two tickets. The next day it came out that it was something to do with Cornelia."

Emma doesn't know what to believe. "Maybe he just blamed it on her?"

"I suppose that could be the case." Roos shrugs, but it's glaringly obvious he has already decided that Cornelia is a killjoy.

"Can you expand on Cornelia's mood changes?"

"You already know about all that, don't you? Since you've talked with others in his circle of acquaintances?"

Emma tries not to look caught by surprise, although she doesn't understand at all what he is referring to. "Know about what?"

"She was admitted to a mental hospital for several weeks. If I remember correctly, it was right before Astrid was born."

"Do you know why?" Emma asks.

"He preferred not to talk about it, but apparently she got hysterical one evening and waved a knife, threatening to kill him. So I'm sure you understand what I thought when he was murdered in his own home."

Emma's skin starts to crawl so much that she has a hard time sitting still. There's no way Roos could know that the murder weapon was a knife. Now they have enough to arrest her, as long as he isn't making this up.

"Do you remember what hospital she was admitted to?"

"Saint Göran, I believe."

Nyhlén asks a few follow-up questions before they get up.

"Thanks very much for the help," Emma concludes. "Please be in touch if you think of anything else we ought to know."

"I promise," says Roos, taking her business card.

47.

Hugo has to restrain himself from rushing up when he sees Emma appear outside the police station. She must have overslept, because she's getting to work after eight o'clock. That's not like her. In the middle of a homicide investigation, she works basically around the clock— or was that an excuse to avoid being with him? Emma's work schedule is the only thing Hugo does not miss about their relationship. He has lost track of how many hours he spent waiting in vain for her. When he thinks back on it, he doesn't understand why he didn't do something meaningful with all the extra free time instead of just playing FIFA. Now the drawn-out wait continues. Hope is still alive.

Only a few meters separate them, but she isn't looking in his direction. She's close enough, though, that he notices something is different. She doesn't walk with the same decisiveness, the same zip in her step, and she seems tired.

When she looks to the side, he gets a glimpse of her face. Her cheeks are rosy, almost a little swollen. Perhaps she has a fever? He hopes it's not something serious.

Emma's back disappears through the entry. Curtain. The scene is past. Yet he is filled with joy at having been able to observe her, if only for a few seconds. Right afterward, her colleague Nyhlén walks past and Hugo turns his head away so that their eyes do not meet.

Usually, when Hugo has had his Emma dose, he can focus on his job awhile, feel the creativity flow. But today, his schedule is much too open, and he's still feeling melancholy and restless. The advantage of running your own company is the freedom to set your own hours, but often it's a problem to fill up the days with meaningful tasks.

Hugo stands there, still waiting. In the best-case scenario, Emma will call when she sees the roses, and then he'll be close at hand. Suddenly, he feels unsure about sending the bouquet. It could reinforce her opinion that he's losing his mind. Hugo asks himself whether there may be a grain of truth; he is aware that it might be seen that way. But all he wants is a chance to talk with Emma, to explain how good everything would be if they started over. There is no one who knows her as well as he does, who knows her good and bad sides. He accepts them readily and is prepared to change—to be more independent, to respect her career choice. To be just the man Emma wants.

If only she'd stop being so stubborn. So duped and blind. Hugo thinks he knows why she doesn't dare see him; she is afraid of hearing the truth. Just as he has this thought, he glimpses someone in a window on Emma's floor. Maybe it's her, standing there looking at him.

48.

Emma tosses the bouquet of roses in the wastebasket. She doesn't look out the window; she doesn't want to know whether Hugo is standing down on the street, waiting for her. She can't let his craziness distract her from her work. It's enough to deal with the nausea. Not to mention Kristoffer's sudden impulse to show her a newly renovated penthouse apartment in Vasastan. Right now, he doesn't seem firmly anchored in reality either, or else he has a few million in the bank she doesn't know about.

Emma waits impatiently for the manager on duty at Saint Göran Hospital to call her back so she can check Bengt Roos's story. Roos's assertion that she waved a knife and threatened to kill Hans might be hard to confirm, but if it's true that Cornelia was hospitalized, they should at least bring her in for more questioning. Obviously, a stay in the hospital wouldn't be something she wanted to come out. Emma sees Lindberg stop outside her door just as the phone rings. She answers before the second ring.

The manager is concise. "A patient by the name of Cornelia Göransson was admitted here at the end of February six years ago. A total of ten days."

Right before Astrid's birth. She repeats the manager's words out loud so that Lindberg will be clear about the situation.

"Who was the responsible physician?" Emma asks, prepared with notebook and pen.

"A woman by the name of Görel Karlsson."

"Can I talk to her?"

"She stopped working here several years ago, but if you wait a minute, I'll see if we still have her contact information." The doctor sets down the phone and is back almost immediately with a cell phone number.

Emma thanks him for his help and looks at her boss. "It doesn't look good for Cornelia."

Lindberg nods resolutely.

"What do we do next?" she asks.

"I'll call the prosecutor," he says, turning on his heels.

Is the meantime, she tries the number for the doctor but gets a this-number-is-no-longer-in-service tone in response. Frustrating, but the probability that Görel Karlsson would remember Cornelia without access to patient records wasn't great anyway. It's more important to hear what Cornelia herself has to say about it. She just needs Lindberg to give her the green light, and after only a few minutes, he is standing outside her door again.

"It's not enough to hold her, but she should definitely be brought in for more questioning, pronto. We'll add surveillance in case she leaves home."

The time is not quite nine, so Emma thinks it's likely Cornelia will be at her new apartment, not at the cordoned-off villa.

The line across Traneberg Bridge winds slowly into the distance. Too bad this isn't an emergency. Then they could turn on the blue lights. Emma daydreams about the penthouse apartment for a moment, toying with the thought that she and Kristoffer could settle down there, however unrealistic that may be. In her mind, she goes through room by room until she comes into the bedroom. On the floor beside the bed stands her old childhood cradle. She looks down and sees a baby there, with some dark-brown fuzz on its head, exactly the same hair color as Kristoffer. She wonders if it will be a girl or a boy. The nausea argues for a girl, or is it the other way around? She doesn't think she'll be able to stand not finding out at the ultrasound in week eighteen. It's too soon to start thinking about a name, but she brainstorms anyway in the backseat and gets stuck on Ines if it's a girl. It's lovely, and a family name besides.

The car stops, and she sees a brick apartment complex. She snaps out of her reverie and is back in the game.

"Second floor, third balcony from the left," a colleague waiting on the sidewalk says, taking out a pair of binoculars.

There are no signs of movement in the apartment. Perhaps they're on their way to Astrid's school. Just as she wonders how long they should wait, she detects something moving past the window. At first, she sees only a big teddy bear, but then she glimpses the girl's dark curly hair.

"Let's get ready to go in."

49.

A sharp ringing makes Cornelia jump. She can't decide where the sound is coming from, but after a short period of confusion she guesses it must be the doorbell. She wonders who could want anything from her this early in the morning. Or is it later than she thinks? Did she fall back asleep? Cornelia searches for her cell phone: ten past nine, and five missed calls. People are so impatient. The doorbell rings again, more drawn-out this time, and then she sees that Astrid is not lying beside her in bed. An icy chill shoots like an arrow along her spine.

"Astrid?"

When she doesn't get an answer, she quickly gets up and searches until she finds her daughter sitting in the window. Thank goodness it's closed.

"Hi, honey. What are you doing here?"

"Just looking out," she states calmly. "Aren't you ever going to answer the door?"

Of course. The front door. The doorbell sounds again, and Cornelia calls that she is on her way. She pulls on the same clothes as yesterday. The same as the day before yesterday too, for that matter. Before she unlocks the door, she looks into the peephole to be on the safe side. You never know what kind of crazy people are running loose. If it's anyone who appears shady, she won't answer it. And if it's Henrik standing there, she intends to call the police.

But it's not him.

Cornelia feels like an idiot when she sees two familiar faces: Emma and Nyhlén. Despite the persistent ringing, it didn't occur to her that it might be the police. Still, what could be so urgent that they are coming to her home now? Cornelia tries to figure out what's going on while she cracks open the door.

"Cornelia, we need to talk with you," Emma says as she approaches the opening. No "hello" or "sorry to disturb you."

"Why is that?" Cornelia truly does not understand a thing. She tries to get an answer by observing Emma, but she is just as hard to read as last time.

"Let us come in, and we'll explain."

Cornelia shakes her head and instinctively tries to push the door shut right in their faces. As if that would stop them. Lightning-quick, Emma takes hold of the door handle and puts her foot in the way.

"I don't understand," Cornelia says weakly. "I came in for questioning yesterday."

"We've gotten information that has led to new questions."

"What did you find out?"

"We'll have to deal with that at the station." Emma looks determined.

"But what about Astrid—can she go along?"

Emma shakes her head. "Unfortunately, that's not possible this time."

Cornelia's courage sinks like a stone.

"Who's going to take care of her?" she says. She backs into the kitchen, and they follow.

"The best thing would be if a relative can step in," Emma says. "Do you have any family in the area?"

"I don't have any close relatives."

Emma glances at Nyhlén. "Will you call social services?"

"Social services?" Cornelia exclaims, putting her hand over her mouth.

"They take care of children and place them with a family pending indictment and conviction."

Cornelia almost blacks out when she realizes what is happening, but she recovers quickly.

"You can't just barge in here and arrest me, can you?" Cornelia is whispering, so that Astrid will not hear. "Astrid just lost her dad, and she needs me more than ever. I'm the only security she has left."

"Unfortunately, this is how it works," Emma responds.

"But I haven't done anything." Desperation is about to make Cornelia hysterical, but she gets no friendly or calming look in return. No consolation. It's only a matter of time before she and her daughter will be separated. She has never before felt so powerless. So incapacitated.

"Can you think of anyone who could be with Astrid for the time being?" Emma asks. Not even the knowledge that Astrid is nearby softens her tone.

There is only one person who knows about her daughter's needs, one person who could help out. "Josefin."

Emma takes a deep breath, and for the first time, she looks embarrassed.

"So you don't have *anyone* else?" she asks.

Cornelia shakes her head. "Can you ask her?"

Emma takes out her phone and goes into the hall to call her sister. In the meantime, Cornelia closes her eyes and tries to convince herself that everything will be fine.

50.

One, two, three . . . Josefin stands in the hall and counts to ten silently. That's the advice she got to keep her from taking her anger out on the kids. But every morning it's the same old story: They refuse to get up, don't get dressed, and don't want to have breakfast until two minutes before they have to leave. Then they get mad at her when they're running late. Today the stress level has reached new heights. They've overslept—and seriously at that, because both she and Andreas forgot to set the alarm clock. The girls' school called at quarter past eight, and now first period is already over.

"I'll be home late tonight," Andreas mutters, sauntering down the steps, and Josefin stops short in the middle of counting when she sees he's about to leave. "Because we're just getting up now, I'll have to work late."

She flares up immediately. "But I have tennis this evening."

"Is it Thursday?" He takes out his phone and stares at the screen, where date and time are shown in black and white. "Damn it all."

"Kids," she says, turning her gaze toward the living room, where the kids are sitting on the couch. "You have to get dressed now. Your teachers are not going to be happy." Her voice sounds much angrier than she wants, but she can't control it. Actually, it's Andreas she's angry at. Partly because he intends to leave, without even helping with the kids, and partly because he refuses to grovel in the dust and admit that he spent a night with his lover. It's gotten so that she thinks he almost believes the lies he's telling.

Andreas puts his hand on her shoulder. "You don't need to yell at the kids just because you're in a bad mood."

Instead of telling him to go to hell, she closes her eyes. *Four, five, six . . .* At any moment, she's going to explode.

"Okay, have a good day," Andreas says. He slips out the door before she makes it to ten. As usual, he's out of there. That's how he solves his problems.

Josefin clenches her jaw tighter and starts counting again. It doesn't help. Nothing is going to change her mood, and the clock keeps ticking. When she sees that the kids have started playing a computer game, she is almost at her wit's end. How could they be so irresponsible? Just when she is about to scold them and come up with a hasty threat to suspend Saturday candy or throw the iPad out the window, her cell phone rings. *What has Andreas forgotten this time?* she thinks. It's not him, though, but her sister.

"The timing isn't great right now," Josefin answers

instead of starting with an enthusiastic hi. "Can I call you later?"

"I need your help." Emma sounds tense.

"I see," says Josefin, and notes that the clock is still ticking persistently when it ought to take a much-needed break.

"Can you take care of Astrid for a day or two until we find another solution?"

Emma's serious voice makes her shiver.

"What do you mean? Now you're scaring me. Tell me what's going on," Josefin says, conjuring up various scenarios. It doesn't take much imagination to think that Cornelia may have been the next murder victim. What would happen with Astrid then? Josefin struggles to breathe.

"We're in Cornelia's apartment. Would you be able to come here?"

"Tell me what happened!"

Emma lowers her voice. "We have to bring her in for questioning."

Then she's alive anyway. Josefin breathes out, but the hair on her arms is still standing on end. What has Cornelia done? She tries to stop the images in her mind of a mother being carried away from her little daughter by the police. Poor Astrid. Josefin shuts her eyes.

"Can you take care of Astrid?" Emma asks. "I wouldn't ask if it wasn't an emergency. Cornelia asked for you in particular."

"Of course I can. I'll come and get her."

"Should we pick you up?"

"It's not necessary. I'll see you there in a little bit. I have the address."

Josefin hangs up and calls Andreas to ask him for help dropping off the kids, but he doesn't answer. As usual, she can't count on him. She goes into the living room to get the children.

"Darlings, if you'll just put on your jackets and come along at once, I promise you a special dessert tonight."

Nine-year-old Julia is the only one who looks up from the game, her gaze cloudy and absent. Josefin silently pleads with her, and the girl seems to snap to attention and realize the seriousness. In a matter of seconds, she has her younger siblings in the hall, and they are all on their way out. True, without having brushed their teeth, but it will have to do.

Andreas still hasn't called back, and Josefin puts the phone in her handbag, trying to bury her disappointment. This is not the first time she has felt alone in their marriage. Alone in solving the emergency situations that constantly arise. Alone in making difficult decisions. Andreas is never available because he doesn't want to take responsibility— that's the only conclusion Josefin can draw. Actually, she doesn't understand why she even called him. She can always explain to him this evening why Astrid is with them.

The children are sitting compliantly in the car. Josefin first drops off the bigger kids, then drives to Anton's school. It was all over in seven minutes. Just as she's at the gate waving good-bye to Anton, her cell phone rings. She hurries to the car and takes off without answering. She doesn't want to risk saying something to Andreas that she will regret later. The phone stops ringing, but starts again after a moment's pause.

Josefin answers angrily. "Yes?"

To her surprise, it's Emma again. "Are you at the building yet?" She sounds stressed.

"I'll be there right away."

"Good. See you."

The sign for Abrahamsberg makes her swallow. Within a few minutes, her friend will be taken away by the police and Astrid must be separated from her mother. And it's all Josefin's fault. If she had just kept quiet when Emma started asking a lot of questions about Cornelia. It must have been because of her that the police redirected their suspicions. A car honks. Josefin looks up to discover that she is drifting onto the wrong side of the road. She swerves and manages to avoid a collision by a hair's breadth. The other driver looks more angry than scared.

"Jesus," she whispers, waving apologetically and forming a "sorry" with her lips.

51.

"Who were you talking to?" Astrid asks.

Emma looks at the little girl, there in the bedroom, at a safe distance from the drama playing out in the kitchen. Cornelia doesn't want to go anywhere without her child, but Nyhlén is doing his best to get her to leave the apartment calmly and quietly for Astrid's sake. On the floor is a basket of toys that seems somehow familiar. Emma has seen the fire-breathing dragon before.

"Your friend Josefin," Emma says, picking up the dragon.

Astrid laughs with an indulgent expression. "She's not my friend. She's Anton's mom. That's his dragon."

"I see." Emma has to think about how to express herself.

"Can I tell you a secret?" Astrid says.

"Please," Emma says, leaning toward the seemingly untroubled child with the lovely curls. When she comes closer, she sees how long the girl's eyelashes are.

"Anton's my boyfriend." Her eyes light up, and she waits for a reaction.

"Wow," Emma replies in an attempt to sound enthusiastic despite the trying situation. As soon as Josefin rings the doorbell, which should be at any moment, they will separate Astrid from her mother. Not something she wishes for any child. Emma notices that she has unconsciously placed her hand on her stomach. She pulls it away. Tries not to be tearful.

"Do you have a boyfriend?" Astrid asks, picking up a plastic dinosaur from the box, exactly like the one Emma gave Anton for Christmas.

"Yes."

"Is he nice?"

"He's really nice, but a little kooky, you know." Emma rolls her eyes and smiles.

Astrid answers her smile and nods in understanding. "Just like Anton then."

Emma had no idea the concept of a boyfriend existed to a six-year-old, but she guesses things must be different nowadays. Children seem more aware of everything at a younger age. Their upbringing is based on the constant flow of information from the Internet and the more advanced children's programs on TV. Emma finds herself thinking it was better before—before cell phones, computers, and social media, where everything is edited and retouched. The doorbell makes her immediately abandon her thoughts and stand up; she's been on pins and needles, waiting for Josefin.

Astrid senses the situation. She is quickly on her feet and gets to the door first, as if it were a fun game.

"Hi," she says with surprise when she sees Josefin.

Emma stands back and nods to her to come in. Cornelia looks at them from the kitchen, pale and red-eyed, and Josefin greets everyone cautiously. The atmosphere is quiet, although not in a relaxing way. As soon as children are in the picture, everyone acts differently, gets much more controlled. But that's only on the surface. At any moment, Cornelia could lash out, and they have to be ready to intervene.

"How kind of you to help out," Emma says, and she can see that Josefin thinks the situation is unpleasant.

She waves to Nyhlén, indicating that it's time to say good-bye. It would be best if Cornelia explains to Astrid in her own words why they must separate, so that the girl will feel secure and not think her mother is being taken away against her will.

Cornelia trudges out into the hall, with her gaze fixed on her daughter the whole time. Emma pretends to be distracted by her phone.

"I'm going to talk with these people," Cornelia tells Astrid, "then I'll come home again. In the meantime, you get to stay with Josefin," she says in a trembling voice. "And Anton!"

Emma waits for Cornelia to explain that it may take some time before they see each other, but those words never come. Either they are too hard to express or Cornelia is convinced that the visit at the police station will be over quickly. But it is important for Astrid to know that her mother may be away overnight or, in the worst case, longer. Cornelia convulsively hugs her daughter, who pulls away in fright. She probably notices that something is not as it should be.

"Shall we go then?" Astrid says impatiently, pulling on Josefin's shawl.

"Come," says Cornelia. "Give Mommy one more hug."

"No. I don't want to." Astrid looks imploringly at Josefin.

"We'll be going soon," Josefin replies, holding Astrid's jacket. "But it would be nice of you to give your mom another hug before we leave."

Briefly, Emma takes Cornelia aside and asks her to be even clearer about what's happening before they leave the apartment. "For your daughter's sake."

When they come back, Astrid already has her jacket on.

"Honey, I'm not sure how long this is going to take," Cornelia says in a nasal voice, apparently struggling to hold back the tears. "You may get to sleep over at Anton's."

"Yippie!" exclaims Astrid. She takes Josefin's hand. "Now let's go."

Josefin formulates a faint good-bye before she turns her back to them and leaves the apartment.

As the door closes, Cornelia looks unhappily at the police officers. "I know what you think, but I'm innocent."

"We'll discuss that at the station," Nyhlén says, friendly but firm.

52.

The car ride to Kungsholmen takes place as if in a dream: Water, cars, clouds, and trains fly past as Cornelia is swept along, and she has no idea where she is, or why. She feels weightless, about to lift off from the ground, leave this place, and disappear. The feeling lingers until she sees two serious, vaguely familiar faces in the car. The driver brakes at a roadblock, and she notes that they have arrived at the plaza at Fridhemsplan. Behind her is the store where she found curtains for a hundred kronor and to the right, the café that serves Stockholm's biggest and tastiest cinnamon rolls.

A guard lets the car through, and it cruises into an endless tunnel. No daylight reaches here, and she wants to get out, but she knows she has no say whatsoever. They are presumably driving under Kronobergsparken. It was just a few weeks ago that she chased Astrid back and forth there; she loves the playground at that park. Cornelia isn't a big fan of playgrounds, but seeing Astrid's delight always overcomes her reluctance. She decides that they should go there again soon, to play tag on the lawn and have a picnic together. As soon as the questioning is over, perhaps in a few hours. Cornelia imagines herself picking up their thermos and filling it with hot chocolate, but she's interrupted when someone taps her lightly on the shoulder.

"We're here," says Emma, neither friendly nor unpleasant, but it's that in-between that frightens Cornelia most. It only reinforces the uncertainty.

Cornelia didn't notice when they drove into the underground parking garage, much less that the car stopped and someone opened her door. Her legs are unsteady as she follows Emma over dirty asphalt through a brick-clad corridor with bare, anonymous walls and fluorescent lights. Claustrophobia makes her quicken her pace, hoping they'll soon come to a more open part of the building.

Farther in, through a door, she hears signs of life. There are scattered voices and ringtones from phones. They stop in front of a simple wooden bench a short distance from what appears to be a reception desk. Two police officers nod in greeting, but as she is about to return the greeting she realizes it wasn't meant for her. Another police officer asks her to turn over her handbag, and she looks at Emma, who nods. For them, these are probably normal procedures, but for Cornelia it is like giving away part of her life. Still, she hands over the bag with her wallet, keys, and cell phone. She has no choice. Then she is shown into a small room with a glass door.

"Do you have any preferences about defense counsel?" Emma asks.

Cornelia barely comprehends what's she's being asked. "I don't think so."

"In that case, we're going to call in a public defender, which may take an hour or so. In the meantime, you can sit here in the holding cell."

Cornelia wants to scream out loud in protest when Emma closes the door behind her and disappears. She doesn't even need to try the door to know it's locked from the outside. Here she sits like an animal in a cage. Anyone at all can walk past and stare in, make all kinds of judgments about her, and she can't defend herself or explain that it's all just a huge misunderstanding. She should be given crisis counseling, not be accused. But the worst thing is, she can't be with her daughter. The only consolation right now is that Josefin is taking care of Astrid. At Josefin's, she will get security and love, just what she needs. And soon Cornelia will be done here, if she just gets the chance to explain herself.

The time passes unbearably slowly. Passersby quickly turn their eyes away when they see her. She can only imagine what they are thinking. She still can't understand why she's being treated like a criminal. Someone must be responsible for putting her here. Could Henrik have made up something that made her a suspect?

Police officer after police officer passes, but no one stops to get her. Doing nothing is even harder when she knows that something awful is waiting. And it's not possible to prepare when she has no idea what she'll be asked. There's a glimmer of hope when she sees Emma approach. Just being able to get out of this cubbyhole is worth a lot, especially for someone who gets anxious in cramped spaces.

"We're ready for questioning," Emma reports, letting her out.

Cornelia has to follow the police officers through a corridor, up a stairway, and along yet another narrow passage, until they stop outside the same interview room as last time. She sits in the same place she sat before, but more than anything, she would like to turn around and run for her life.

53.

"No one broke into the house. You wanted a divorce. And your fingerprints are on the murder weapon." Nyhlén falls silent and then fixes his gaze on Cornelia, who sits as if petrified alongside the public defender, a woman in her fifties.

Because Cornelia is a friend of Josefin, Emma has to be an assistant during the questioning instead of leading it. In the adjacent observation room, Lindberg is scrutinizing every syllable, just like the first time. The more eyes and ears there are, the greater the chance of picking up any discrepancies. The only clue in the room suggesting that others can watch is a small opening on the opposite wall.

"There's an explanation for all that. Someone must have stayed behind after the open house. Astrid saw a man in her room that night—you already know that. And as far as fingerprints go, that's not strange, because it was our knife. I use it practically every day when I'm cooking."

"But there were no other fingerprints on the murder weapon, except yours and Hans's," Nyhlén says.

Cornelia's desperation cannot be mistaken. She is going to have a hard time getting out of this, and she seems to have realized that. Emma wonders how much it will take to crack her.

"If I hadn't asked for a divorce," Cornelia says, "sooner or later a knife would have ended up in me. Hans was crazy. He hit me all the time, over and over again. Nothing could stop him once he got going. I'm honestly surprised that *I'm* the one sitting here today."

"So it's not the case that you wanted revenge because he had a mistress?"

Cornelia looks nonplussed. "Now I really don't know what you're talking about."

"So you didn't know there was another woman?"

"No, but it doesn't surprise me a bit," she says, sighing heavily. "Hans wasn't like other people. He had no boundaries. I guess that was also why he didn't hesitate to use violence."

"But why didn't you ever report the abuse?" Nyhlén asks. "I don't understand that."

Cornelia shakes her head and then rests her forehead in her hands. "It's not that easy. Every time it happened, I was going to report it, but I changed my mind at the last moment. I knew it would only make the situation worse. That it would only provoke him."

"You could have asked for help," says Nyhlén, but he gets only a snort in response.

"I couldn't take a chance. The risk of retaliation was too great. Imagine having to live under the same roof as your assailant. How are you supposed to protect yourself—and your child? For Astrid's sake, I kept quiet."

"But how can we trust that your assertions are true when there are no police reports?"

"You think I'm just making it up?" With a look of indignation, Cornelia turns toward the public defender. "That's just crazy!"

The attorney neither contradicts nor agrees with her, but simply stares at her red nail polish.

"No one is saying that," says Nyhlén. "But for your sake, it would be good if there was some sort of proof."

"Astrid is the only one who has seen it happen. Unfortunately." Cornelia looks distressed.

"But she's a child. Your own, besides. Not exactly star witness from a prosecutor's viewpoint."

"I told Josefin what happened, but I already told you that."

Nyhlén nods. "But did she *see* anything?"

"Not when he hit me, if that's what you mean."

"No, I'm thinking more about bruises. Have you ever shown your injuries to Josefin?"

Cornelia shakes her head weakly. "Over the years, I've learned to conceal them well. I was ashamed of how my body looked—like a paint-color chart."

Emma looks for uncertainty in Cornelia, but she doesn't find any.

"What did you actually feel for Hans?"

"Fear."

"Hatred?"

"More fear than hate. I was scared to death of him."

Nyhlén pauses for effect, and Emma understands what this means. Now is when Cornelia's future will be decided. Emma glances toward the glass pane to the observation room, and wonders whether Lindberg is listening extra carefully.

"Can you tell us what happened at the end of February six years ago, when you were pregnant with Astrid?" Nyhlén asks.

Immediately, Cornelia turns pale and starts to shake. It takes a while before she is able to collect herself.

"Who told you that?" she whispers. She appears to be struggling not to fall apart again. "No one knew about it except Hans."

"Where the information came from we can't go into, but you do understand what I am referring to?"

The anxiety in Cornelia is tangible. "When I was admitted to Saint Göran?"

Nyhlén nods. "Tell us what happened."

"Do I have to?"

"It would be best," Nyhlén says. The attorney nods.

"I haven't ever talked with anyone about it, because it's so painful to think about."

"I understand," says Nyhlén.

"Do you? So you can relate to what it's like to wake up in the middle of the night because someone is holding down your arms and kneeing you in the stomach with full force? Someone who is your husband, who has decided to kill his unborn child?"

Emma automatically takes hold of her stomach.

"He was reeking of alcohol and screaming at me. I tried to wriggle loose, but because I was pregnant, I wasn't flexible enough. It was a miracle we survived, Astrid and I. The next morning I didn't know whether she was alive. I felt no kicks from her for several hours. It's not possible to put into words how desperate I was. And afraid that Hans would prevent me from calling for an ambulance. But he left me at home and didn't come back until several hours later when I was at the ER. He must have told them an incredible lie, because it ended with me being admitted to the mental ward. More or less as if I was crazy and went berserk at home and hurt myself," Cornelia says, shaking her head at the memory. "But at that moment, I felt so much relief about not having to go home that I didn't try to fight the decision. I didn't bother to protest either when the doctor asked whether Hans's statements were true, that I had fallen on the stairs. The hospital was my free zone. I felt safe there, because no one could hurt me anymore. I told the truth to a psychiatrist there, and that was why I got to stay as long as ten days. But Hans never found out the reason for the extension, and I strongly doubt it was noted in my patient record."

"Why not?" Nyhlén asks.

"Because I said I'd tell them only on that condition."

Not a single time does Cornelia get stuck, even though

she is agitated. That tells Emma the story comes from the heart and it's painful for her to put into words. On the other hand, the short-haired woman opposite them may be a talented actor, or a pathological liar. Emma has seen it all. She tries to maintain her objectivity in the assessment, but she can't help being affected.

"I know what you think, but I would never kill Hans."

"But you're not particularly sad that he's dead?" Nyhlén asserts.

"No, I'm not," she answers with a steady gaze.

Nyhlén looks at Emma. "Do you have any more questions?"

"Yes, I'm wondering about that life insurance again. It's certainly strange that it wasn't taken out until January of this year. Why not until so recently?"

"I wish I had a good explanation, but there isn't one."

"But you do understand that it worsens the suspicion against you since you knew you would get several million if your husband died?"

"Yes."

"So it isn't the case that you hired someone to kill Hans?" Emma asks.

Cornelia looks like she can't believe her ears. "Hired? No!"

"But you had no problem hiring a shill to bid up the price of the house?"

"That wasn't my idea." Cornelia bursts into tears. She's crying so hard her snot is running.

"Let's take a break here," says Nyhlén with a worried

look toward the adjacent room. "We'll return in a little while."

Then they leave Cornelia and the attorney in the interview room with a pile of tissues.

54.

I t feels like an eternity before Emma and Nyhlén come back into the hideous interview room. Cornelia doesn't know how to interpret their solemn expressions, and the public defender is of no use whatsoever, with her indifferent, verging on completely absent attitude. She gives off the impression of someone marking time just to have an excuse to send an invoice.

A scrape from a chair leg makes Cornelia tense up. Soon she is going to find out if this nightmare is over. The police officers sit down in the same places as before, but with a changed posture.

"Sorry it took so long," Emma begins. "It took a while to get word from the prosecutor."

So it wasn't an easy decision, Cornelia thinks.

"Did you get hold of my psychiatrist from Saint Göran?" she asks, to put off the judgment.

"We're still working on that," Emma says, turning toward

Nyhlén. That small gesture is enough for Cornelia to understand that it's bad news. If Emma wants to turn over the floor to her colleague, it must be something that's hard to say. The realization smarts like an unexpected wasp sting.

"The prosecutor has decided there's probable cause to have you held," Nyhlén says.

It's impossible to take in. She twists and turns the words, reconstructs the sentence, tries to understand its meaning, but it's not possible.

"What does that mean?" she forces herself to ask.

"It means you're under arrest," Nyhlén answers with a steady gaze, "suspected of the murder of Hans Göransson."

Suspected of murder?

Her vision fails her, and she has to focus on something concrete in order not to lose consciousness. Her gaze fastens at last on the white curtains with green leaves. Or do they really depict leaves? She's unsure about what she is seeing and where she is. Why the windows are equipped with bolts and no sound penetrates the panes.

"Cornelia?"

She hears her name and turns toward the police officers. Neither of them is in uniform. Nyhlén is casually dressed in a cotton shirt, and Emma has a V-neck T-shirt in shades of green. And the attorney is too made-up to be for real. Her dress is more suited for a gallery opening with bubbly and canapés than a police interrogation with a murder suspect. The police continue to observe Cornelia, encouraging, even pleading. They probably hope she will confess to the murder.

Then they'll have to wait, because that will never happen.

The attorney clears her throat, and it occurs to Cornelia that this woman will soon get to leave the police station. But she will stay here behind a locked door. Alone, without contact with the outside world. Far away from Astrid.

"But I can't stay here. My daughter needs me." Cornelia's voice barely holds, but she doesn't care how pitiful it sounds.

Emma lowers her eyes. "It will work out. She's with Josefin. We'll make sure she's doing fine."

"But I *will* get to see her soon, right? I have to give her an explanation."

"Not now."

"When?"

"That depends on how all this develops."

When the police officers leave the interview room, the public defender starts rattling off various clauses, obligations, and rights, but for Cornelia it's all gobbledygook. Everything is spinning and out of focus, except for the image of Astrid's face, with the apple-round cheeks and curly hair, the mischievous expression and long eyelashes. The baby fat on her stomach, the loose tooth in her lower jaw. Astrid will soon be wondering why her mom isn't coming home.

Cornelia feels betrayed and tricked. She can't stop the tears. The police said that she would be brought in for questioning, but no one said anything about the risk of her being held for murder. If she'd known that, she never would have gone along voluntarily, much less told her daughter to her face that she'd be home soon. She wants to howl out her frustration, to scream at the attorney to do something instead of just sitting there fingering her leopard-skin-patterned eyeglasses. Doesn't the bitch understand that the prosecutor is making a mistake, that she's innocent?

But common sense kicks in, making Cornelia remain silent and follow along compliantly when two police officers lead her to the jail. Her feet do not want to cooperate as they lead her across the cracked green linoleum floor and down a stairway. She stumbles and is clumsier than ever. They have already taken her phone and keys from her, but evidently that wasn't enough. Now they force her to take off her belt and remove her shoelaces too. They might just as well tear off her pants, blouse, and underwear while they're at it. She feels more exposed and abandoned than ever. It's like being subjected to an assault.

"You'll have to take off your necklace too," the police officer says, and that is too much. She has worn the piece of jewelry with Astrid's name on it ever since she made it, the day after giving birth. The name has its own special place, in the little hollow where her collarbone meets her throat. And she has always sworn that she would never take it off.

"Do you need help?" the police officer asks impatiently when he notices she's making no effort to undo it. It's not worth trying to explain why. She offers no resistance when his broad fingers scratch her on the back of the neck reaching for the lock. Strong male hands make her stiffen with discomfort, and she holds her breath until he is done. Hopes that the chain held.

"Can I keep a picture of my daughter anyway?" she asks quietly.

A glimpse of empathy is reflected in the police officer's eyes, then he looks inquisitively at his colleague. "That shouldn't be any problem, right?"

His colleague shrugs to indicate that he doesn't care.

"The photo is in my wallet, which I've already turned in."

"We'll arrange it."

After a while, the police officers come back and she takes the postage stamp–size picture with ragged corners without meeting Astrid's skeptical gaze. When it was taken at school last fall, Astrid was not at all in the mood. The photographer wasn't either, judging by the result. Cornelia closes her hand, afraid to lose the only tangible reminder of why it is worth continuing to struggle. She has no idea what is awaiting her in jail; she has never set foot in a place like that before.

As they continue toward her cell, she stumbles and the photo flutters away, landing right where one of the officers was about to set his heavy boot with all of his weight. He moves so that Cornelia can pick it up, and when she tries to wipe away the dirt she meets her daughter's sullen expression. She swallows and looks away. What will Astrid think of her?

55.

The kids are jumping on the trampoline in the yard while Josefin wanders around inside, restless, without getting anything done. It's a bad sign that the questioning is taking so long. She texts Emma asking her to call as soon as she knows how it's going. Andreas is conspicuous by his absence. He's probably fully occupied screwing around in the conference room at work.

The shrieks of delight outside the window suggest that Josefin can sit down at the computer instead of serving as playground monitor. She clicks onto a news site to see if the article about the open-house murder has been updated. The latest is that a suspect has been brought in for questioning; thank goodness it doesn't say who.

As long as it doesn't come out, Josefin will feel somewhat less guilt-ridden. The last thing Cornelia needs now is to be called a murderer. It's impossible to imagine what it would be like to be wrongly accused of such a horrifying crime. Josefin thinks about the loathsome way the tabloids treated that pediatric doctor at Astrid Lindgren Children's Hospital before he was acquitted. The media ought to be ashamed of witch hunts; they're unforgivable. What if Cornelia is subjected to something like that?

Josefin once again thinks about the claims of domestic violence, and her newfound doubt flares up again. But what about the fact that Cornelia chose to cut her hair short so that Hans couldn't drag her with it again? She wouldn't just make that up, would she?

When Josefin gets off the computer, it strikes her that it has been quiet outside for a while. She peeks over toward the trampoline and sees the children's shoes still under the ladder, but no one is there. It's much too cold for barefoot play outdoors, and a faint whispering from the bathroom in the basement implies that they have gone inside. But silence is usually associated with some form of mischief—that much is clear to her. So she goes down to see what's going on.

The bathroom door is shut and locked, so Josefin knocks. "What are you doing in there?"

"Nothing," Anton answers, giggling in contradiction.

"Open up, please," Josefin says. It's better than her picking the lock from outside. A measure she wants to resort to only in an emergency.

After further exhortations and threats of no dessert, the lock is turned.

Josefin is met by scissors on the floor and a bed of shorn-off dark-brown curls on the tiles.

"What have you done?" Josefin exclaims, staring at the pile on the floor. "Astrid, your lovely hair!"

The children's conspiratorial looks are erased.

"I want to look like Mommy," she answers.

How will Josefin explain the jagged haircut to Cornelia? In some places it's cut off right next to the scalp, impossible to rescue. Astrid looks in the mirror with dismay when she starts to realize what they have done.

"I changed my mind," she says, bending over to gather up her hair. "Help me put it on again. Do you have superglue?"

Josefin steels herself not to let her rising panic rub off. It's just hair, after all.

"Do you want to play Kinect?" she says in an attempt at diversion.

The kids nod and rush upstairs, shouting happily. Josefin follows. She'll have to clean up later. Just as she is coming into the living room, her phone rings. She hushes the children before she answers.

"Hello. This is Thomas Nyhlén from the county detective unit violent crimes section. Am I disturbing you?"

Josefin's hands start shaking when she realizes she's going to get the information she's been waiting for. Her gaze is drawn toward Astrid. *Will she get to sleep with her mom tonight?* Josefin closes her eyes, takes a deep breath, and leaves the room.

"Thanks for calling. How's it going?"

"The prosecutor has decided to have Cornelia Göransson detained effective immediately, which means that she will be with us for a while."

Josefin collapses like a stone, landing on her tailbone on the hard floor. "Is that true?"

Nyhlén's answer is heard from far away, as if he is calling from the other side of the globe, and she jots down the attorney's contact information on the back of a receipt. When the call is over, she starts counting to ten, thinking maybe the technique would work in a panic situation too. Her head feels strangely empty, as if life were put on pause. She has to get control of herself. *Kinect it is, yes. Time to get up and act as if everything is just the way it should be.*

"Was it Mommy?" Astrid asks when Josefin comes back to the room. She pulls on a long strand of hair that escaped the sharp scissors.

"Yes," Josefin lies. "She said it's okay if you sleep over. Fun, huh?"

The news makes Astrid light up, and she takes hold of Anton's hands. They jump around in a joyful dance. Josefin tries to play along, but both her smile and movements get stuck along the way.

56.

"How did Josefin sound?" Emma asks as soon as Nyhlén has hung up. Lindberg had insisted that she shouldn't be the one to call her sister and report the prosecutor's decision.

"Sad," he answers. "But that's understandable."

"How did it go with Astrid?"

"She didn't say anything about that. If there's a problem, I'm sure she'll call you or the attorney," he says, looking absentmindedly at his watch. "One-thirty coffee break. Are you coming?"

It is noticeable to Emma that the phone call was just like any other for Nyhlén. No contradictory emotions are circulating through him. Although she hardly wants to admit it even to herself, she is affected. Without any great enthusiasm, she goes with her colleagues to fill her cup with good fresh-brewed coffee, not the usual vending-machine sludge.

Her coworkers look relaxed, like they have everything

under control. When she passes the bookshelf in the break room, she is reminded that she can't bear to read murder mysteries anymore, because she lives them around the clock. She can't leave her job simply because she goes home; at night, she often lies awake in bed going over her current case. It's true that the plot in books is often more exciting than what happens in real life, but not always. Sometimes she and the homicide investigation team dig up leads that no one would ever expect. But not in this case. Here, they've rejected one lead after another until only Cornelia remains. Emma wishes she felt convinced that the prosecutor made the right call, but doubt has started to grow.

Emma takes a cup from the cabinet and a piece of sponge cake that someone has set out. She sits down beside Nyhlén on the curved gray-and-red couch but feels immediately too antsy to sit and chat.

She gets up. "I'm going back to the office to read through the interviews from the door-to-door," she says.

Nyhlén looks up with a perplexed expression. "You just sat down."

"I'm too restless for a coffee break."

A pile of printouts is on her desk with a message from Lindberg to look at them when she has time. She skims through the first sheet from the Västerort Police interview of the Göransson family's neighbors in Bromma. But before she has finished reading, she is interrupted by a call, which she answers when she sees it's her father.

"You've arrested a suspect," he observes, as usual without

any introduction. A county police chief apparently has so much to do that he doesn't even have time to think about how his daughter is feeling. Not even when he knows she's pregnant.

"Everything indicates that the victim's wife committed the murder," Emma says, "but she denies it."

"In seventy-two hours, you can get her to talk, right?"

"We hope so."

"Good," he says, hesitating before he continues, to Emma's surprise. "Considering the circumstances. Your mother has told me how you're doing."

"I'm doing just fine," Emma says, to prevent her father from getting into whether she's capable of working in her condition. She wonders where his sudden consideration comes from and hopes Lindberg hasn't discussed the case with him.

"Are you sure?"

"Yes, and if there isn't anything else, I have to get back to work now," she says. "We have a lot to do."

"Okay. Bye now," says the man who soon will have to give up his esteemed title and retire, a change she knows he's trembling at the thought of. She wonders what will happen to him as an individual when he loses this significant role. Perhaps he'll appreciate simply being a grandfather. Emma laughs at that absurd thought. Of course he's not going to be content with that.

Since she was interrupted anyway, she figures she might as well give Josefin a call. She doesn't feel like talking to her, but it would be just as well to get it over with.

"Hi. I heard about Cornelia," her sister says. "Is there anything new?"

"I can't give you more information than you already have."

"But what does it mean? Do you really think she murdered Hans?"

"We wouldn't have held her here without probable cause. How is Astrid doing?"

"She's doing fine." Josefin now sounds out of sorts.

"And you?"

"To be honest, I haven't had time to check," she answers. "It makes no sense to me that Cornelia isn't coming home."

Emma tries to distract Josefin. "Good thing you have Andreas, so that you're not alone with all this. I can't imagine better support."

Josefin's voice falters as she mumbles something evasive about having to help the kids with something.

Emma is grateful that the call is over quickly. Now she can devote herself to the interviews with the Göranssons' neighbors. With a little luck, someone may have observed a seemingly irrelevant detail that in reality is quite significant. She reads carefully so as not to miss anything in the thick bundle of papers. So far, no one has heard or seen anything strange during the night of the murder, or the night before. No unfamiliar cars on the street or shady characters wandering around. At least not as far as anyone knows.

If Cornelia was involved in her husband's death, something should seep out in the questioning with her, perhaps as early as tomorrow. Especially if they pressure her. No one sleeps well in jail, and most likely she'll wake up weak and downcast. Then perhaps a confession will come.

57.

The drab cell is so small that Cornelia has nowhere to sit other than on the cot. When she tries to smooth out the wrinkles in the blanket, it gives off a musty odor mixed with sweat. She tries not to think about whether it has been laundered or not, much less who slept here before her and why. She wonders how long Hans had been unfaithful but realizes she actually doesn't care. The main thing is that he can no longer get at her. Her gaze wanders around the urine-colored walls, which are decorated with inscriptions along the lines of "Fuck the police" and expressions of discontent and anger toward life in general. Cornelia can't figure out how people managed to scratch things into the wall. What did they use? She runs her fingers over a heart that someone carved beside the bed. The only sign of love in this room.

Automatically, her eyes are drawn to the photo of Astrid, and she feels pressure in her chest. Her throat is getting drier with every second. The walls feel much too close. Her anxiety is attacking from all directions, and her pulse is rushing so that it pounds in her ears. How could she bring a small child into the world with such an awful person as Hans? Cornelia already had a taste of who he was and what he was into; she understood that she had created a bottomless hell for herself. Even so, she didn't terminate the pregnancy. She was irresponsible, naive, stupid.

At the same time, the result of that pregnancy is the only tangible evidence that Cornelia has succeeded in something in life. She tries to linger on that last, positive reflection, but she doesn't succeed for very long. She is tormented by the thought that she may be behind bars for good. They will probably have to place Astrid in a foster family somewhere far from here, maybe in the countryside. Her brother couldn't take care of Astrid when he still lives at home. Besides, she would never let Astrid set foot in her parents' house. Cornelia gets tunnel vision when she thinks about losing her child, and her air passages constrict; there is only peeping and hissing when she tries to breathe. The room seems to be getting even smaller. She staggers up from the cot and shuffles over to the metal sink to slake her persistent thirst, but there's no room for her head under the faucet. She captures a little splash with her tongue and laps it up like an animal.

Powerless and overwhelmed, she makes her way back to the cot, cursing herself for not keeping her nerves in check. She can't allow her thoughts to get carried away. It's just so hard not to when there is nothing to pass the time with. There are no books or TV, only her imagination. She imagines a young guy with tattoos and scars on his shaved head. For her, this is a person who could end up here—not a young new widow without a criminal record from one of the nicest parts of Bromma. The most illegal thing she has done in her whole life was to run a red light on her bicycle. And swipe apples as a nine-year-old. She is an honorable person, but the suspicious gaze the guards here gave her could not be mistaken. To them, she's like all the rest. Someone who deserves to be locked up.

The lackluster public defender isn't going to lift a finger for Cornelia's sake; that much came out of the little time they had together. The first thing Cornelia must do tomorrow is demand a new attorney. Someone with a positive attitude—about her job and her client. Someone who will look out for Cornelia's best interests, who understands how unreasonable the situation is. It might take time to find a replacement, but it would be worth the wait. Just so she escapes that bitch, who isn't the least bit interested in getting her out of here.

58.

Emma is not satisfied when she leaves the police station, even though she has worked late to read through all the door-to-door interviews. The Västerort Police talked to all the neighbors except the ones who live right next door. Every time the police knocked on Kerstin and Staffan Svärd's door, they weren't at home. That in itself is enough to arouse Emma's curiosity, and she intends to start where her colleagues in Västerort were forced to give up. She has already tried calling a few times but only got the answering machine. The hunt for the psychiatrist Görel Karlsson is also turning out to be a problematic task, despite all available databases. The woman no longer appears to be active in the field. But sooner or later, they always manage to track down the majority of people. It's just a matter of being creative.

Fifteen minutes later, when Emma is standing outside the door to her apartment, she hears the entry door open and quick steps approaching on the stairs.

"Hi," Kristoffer calls, noticeably out of breath, and hugs her.

The embrace turns into a long kiss. Emma manages to take out her keys and unlock the door as together they back into the apartment. Firmly, he pulls off her jacket and feels his way under her sweater. His hands are so cold that she gets goose bumps. When she notices he hasn't pulled the door closed behind him, she takes a few steps to reach the handle. Kristoffer follows along, and she shuts the door. Now she can relax and try to enjoy.

She really wants to let go of work for a while, but after this kind of day, it's hard to do. She lets Kristoffer lead, and he gets her bra off. Her breasts are swollen and sensitive, but she doesn't say anything as he caresses them, afraid of sabotaging the mood. She doesn't even bother to suggest that they go into the bedroom instead of standing in the unfurnished hall. When he gently works his fingers inside her panties, she finally lets go of everything else and longs for him to take off the rest of her clothes. She doesn't need to wait very long before he eases her down on the floor and brings her legs up toward the ceiling.

A sharp telephone ring makes them both freeze. They let it ring, but the mood is gone, the moment where nothing existed other than their two bodies. They complete the sexual act they had started anyway, but it's more goal-oriented than impassioned now. Afterward, Emma is bothered by lying on the rug in the hall alongside Kristoffer's foul-smelling boots, about as unromantic as you can get.

As Kristoffer goes to the bathroom, Emma gathers up

her clothes on the floor. After a while, he looks out with a content smile. For her own part, she feels shy, like she does every time they have sex. Perhaps she is always going to be a little embarrassed afterward. He helps her to her feet before he continues to the living room with his cell phone. Emma is looking forward to some peace and quiet during a hot shower. But just as she has covered herself with shower gel so that there is lather all over her body, there is a light knock at the door.

"May I come in?" Kristoffer asks.

"It's open," she replies. She sees by his look that he is no longer as cheerful.

"Someone from the board of the allotment gardens called. They've discovered a leak at my cottage, even though the water's not even turned on yet. Fucking unbelievable."

"What are you supposed to do about it?"

"I have to go and see if I can solve the worst of it myself. If I can't, I'll just have to call a plumber."

"So you have to leave right now? Can't it wait until tomorrow?" Emma is disappointed. Won't they ever get to be together like a normal couple? Just sit on the couch and talk. Eat chips, watch TV, and take it easy. Without phones buzzing and beeping all over the place or leaking pipes calling for attention.

"Do you think I want to? I'll be back as soon as I can."

"I guess I'll have to eat alone then," Emma says. "You know, I'm so tired I don't think I have the energy to stay up until you get back. Maybe it's better if you stay at your place tonight."

"Knock it off. I'll hurry. I'll call on my way back."

"Do that. Then we'll see if I'm awake," she says, turning on the water and taking a deep breath before she brings the shower nozzle to her head.

That darned garden plot. Emma doesn't understand why he keeps it.

59.

The little garden is not neglected, but it doesn't give the same cozy impression as the neighbors', with its straight-as-an-arrow flower beds and precisely pruned apple trees. Hugo turns around to be certain no one has seen him outside the white gate. If that were the case, he'd have to keep going and return at a better time. As if he were just out for a walk. But no one is around, so he decides to break in. This is easier said than done; the gate's handle jams and refuses to budge. He pulls on it with force, and then the piece-of-shit gate comes completely off. Surprised, Hugo stands with the gate in his hands and looks around, worried. It takes no great exertion to put it back in place in the rusty brackets, but it's somewhat crooked now.

Emma may be ignoring him these days, but she used to talk to him occasionally after they broke up. Hugo doesn't remember in what context she mentioned Kristoffer's allotment garden in Stora Mossen, but he's glad he filed that information away. It wasn't hard to locate, since she posted a picture of the cottage on Facebook at one point. All the cottages in the area are different, but Kristoffer's is one of the nicer ones. Someone has recently fixed it up—painting the red wood paneling and putting on a new metal roof. Is he so handy, that smarmy guy? Hugo has a hard time believing that.

As he approaches the steps to the front door, he wonders why in the world Kristoffer has this place. Sure, it's sweet, but what use is it? Is he interested in gardening, or did he buy it for another purpose? Alarm bells are ringing deafeningly loud in Hugo's head. A man like Kristoffer isn't the type who makes his own elderberry juice, so Hugo is determined to find evidence that something isn't right. Evidence that hopefully will make Emma reevaluate their relationship and leave Kristoffer for good. But that would require something exceptional, and so far he has no idea what he is searching for.

Hugo peeks in through a window and sees a table and wooden bench like his grandmother had in her kitchen. An extendable one that you can sleep on if you're skinny as a stick and very short. Basically, if you're a small child. On the table is a pile of flyers and drawings, work gloves, and an empty paper muffin form with a collection of crumbs around it. The angle from this window isn't the best, though, so Hugo moves to the side of the cottage to get a better view. The window frame is damaged—someone must have tried to get in—but the glass is still intact. He gets a glimpse of a kitchenette, but not much else, other than a coffeemaker and saucepan. *That's it?* he thinks miserably. *What good was it coming out here?* But what had he expected?

He walks around at random in the garden and tugs at a padlock on the nearby shed. The lock pulls opens with no effort at all, and he feels his pulse rise as he steps in. The space is no bigger than a small elevator. On the shelves gardening tools and seed packages are jumbled together. Something stinks, and Hugo sees shears sticking out of a bowl filled with a fluid that smells like paint thinner.

A faint rustle somewhere in the vicinity makes him stop in his tracks. It sounded exactly like the stubborn handle of the gate. Instinctively, he pulls the shed door shut and listens. It sounds like a man is talking on a phone and, even worse, the voice is coming ever closer. Hugo stands completely still, but it's not easy. Particularly when he realizes the voice belongs to Kristoffer. If he goes around the corner and sees the open padlock to the shed, it would mean the end for Hugo. The ultimate evidence that he, not Kristoffer, needs psychiatric care.

"Yes," Kristoffer says. "I see that the hose has come loose from the pipe. Hopefully. I have extra gasket rings and hose clips somewhere. This isn't the first time this has happened." Kristoffer sighs, and Hugo stares, standing by the shelves as if paralyzed.

A key in a lock. A creaking door being opened. That means Kristoffer is inside the cottage and Hugo has the chance to slip away. But it is as if his feet have frozen solid in the ground. His survival instincts fail to function, and he stands there, unable to move—not even to scratch his back, where he notices something is itching. Besides, the garden is too small for him to be able to avoid discovery if he tried to leave. He has no choice other than to stay put and keep his fingers crossed that Kristoffer will find what he needs in the cottage. There are no bags of gaskets in here, and he ought to know that.

Hugo's breathing is so labored now that he thinks it must be audible at a distance of several hundred meters. It strikes him that hiding is something he has always done with enjoyment mingled with terror. Hide-and-seek was a game he both feared and loved. The nerve-tingling feeling of knowing that someone is looking for you, the fear of being found first, is unbeatable.

When Hugo's courage is starting to run out, he hears crunching on the gravel outside.

"It's all taken care of," Kristoffer says. "Thanks for calling."

The steps die away, but Hugo doesn't dare take a chance and come out. After another ten minutes, he carefully cracks open the door and peeks out through the gap. He sees that the gate is closed, but he can't decide what that means. Kristoffer could be just around the corner, prepared to expose him. *But why would he do that when he doesn't even know I'm here?* He dismisses the thought. As quietly as he is able, he leaves the shed and then runs quickly away.

60.

FRIDAY, APRIL 4

It's just past midnight, but it is impossible for Josefin to wind down after this intense day. It doesn't matter that she is completely worn-out. Sleep will not come. Andreas doesn't share her problem; he is breathing heavily and loudly, which means he's fast asleep. But as long as he sounds like a hissing snake, there's no way she'll settle down.

This particular part of their relationship she'd be happy to escape, and she thinks with schadenfreude about the new woman. The one whose identity Andreas will not reveal. The one he refuses to admit that he has slept with. Josefin pushes him, harder than usual, to get him to change position. He grunts, turns his back to her, and is quiet for the moment. But that still doesn't help. Now she is concentrating on every breath he takes just to assure herself that it's not really bothering her. Then the hissing snake is back, and the only thing to do is to observe that he is hopeless.

She thinks about her parents, who sleep in separate rooms, avoiding such torment during the night. For Andreas, such a step is inconceivable in a marriage, at least a happy one, but Josefin wouldn't hesitate a second if he would go along with it. When she convinced him to have separate blankets instead of a single one, Andreas started muttering about couples therapy. So it was hardly the time to point out that she'd like a room of her own. She wants to be in peace at night, to breathe fresh air and have quiet around her. Read as long as she wants. Not have to take into account, and feel controlled by, the needs of someone else. Especially when that someone else is fantasizing about another woman.

Astrid fussed until eleven o'clock, when she fell asleep from sheer exhaustion on the extra bed in Anton's room. She hasn't said very much about how she's feeling, but surely she understands more than she has expressed. Children have an exceptional capacity to sense moods, however well adults think they're hiding things. Josefin doesn't want to think about what things will be like for Astrid if Cornelia is found guilty and gets a long prison sentence. There is nowhere for her to go; a foster family will be the only choice. Josefin can't take care of yet another child, especially now that her marriage is so shaky. Three is already too many sometimes.

It's hard to stop dwelling on it once she starts, though, even when she sees it's twelve thirty and she knows that the alarm clock is going to ring at a quarter to seven. She can only dream of Andreas getting up in the morning and taking care of the kids. Fixing breakfast, packing sports clothes and homework, driving them to school, and letting Josefin sleep in. It did happen *one* time, when she was knocked out with a high fever.

Fatigue finally starts to creep up on her, and Josefin almost becomes exhilarated when she realizes she is on her way into much-needed sleep. Her body is in a resting position and her pulse is on low. But just as she is about to fall asleep, she hears a howl from Anton's room. Josefin throws off the blanket and rushes in.

Astrid is sitting up in bed with her eyes wide-open. "Make him go away!"

She points toward the door, but there is no one there.

"There, there, Astrid. Everything's okay," Josefin says, starting to go over to her bed, which turns out to be a bad idea.

"Stop," Astrid howls even louder. She waves her arms around wildly to protect herself from something that Josefin can't see. "No! Don't touch me!"

Josefin tries to say a few more calming words, but the girl can't be reached, despite the terror in her eyes. It hurts so much to see her yelling incoherent sentences and not be able to do anything to put a stop to it. And at any moment, she's going to wake Anton, who strangely enough has slept through it so far.

Josefin tries again to help, but when she places her hand on Astrid's cheek, the girl pulls back in terror and flings herself farther up in the bed, as far away as possible. Josefin sits carefully down on the edge of the bed and reaches toward her, but again regrets her impulse. The loud howling is back, and now Anton is sniffling.

Josefin jumps when she sees someone standing in the doorway. She breathes out again when she realizes it's Andreas, on his way into the room. He goes over to Anton and tucks him in.

"You scared me," Josefin says to Andreas.

He nods toward Astrid. "Night terrors. Just like Julia—do you remember? There's nothing you can do. It's best to let her be until she settles down."

Night terrors. She had completely repressed that, but now she remembers how upset they were the first time it happened. Nothing they tried helped. Then they read on the Internet that you should never wake the child. That the next day the incident will be forgotten. At least by the child.

"Don't you think it could be just a nightmare?" Josefin whispers.

"You can't make contact with her, can you?"

Josefin shakes her head. "She's afraid someone will take her. Her reaction was so realistic at first, I thought there *was* someone in the room."

Andreas picks up Anton, who is having a hard time falling back asleep. "You can sleep between Mom and Dad," he says. "I'll carry you."

Josefin can't bring herself to leave Astrid alone in the room, where she is still sitting with a terrified expression. Even if Astrid isn't aware of her presence, Josefin doesn't want to go until she is certain that the girl has fallen back asleep.

Once again, Astrid screams desperately, but this time Josefin is prepared and her heart doesn't race to the near-bursting point. After a while, the little girl sinks down with her head on the pillow and makes one last whining sound, as if the struggle is over and she doesn't have the energy to fight back anymore.

61.

A cry of despair wakes Cornelia. She is rocking in and out of a troubled sleep, and when she opens her eyes for the hundredth time that night she is still surrounded by darkness. Even though she can't see where she is, she knows by the smell that something is different. She fumbles for her cell phone to see what time it is, but it's not on the nightstand. Strange sounds come and go outside.

Then yesterday's police interrogation and the decision to arrest her hit her like a blow to the face. The trip through the corridors, the pat-down. A door that opens and closes. The click of a lock. The mere knowledge that she can't leave here is frightful. She sees a crack of light from the door, goes to it, and bangs hysterically with both fists. No one reacts. Tries again, now with less force and determination, like a boxer who knows he's losing but still has to fight. Because she knows how meaningless it is, that it doesn't matter what she does.

"Shut up," she hears someone yell. At least one response. She is not alone.

Slowly she sinks down to the floor and takes hold of her head. A pounding ache, starting from the back of her neck and radiating up toward the top of her head, is there along with the image of Astrid. Cornelia imagines her lying awake in the middle of the night, longing for her mother.

It's all too unbelievable to be true. Someone must have said things to make the police direct their suspicions at her. But who, and what? Did she dig her own grave by not mentioning the hospital stay? But why should what happened six years ago have any significance? It must be something else. *Josefin?* Cornelia breaks into a cold sweat at the thought of her name. Josefin is the only person Cornelia dared to confide in about the domestic violence, but she was nothing but supportive through the separation, giving her the courage she needed to break up with Hans. What could Josefin have said to Emma that didn't sound good? That she's lying about the abuse? That can't be. Josefin doesn't wish her any harm.

Suddenly, Cornelia feels guilty for letting her thoughts run away. It must be one of Hans's friends who told police about the time at Saint Göran Hospital but completely distorted the story. Gave an incorrect picture. She was just there to survive, nothing else, but she realizes now that Hans must have said otherwise.

Cornelia doesn't have the energy to be angry anymore. But the possibility that Emma and Nyhlén don't believe her stings almost as much as Hans's blows. Sure, the police have to do their job, but their accusatory way of asking questions is almost unforgivable.

They have ninety-six hours at their disposal to get her arraigned, but they'll never succeed. And once she's out of this place, she's going to sue the whole bunch. They'll regret what they've done. Cornelia isn't going to give Josefin's sister a break. It will be all or nothing, but she can live without Josefin's friendship if that's what it comes to. It's all about getting satisfaction.

The smartest thing for her to do now would be to try to sleep through the last hours of the night, but Cornelia is much too agitated for that. She is seething with the injustice. She is a victim, not a criminal. She grits her teeth and, as best she can, tries to focus on the fact that at least Astrid is fine. She must be excited about having a sleepover with her best friend. Although soon she's going to wonder what's going on and when everything will be as usual again. No one has bothered to tell Cornelia when she will get to see her daughter, and what is going to happen when it gets light in a few hours.

62.

It was surprisingly simple to get in through the basement door. Almost too simple. *I ought to become a burglar,* I think.

Now it's crucial not to make any mistakes.

The drawback with an unfamiliar house is that I don't really know the layout and the opportunities for escape. On the other hand, I probably won't be in a hurry to leave, considering that no one is going to be capable of running after me.

When I reach the hall and round the corner to go to the next staircase, the one to the top floor, something happens that is not part of the calculation at all. An ear-splitting, almost insufferable siren goes off. It's so loud it cuts through my whole head. A box on the wall is blinking madly, and a light goes on upstairs. Suddenly, the home phone starts ringing too, but I just stand there, paralyzed.

Take it easy, I tell myself. Presumably, it's the security company, wanting to know what's happening—whether it's a false alarm or a situation requiring an emergency response. *It will probably be at least fifteen minutes before anyone gets here.*

"The police are on their way, so don't do anything stupid." The man's voice from the top floor is just as harsh as I remember it.

A personal attack alarm with a direct connection to the police. Naturally, he has spared no expense. I'm probably not the only one who wishes him harm. Strange, though, that he hasn't installed an alarm in the basement too, that I even got this far.

It sounds like footsteps on the stairs, but I'm not certain. The siren drowns out all other sounds, and it's hard to make out what is what. I realize how close I am to getting caught and going to prison.

In a few seconds, I'm at the back door and turning the knob, but it's secured with a lever tumbler lock and the key isn't in it.

All the windows are locked. I'll have to go out through the terrace door. I rush there, no longer bothering to be discreet. Now it's just about getting out of here alive. It wouldn't surprise me if the owner was armed.

The handle is tricky, but I manage to get the door open at last and hear it slam shut behind me. Then I run for all I'm worth, without turning around.

63.

Benjamin knows it's safest to stay upstairs while waiting for the security guards and police, but pride wins out over common sense. The person, or persons, who broke in isn't going to get away, damn it. No fucking intruder is going to break in here without consequences. He turns on all the lights in the whole house, room by room, trying to ignore the painful noise cutting into his ears. Helena, panic-stricken, has locked herself in the storage space under the eaves. He'd thought she was tougher than that, but he admits to himself that he's jittery too. Not at all as self-confident as he tries to convince himself.

Tensely, he approaches the living room and flips the switch for the ceiling light. Unfortunately, the designer Kotten lamp doesn't illuminate the room like a searchlight, but it's good enough to see that there is no intruder here. He lets his gaze run along the fancy dado and up toward the stucco work in the ceiling without seeing any sign of a break-in.

Then he goes by way of the serving entrance toward the social spaces of the house, around the kitchen island and farther in the library. Not a trace of damage or theft. Only the basement remains. Maybe someone has managed to crawl in through one of the narrow windows and down into the hot tub.

Benjamin is no longer afraid, just hopping mad. Angry at being awakened in the middle of the night, frightened like a little snot-nosed kid. He turns on the custom-made cable lights along the basement stairs. When he has searched through the slightest corner to find something that may have caused the alarm, there is a knock at the door. So now they get here, half a century from when the alarm was triggered. The burglars have already made it to the Arctic Circle at this point.

"Securitas," he hears, and he goes up to let the guards in. They quickly silence the alarm, but it continues to echo in his ears for a long time.

Shortly afterward, the police also arrive at the scene while some worried neighbors stick their curious mugs out their windows. *Don't they have anything better to do?* Benjamin thinks as he tries to shake off his anger.

"False alarm," he calls from the doorway to calm the elderly couple coming out in the middle of the night to see what's going on.

It doesn't take long for the guards and police to draw the same conclusion—there is no intruder in the house.

"The terrace door is unlocked, though," says one of the guards, and Benjamin has to go there to see if it's true. He usually makes sure everything is locked before he goes to bed. But perhaps Helena's seductive smile made him think about other things. Could he have been careless and given the intruder an easy way in—and out?

When the police and guards finally leave the house, Benjamin collapses in bed alongside Helena, who has ventured out from her hiding place.

"Maybe you ought to contact Inspector Sköld or her associate," she says.

Benjamin is wide-awake again. "Why should that be of interest?"

"I don't know, but what if this has a connection with the murder of Hans Göransson?"

Helena is sitting curled up against the wall, looking frightened. The light from out on the street produces unflattering shadows on her face, and he is suddenly starting to wonder about her.

"What could they do about it anyway? The police have already been here, and all they found was an unlocked door, which evidently I must have forgotten to close because you occupied me with something else."

"Don't blame me," she says. "But what triggered the alarm, do you think? Do you think someone was in the house?"

"A fly, maybe—what do I know," Benjamin says to calm her. Even though he didn't say so to the police, it's obvious to him that someone was in the house.

Helena snorts. "Hardly."

"It's quarter past three. I think the detectives are asleep by now, and we should be too."

He turns off the lamp so Helena will understand that the discussion is over.

64.

Emma wakes up with something caressing her lovingly across her belly. A big warm hand.

Kristoffer smiles at her. "Good morning, beautiful."

"What time is it?" Emma asks, fumbling for her phone.

It can't be morning already. She's much too tired for that, and the nausea is back. She just wants to sink back into sleep again, but she knows that's not an option.

"A few minutes past seven."

In half an hour, she has to be at work to question Cornelia Göransson again. But the sooner, the better. Emma holds no hope that the case against Cornelia will clear up unless there is a breakthrough. It's crucial to find the psychiatrist and the next-door neighbor as soon as possible—Hans's ex-wife too, who suddenly seems impossible to get hold of. Still, Emma can't quite make herself get out of bed yet. And when she picks up her phone, she sees a new text from Hugo, which doesn't make her any more energetic. She deletes it without reading it.

"Why the worried frown?" Kristoffer asks, trying to smooth out her wrinkled forehead. "It doesn't suit you."

Emma smiles. "I forgot I was at home and not at the police station."

"That can happen. But *I* would never let my personal life get mixed up with work."

Emma laughs out loud but quickly turns serious. "Although I do need to practice letting go of work when I'm off."

She has almost seven months to practice, but she thinks it will get easier once she's completely disconnected from ongoing investigations. Parents who are physically present but mentally absent are terrible role models, and she doesn't intend to be that way. She also doesn't intend to live apart from the father of her child.

"How's it going with the apartment, by the way?" Emma says, fantasizing about decorating one of the bedrooms in the dreamlike four-room as their child's room. She imagines the baby lying under the exposed beams of the slanted ceiling with built-in spotlights. She could hang an interesting mobile there, with little figures twirling around, so that the baby is occupied with processing new impressions instead of crying.

"What do you mean? I have something like five properties out at the same time."

"The *penthouse* apartment." Emma rolls her eyes.

Kristoffer gets up and answers with his back to her.

"Sold. I thought you weren't interested. Or did I misunderstand you?"

"Are you joking?" Emma says. "I just said it seemed expensive. You could have asked first before you let it go. So now I've been dreaming about it for no reason."

"An offer came in that the seller couldn't resist. Sorry I forgot to tell you," Kristoffer says in a businesslike voice. He turns around. "Don't sulk now."

"I'm not sulking, just surprised. And disappointed. It would be nice if we were living under the same roof when the baby arrives."

"There are loads of apartments—don't worry. And we already have two, plus my allotment garden cottage."

Emma laughs dryly to indicate her dissatisfaction. "Thanks. I feel better already. My goal has always been to live in a one-room cottage with no indoor plumbing. Handy when you're going to change diapers too."

"You're so demanding," Kristoffer says, winking seductively before he leaves the bedroom.

Emma burrows her head down in the pillow again. How is she supposed to react when first he gives her a private showing and then sells the apartment without informing her? Kristoffer sees new homes come on the market every day; he's probably not emotionally involved. But he ought to understand that it's different for her. In protest, she stays in bed until Kristoffer comes back from the shower.

His aftershave smells so pungent that she wrinkles her nose.

"Please, can you take it easy with anything strong-smelling?"

"Still grouchy?"

"More like nauseated."

"But chin up now, honey. I'll scrape up a few more apartments today if you think that will help." The sarcasm in his voice is in high gear.

"For nausea, I prefer vitamin B12," she says, hoping he leaves soon.

Emma totters into the bathroom on shaky legs, takes a vitamin, rinses her face, and washes under her arms. That will have to do. She can shower another day. She doesn't have time to await a more lively facial color either. She has to get some breakfast and take off.

Kristoffer is waiting for her outside the bathroom door, completely naked and with a sturdy morning erection. "You forgot to say good morning."

"Good morning," she says guardedly, heading for the refrigerator. She doesn't have the energy for his constant sexual innuendos. Especially not when she has to struggle to keep down yesterday's dinner.

But Kristoffer is not one to give up. He slips after her and hugs her from behind as she is taking out the milk carton, then presses himself playfully against her rear.

She can't keep from laughing at him. "If you just had a little more hair on your body, I would've thought it was a dog grinding."

"Must you punish me?"

Emma turned around. "You know how I'm feeling."

"Finally, eye contact," he replies. "I love you, Emma."

"And I love you. Most of the time."

He holds her gaze for a few seconds before he leaves to get dressed.

After a while, he returns in his stylish real-estate-agent suit, with a completely different, serious image.

"How's the investigation going?" he asks, serving himself coffee. He is about to put the carafe back in the coffeemaker, but stops and looks at her first. "You don't want any, do you?"

"I wouldn't mind a little."

"Are you making progress?" he asks, filling her cup to the brim.

"Yes."

"But the wife has been arrested?"

Emma wonders how that information got out. "What makes you think that?" Emma says.

"Just from reading Flashback online. Everything's there and a little more. All the real estate agents are eagerly following the story."

"Don't believe everything you see there."

"Of course. I'm not that dense," he says, raising his eyebrows. "But is she the one who did it?"

Emma lets the silence speak for itself.

"Okay, okay. I'll have to be content with the gossip sites for now," he says.

"Like everyone else," she says, smiling at his sullen expression.

Kristoffer gulps down the last of his coffee and sets his mug in the sink.

"What a hurry you're suddenly in," Emma says. "Where are you going?"

He kisses her on the forehead. "Just a photo shoot. But I want to be there on time so the photographer doesn't have to wait."

65.

Hugo can barely contain himself, standing there like a kid on Christmas morning. It will be so interesting to see the reaction when the real estate agent shows up.

A woman's voice calls to him.

"Excuse me, but are you the photographer?"

He turns around and smiles broadly when he discovers a woman in her forties looking out the front door of the house that is to be sold. "That's right."

"Come on in. I'll put coffee on," she says and waves to him to hurry. "It's really chilly out today."

He hadn't even thought about the weather, but he shivers as he comes into the hall and sets all his camera bags down on the floor. "It really is. I intended to wait for the real estate agent outside, but it's colder than I thought."

"Almost freezing in April," the woman mutters, shaking his hand. "Smilla Westberg."

"Unusual name," he answers. "Hugo Franzén."

"Pretty unusual too," Smilla says with a laugh. "Coffee?"

"That would hit the spot."

Hugo doesn't want to ask, but he wonders whether Smilla is planning to be at home during the photography session. It seems that way, because she fills the coffeemaker to the point of overflowing. Actually, it doesn't matter if she's here, even if he had imagined a different scenario.

"Is it okay if I look around for some good shots?" he asks.

"Naturally," she says. "Make yourself at home."

Hugo has no problem getting acclimated to the beautifully furnished home. Ornate details testify that the house is old. His eyes land on the animal-skin chaise longue, and he can't resist going up and touching it.

"Pony," he hears a voice behind him say, and he spins around.

Smilla's smile goes from polite to flirtatious. "Are you in the mood to try it out?"

He's not sure exactly what she means by that, and he gets nervous when she approaches. Her generous cleavage makes it hard for him to look anywhere other than right down into the gap.

"That would be nice," he answers, wondering what will happen now, just as there is a knock at the door.

Smilla turns on her heels. "That should be the real estate agent."

Hugo sits down and leans back against the cylinder-shaped pillow, which is a perfectly designed neck support. If it were up to him, he'd lie here until someone tore him away by force. His body conforms itself to the flexible base as he hears Smilla welcoming someone out in the hall. Hugo knows who this someone is without needing to look. He is in no hurry to get up and say hello; after all, they're going to spend the next few hours under the same roof.

When he and Emma find their way back to each other, he will get a similar chaise longue upholstered in some other material—fabric is probably the safest. There will be no talk of pony, or Emma would have a fit. Hugo laughs when he thinks about his favorite horse enthusiast, the most wonderful woman on earth. He fishes his cell phone out of his pocket to see whether she has replied to his latest message. Not yet. Perhaps it didn't send? Hopefully, he goes into his sent messages and double-checks. Yes, it was sent over an hour ago. He puts the phone back and tries to pep himself up. Emma is probably still thinking everything through. She's not going to ignore him forever. Deep down, she has to know that the two of them are meant for each other. They just had some bad luck along the way.

From in the kitchen, he hears ringing laughter and a refrigerator door closing.

"Coffee's ready," Smilla calls.

He's here to work after all. Might as well stand up and get the preliminary greetings over with. On his way to the kitchen, he puts on an innocent smile.

"Well, hi there," he says, trying to sound surprised.

Kristoffer turns around, and his face darkens. "What are you doing here?"

"I'm the photographer," he answers, as if that were obvious.

"There must be some mistake. I booked Hasse."

"Hasse had to be somewhere else, so I offered to fill in. Sometimes we help each other out, as colleagues."

A modified truth. When he talked with his colleague yesterday, it came out that he was going to work with Kristoffer today, and Hugo convinced him to trade assignments. Hasse spent no time on unnecessary questions. Quid pro quo.

"Is there a problem?" Smilla asks, who must have sensed the chilly atmosphere in the room.

"Absolutely not." Kristoffer smiles disarmingly. "This is going to be the best photography session ever."

Hugo nods. "Then I think we should get started."

66.

On her way up in the elevator, Emma composes a text to Hugo, but she deletes it and starts over again. She doesn't know how to express herself so he will understand. She has to get him to accept that she has moved on and doesn't want any contact. She considers arranging a meeting with him. Then the pregnancy would speak for itself. Soon she and Kristoffer are going to be a family. Emma feels all warm inside as she thinks about the little being growing in her belly. Someone who will be a separate individual, yet a combination of his parents.

The elevator stops and she steps out. Hugo is going to be crushed when he finds out. It would be kinder to break the news to him in person. She deletes the message and calls Josefin, who has been trying to reach her.

"Hi. How's it going?" Emma asks.

In fifteen minutes, it will be time to confront Cornelia

again, and she needs to prepare herself, at least skim through yesterday's questioning first.

"Everyone's alive anyway." Josefin sounds pitiful.

"Is it that bad? What's going on?"

"Astrid had nightmares all night. I've been running around between bedrooms like a scalded rat, trying to console crying children."

"Then you've got today's interval workout done," Emma says, but she regrets her attempt at humor right away.

"Knock it off. I'm not ready to laugh at the misery."

"How is Astrid doing now?" Emma asks while she sits down at the desk. With a sigh, she looks at the pile of papers waiting.

"She's back to her usual self this morning, but last night . . . she scared the life out of me with her screaming. At first I thought someone had broken in and was about to kill her. It sounded that bad."

It strikes Emma that no one considered that the entire Göransson family might be in danger. Nothing suggests that, but perhaps the police are in the dark. And now Astrid is staying with Josefin. She almost blacks out as her imagination gets the best of her. What if someone stayed behind after the open house and killed Hans during the night? What if that "old man" Astrid said she saw really exists? And what if he is planning to come back to put an end to the rest of the family—and anyone else who might get in the way?

"Hello? Are you still there?" Josefin asks.

"I'm here," Emma answers. "What did Astrid say? Did you get any idea what she was dreaming about?"

She'll have to discuss the possibility of a threat against the whole family with Nyhlén later. But if the entire family were targeted, why wouldn't the perpetrator have killed them all at once? Cornelia and Astrid were sound asleep, and would have been hardly able to put up resistance anyway.

"She acted as if someone were coming to take her away, and she kept screaming for help. It seemed so real."

"It's not strange that she'd be having nightmares."

"True, but this was something else. More like night terrors. Do you know what that is?"

"Never heard of it."

"Ask Cornelia about it—if this is something that has affected Astrid before, it would be good for us to know."

"I'll do my best to find out."

"Astrid asked about her mother this morning. Do you know when she'll get to see her?"

Emma sighs heavily. "Not as long as she's under arrest. I have to go now. Hugs."

67.

As soon as she enters the interview room, Cornelia has a premonition that a critical point is within reach. She'll have to put all her cards on the table. The last thing she wants is to get herself tangled in more strange lines of reasoning that will only lead to more questions. She has nothing to hide. The curtains in the room are fluttering from the draft, and in some strange way this gives her hope.

Unfortunately, her defense attorney seems more interested in her cell phone than in her client's fate. Cornelia sits down and waits for a greeting, which doesn't come. Instead, the two of them sit silently side by side, waiting for the police. As soon as the door opens and Cornelia sees Emma, she gets up.

"How is Astrid?"

"Sit down," the attorney says firmly. "I'll talk with Josefin Eriksson later today and ask her how your daughter is doing. That's not the job of the police."

Feeling totally wronged, Cornelia sinks down on the chair again and looks at Emma. "May I please see Astrid today?"

"Let's take one thing at a time," Emma answers.

The attorney mutters something about getting started with the questioning, and Emma and her colleague nod.

"I want to get out of here. I haven't done anything," Cornelia sobs, unable to hold in the outburst. "I'm innocent, and my daughter needs me."

"Save your energy. The questioning hasn't even started," the attorney says acidly, pushing up her glasses.

Cornelia wants to scream that they should send that bitch out headfirst. She would rather have no attorney than one who is openly contemptuous.

"Shall we get going?" Emma asks.

The attorney nods and takes a not-so-subtle look at her watch.

Cornelia can't take it anymore. "I want to change defense counsel."

The woman beside her sighs deeply. "Is that the thanks I get for coming all the way here? If you only knew about my tight schedule."

"You have the right to change," Nyhlén says, "but that means this may take longer."

"I thought you couldn't hold me longer than ninety-six hours."

"Until the prosecutor makes a decision about arraignment," Emma says. "That's correct."

"Then I want to replace her, thanks."

Cornelia breathes out when the woman gets up and leaves the room without saying a word. Emma appears to want to say something, perhaps apologize on the defense attorney's behalf, but she remains silent.

"In the meantime, what can we work on?" Emma says, looking at Nyhlén.

"When can I see Astrid again?" Cornelia says.

"In two days at most, regardless of what happens," Nyhlén says. "In the remand prison, you get to have visitors, in contrast to the jail."

Two days. Forty-eight more hours without Astrid?

"Does she suffer from night terrors?" Emma asks suddenly.

Cornelia doesn't know what she's talking about. "What's that?"

"Night terrors."

"I've never heard of that. Why do you ask? What happened?" Cornelia is about to stand up again.

"Astrid is fine," Emma says, raising her hand in a gesture that means Cornelia should stay seated. "She just had a bad dream."

The little strength Cornelia still had runs out. She doesn't know how she can bear any more. Not when Astrid is having horrible nightmares and she isn't there to console her. It's just too much. She has to be able to hold her child, to tell her that soon, soon everything will be back to normal again.

"What can I do to speed up the process?" Cornelia asks, as collected as she is able to be. "Astrid needs me."

"Tell the truth," Emma says without moving her gaze away. "Tell us what happened."

The truth. Cornelia wonders what that's supposed to mean. Because if she were guilty and confessed the murder, she wouldn't get out to be with her daughter for many years.

68.

Josefin doesn't feel she can leave Astrid and Anton at school when everything is so turbulent, but she is going crazy having them at home, especially indoors. It's as if the limited space turns them into little monsters that have to climb on the walls, tear down the wallpaper, shriek and make a racket. A change of environment is needed immediately if the house is going to remain intact. She decides on a stroll to the playground. When Josefin goes up to Anton's room to interrupt their play, she overhears their conversation and feels pressure in her chest.

"My daddy's dead. Is yours too?" Astrid asks in a voice that doesn't reveal any feelings.

When Anton doesn't answer, she continues. "He's never at home, so he's probably dead too."

Josefin sees Anton's face distorted by worry, but she slips into the room just in time to straighten out the misunderstanding. "Anton's dad is at work, Astrid. He's not dead. Most dads are alive. And work."

"Not mine."

"I know that, honey. Are you sad about that?"

"Yes," she answers quietly, fingering her dirty sweater. She hesitates before saying anything else. Then it comes. "I miss his phone."

Josefin doesn't know if she should laugh or cry. If Hans could hear his daughter now, he'd turn in his grave. Or rather in the morgue, because he's probably still there, waiting for burial.

Once they're outside, Josefin lets the children run ahead, on the condition that they look carefully in both directions before they cross the street together, hand in hand. Josefin is convinced that even young children need to be given some independence, but she never lets them out of her sight. She walks a few meters behind them, making sure no cars are coming.

Astrid gets to the tire swings first. *Thank goodness they manage to get going by themselves nowadays.* All Josefin needs to do is sit down and observe. The spring sun peeks out, and she tries to enjoy the moment.

It doesn't take long before fatigue catches up with her and she feels drowsy, almost about to fall asleep. Then her thoughts drift to Cornelia, and she is wide-awake again. What could she possibly say to the police? Josefin can't believe that her friend stabbed her husband in the chest. The desire to kill him has probably been there over the years, but Cornelia isn't so stupid that she would risk ending up in prison. Not when she has Astrid.

Sure, Cornelia acts hastily and nervously sometimes, but that's understandable considering the chaos she has lived in. When they had coffee at Park Bakery the last time, Cornelia wanted to sit in the corner to keep an eye on her surroundings. The explanation was that she wanted a clear view so that no one could surprise her from behind. That, if anything, seemed like a sign of vulnerability to Josefin.

A yell interrupts Josefin's thoughts.

"I'll kill you!" Astrid throws herself over Anton, who falls down defenseless on the ground.

Josefin is quickly on her feet, pulling them apart. "You don't say that, Astrid."

"He threw sand," she says.

Children have an exceptional capacity to change activities at the speed of lightning; a moment ago, they were swinging together. Josefin didn't even see when they jumped off the tires, let alone how the quarrel started. Anton is shaking with fury and Josefin consoles him, but she senses that she can't take sides, however mean the words that come out of Astrid's mouth. It's important to show that she doesn't automatically think her own child is always innocent. And right now Astrid doesn't need to be scolded but hugged.

"I want to go home," Anton says over and over again, clinging harder to his mother.

"There now. It'll work out."

Anton refuses to let go, and when Josefin at last succeeds

in freeing herself she doesn't see Astrid anywhere. Just what she needs.

"Astrid," she calls, then looks at Anton. "Did you see where she went?"

He shakes his head. "And I don't care either."

Josefin calls again, louder this time. A dad with a child on a bicycle is coming toward the park, and Josefin asks him if he has seen a six-year-old girl with dark, unevenly cut hair. He shakes his head.

If she left, she can't have gone far. She'll have to try to coax her.

"Astrid, we're going home for ice cream now," she calls, but without response from anyone other than Anton, who lights up. Josefin doesn't even know if they have ice cream at home, but she'll deal with that problem later.

If Astrid went into the woods, she may be headed for the water. That insight makes Josefin's pulse pound harder. She takes out her phone and calls Andreas while she scans the area with her eyes. It goes straight to voice mail. What did she expect? Panic is well on its way to taking over completely; at any moment she's not going to be able to think rationally. She goes toward the bushes where Astrid was standing just now and looks behind them to be on the safe side. The father of the child on the bicycle asks if he can help out.

"It would be great if you could search along the path. The girl's name is Astrid. She has a red jacket and brown shoes," Josefin says, exchanging cell phone numbers with the man.

"We'll go up into the woods and call," he says.

"Then I'll go toward Alviksvägen."

How does an angry child think? Presumably not at all, simply acting in rage. They are only several blocks from home, so now Josefin wonders if Astrid may have headed back there. But it's doubtful she would find the way by herself. Best to get out to the road as quickly as possible. An accident could happen there. Her heart rushes, and she starts running. Anton falls behind but keeps up as best he can. She has a bad feeling inside that she's not going to see Astrid along the street, and her anxiety increases when she discovers she was right. No solitary girl as far as the eye can see. Josefin looks toward the meadow again. No Astrid there either. Her phone rings, and Josefin hopes it's the father she met in the park.

"Hi," Andreas says. "Did you just call?"

"Astrid disappeared from the playground. I can't find her."

"What do you mean disappeared? How did that happen?"

"I'll explain later," Josefin says. "Anton and I are going to their school to ask for help."

"Have you called the police?"

Josefin stumbles on the edge of the sidewalk. "The police?"

"A missing child . . . it can happen quickly."

She didn't want to hear him develop this line of reasoning. "Can you come home?" she says.

"I'm already on my way."

When they've hung up, Josefin calls Emma, however

unpleasant she fears that may be. In her mind, she is preparing a speech in her defense. All she wanted was to help out with Astrid, and then this happens.

Thank goodness Emma answers immediately. "Hi, Josefin. I can only talk briefly."

"Astrid is gone," she says while she hurries on. "She disappeared from the playground a few minutes ago, and now I can't find her."

Josefin hears that she sounds as anxious as she feels.

"Take a deep breath. Where did you see her last?"

"In the playground in the park right above the beach—Solviksbadet. The children got into an argument at the swings, and I went over to help them sort it out. For a few seconds, I didn't have my eyes on her, when I was consoling Anton, and then she was just gone."

"Were you alone in the park?"

"Right then, yes." A shudder sweeps through Josefin. What was Emma trying to suggest by that?

"Keep searching. Contact the school and ask them to keep an eye out. She may be on her way there. Are there any other places she could conceivably want to go?"

"Not that I can think of. Andreas is coming home to see if she went back to our house and a dad we ran into after she disappeared went toward the woods to search."

Anton has caught up with her and is panting from running so fast.

"We'd better hang up now so you're available in case someone tries to get hold of you," Emma says. "I'll get the police there as soon as possible."

69.

A patrol car outside the Brommaplan subway station answers the call and drives the four kilometers to Smedslätten. Practically enough, they already have a picture of Astrid to send out, because she figures into the investigation of her father's death.

Emma and Lindberg discuss how they should handle this unwelcome news with Cornelia. Should they inform her now, that her daughter has disappeared, or is it better to wait until they know more? Even though Cornelia has the right to information about her child, it seems cruel to give her such news in her cell, where she sits without being able to do anything.

"How long has the girl been gone?" Lindberg asks.

"Just fifteen minutes."

"Then let's focus on searching first and avoid creating unnecessary chaos. Because there's no known threat against the family."

"Not that we've identified so far anyway," Emma replies. "What do you mean by that?"

"Just something that struck me before, when I was talking with my sister. What if someone *is* after the family?"

"That's highly unlikely," Lindberg says. "Then they wouldn't have survived the night of the murder."

"That's what I thought too. Unless we're dealing with a really sick character, who thinks this is all just a game."

Lindberg shakes his head firmly. "Get back to me as soon as you have any news about the girl."

Emma goes to her office, ill at ease. If it turns out that someone does want to injure the rest of the family, the police have done a poor job by not understanding that and, above all, depriving the wrong person of liberty. If only she could just get hold of the psychiatrist at Saint Göran to confirm that Cornelia is telling the truth. Emma is about to make another attempt to call the Göranssons' next-door neighbor, but then she sees that Kristoffer has tried to reach her. He left a voice mail and a text message, both with the exhortation to get in touch immediately. She should have time for a brief call to him, even if he isn't top priority at the moment.

"Good of you to finally call," says Kristoffer, his voice sounding somewhat cold. "You have to have a talk with that creep. I can't put up with it anymore."

Emma is trying to follow along. "Are you talking about Hugo?"

"Damn right I am. Who else?"

"Okay, but perhaps you don't need to yell at me because you're angry at him. What's he done now?"

"He's everywhere. I'm going crazy! And that's exactly what his goal is. Besides ruining my open houses, he showed up at a photo shoot today. Just like that."

A man has been murdered. A child is missing. And Kristoffer calls to whine to her that Hugo is being troublesome? Emma doesn't know what to say; after all, shouldn't he be the one to tell Hugo to go to hell?

"I have too many other things going on," Emma says. "You'll have to resolve this on your own."

"Well then, maybe I should let him win the battle."

Her stomach tightens when he says that. "What's that supposed to mean?"

"Oh, nothing," Kristoffer says, hanging up.

Emma tries to shake off the irritation that has managed to rub off on her in such a short time; the call took only a minute. Right now she's most annoyed that Kristoffer is making such a big deal out of it. Why not just ignore Hugo? Not let himself be affected. "Idiot," she says under her breath.

"Did you say something?" Nyhlén asks from the doorway.

Emma sighs. "Man or mouse—sometimes I wonder."

"Are you talking about me?" Nyhlén says, laughing, although somewhat tentatively.

Emma and Nyhlén have a hard but honest way of talking to each other, and the jokes usually come thick and fast. Sometimes they miss the mark, but they need humor to cope with the job. But before she can throw him out with a cutting remark, the phone rings. When she hears

Staffan Svärd introduce himself, she signals to Nyhlén to stay.

"Hello. Thank you for calling," Emma says. "We've been trying to reach you for a while."

"We've been gone for a week," Mr. Svärd answers. "We turned on our phones when we came home again. Otherwise, you never know how expensive the phone bill will be when you're abroad."

A week? Then they can't have seen or heard anything the night of the murder. Emma sighs until it occurs to her that it's possible they observed something earlier that could turn out to be significant.

A faint child's giggling on the other end makes Emma stop short.

"Do you have small children?" she asks with surprise, because she knows that both of them are over seventy-five. But perhaps a grandchild is visiting.

The man laughs. "Oh, no, we've been retired for many years. It's our little neighbor girl, who came over for a snack. She's so sweet."

"What's her name?" Emma asks, fixing her eyes on Nyhlén. *Say it's Astrid,* she thinks.

"Astrid," he answers, lowering his voice.

"But you wouldn't believe what the girl's hair looks like right now. It's a total mess. What could have happened to her, I wonder. She just shakes her head when I ask. Oh well. That's not something you need to concern yourself with, of course."

Thank God she's safe and sound, Emma thinks. "How

nice to hear that Astrid is with you," she says. "Would you please see to it that she stays there? You see, we've been searching for her. My colleague and I are leaving now, and we'll be at your house within fifteen minutes. Okay?"

"That's just fine. It's no trouble at all," the man says politely, but at the same time he sounds confused.

It seems he has no idea what happened in the house next door.

70.

When the teacher says it's not like Astrid to run away, Josefin has a desire to strangle her. Her guilty conscience doesn't need any more fuel; it's burning just fine anyway. Good thing they're just talking on the phone, so that the woman can't see Josefin's expression. This is the third time now the staff has called, and Josefin asks them to call back only if they have good news. Then she calls Emma. Voice mail. Andreas has made it home, but there's no trace of Astrid, and Josefin has recounted the course of events for the police officers in the patrol car. The father who was going to check in the woods reported back that unfortunately he didn't seen a girl in a red jacket. But Josefin is still hopeful they will find her soon.

When she's halfway past the beach at Ålstensängen, her phone rings.

"The girl has been found," a police officer says, giving an address near Cornelia's house.

"Thank God. I'll be there in five minutes," Josefin says. She shudders when she thinks about Astrid walking all that way by herself. Presumably on the path through the woods, otherwise some outsider would have reported a solitary six-year-old on busy Alviksvägen, where many drivers exceed the speed limit and then some. Josefin knows the path well, because of her trail runs. Off the trail, the terrain is big and bushy, and treacherous.

At the moment, the kilometer plus to Cornelia's old neighborhood is tough going because of Anton's flagging energy. Even if common sense says that the situation is no longer dire, Josefin wants to get there as quickly as possible. Give Astrid a hug and say that she was very worried when she disappeared. But when they turn onto the street and Josefin sees the neighbor's house, all tension lets go. Her legs are about to give way as she stands at the door catching her breath.

When she rings the bell, a man opens the door with Astrid at his heels. The girl looks sullen. Anton hides behind Josefin's legs. It's clear the children have not made up yet.

"Hello, my little friend," she says, getting down on her knees to be on the same level as Astrid. "I'm so happy to see you."

"Sorry," Astrid whispers. "I'm a monster." She hits herself hard in the stomach with a clenched fist.

Josefin takes hold of her hand and picks her up. "Don't say that. You aren't at all."

"It's my fault that Daddy died. My fault."

It is distressing to see her punishing herself. Poor little girl.

"No, it's not. Not at all," Josefin says.

The neighbors exchange perplexed glances, but she will have to deal with their speculations later. First, she has to try to understand why Astrid ran away.

"Why did you leave the playground?"

"I wanted to go home to Mommy."

Of course.

"But Mommy wasn't home, and the door was locked," Astrid says. "So I knocked on Kerstin and Staffan's door."

"It was good you did that," says Josefin.

Astrid looks thoughtful. "Maybe Mommy is at that new place? In the apartment."

"I don't think so." Josefin trembles at the thought of where the conversation is heading.

"So where is she? Why did she just leave me?"

Josefin ignores the neighbors' increasingly inquisitive looks.

"She'll be home again soon. I promise," she says, and at the same time bites her tongue. But what should she say? It's probably better to keep Astrid calm instead of telling the truth—that perhaps her mother is never coming home. Well, if it turns out that way, Josefin will just have to admit she was wrong.

But she can't bear to think that far ahead right now.

71.

Kerstin and Staffan Svärd look shaken. They start to move aside the luggage blocking the entry.

"Don't worry about that. We'll get past," says Emma, shaking hands with them. Then she greets Astrid, who doesn't answer when spoken to. In fact, she doesn't even give Emma a glance. Anton, on the other hand, happily jumps up into her arms.

Josefin seems surprised. "Everything's under control," she says. "You didn't need to come."

"We're here to speak with Mr. and Mrs. Svärd too," says Emma. "Did you say anything about Hans?"

"Astrid told them herself."

"Okay. Do you need help with anything? A ride home maybe?"

"Andreas will be here any minute to pick us up, but thanks anyway."

Emma and Nyhlén choose to wait for the questioning

until Josefin and the children have left. It shows on the Svärds' faces that the commotion is too much and that they're having a hard time making sense out of everything.

Thank goodness Andreas shows up shortly. Emma greets him, but he looks so worn-out that she backs away. Not a trace is seen of his usual positive attitude. At first, she thinks he's not feeling well. But when Josefin meets him in the hall with the children, Emma sees that something else is wrong. Their awkward hug feels forced, and they don't exchange many words. Hopefully, it's not anything serious.

As soon as Josefin and the children have left, there is calm in the house. Emma goes into the kitchen and sits down with the others. She almost laughs when she sees how transparent Nyhlén's face looks compared with the two returning foreign travelers, who look like gingersnaps just out of the oven.

"So you've already heard about Hans Göransson?" Emma says.

"It's so awful," Staffan says without looking particularly sad. "A week ago, we were talking to him by the hedge that separates our yards. And now he's dead."

Kerstin shudders and pulls up her poncho, which had slipped down over her back.

"Do you remember what you talked about?" Emma asks.

"He told me they'd soon be showing the house and wondered if we would be around then."

"What did you say?"

"That we were leaving for our apartment in the Canary

Islands," Staffan says, nodding toward his wife. "We go there three times a year."

Kerstin sits quietly alongside, looking almost as shrunken-up as the withered flowers in the windows. Either she is shy or else she's used to her husband speaking for them.

"Did he say anything else?"

"We got on the subject of the pine tree right on the property line. I used to be a forester, so I could see that it's dying," says Staffan, pointing out the window at a stately tree. "But Hans didn't seem to want anything to do with that."

"How did the conversation end?"

Staffan thinks. "His phone rang. So we never came to any decision concerning the tree—whether it was to be or not to be."

"How would you describe Hans as a person?" Emma asks. She looks at Kerstin to begin with, but Staffan gets there first.

"A conscientious neighbor who didn't create any problems."

"Kerstin?"

She winces. "Yes?"

"What opinion do you have of Hans?"

"I don't really know," she answers.

Emma's curiosity is rising. She senses that Kerstin is trying to evade the question, but she doesn't intend to let her off so easily. "It's important for the investigation that we get a complete picture of him, even if talking about it may be uncomfortable."

"You mustn't pressure Kerstin," Staffan says. "She has a weak heart." He places a veined hand protectively over his wife's.

Emma imagines Kristoffer and herself as elderly. Will they be sitting together in a villa somewhere in the suburbs looking out for each other, like this couple is doing? She has a hard time imagining that Kristoffer will ever sit still longer than a minute or two.

"What impression do you have of Cornelia?" Emma asks. They can come back to Hans later.

Kerstin gives a sad smile. "A troubled soul. She hasn't had it easy. Cornelia was only a child when she and Hans met."

Staffan nodded. "And then little Astrid came into the world."

"What do you mean that Cornelia hasn't had it easy?" Emma gives Kerstin a look of encouragement.

"Hans was no gentleman," she replies, stopping short. "But you shouldn't speak ill of the dead. No, it's not right."

"Still, it may be of the utmost importance that you tell us what you know, so I have to ask you to continue anyway." Emma's patience is wearing thin, and she has a desire to squeeze the truth out of the old woman.

"Well, I don't like to say so, but his way of addressing her when he thought no one else was listening, my goodness. Such mean words and such deep contempt—for his own wife. Sometimes I heard more than I should have. Oh, how afraid I was many times that he would discover me sitting on the porch. I didn't dare move until he had gone inside."

Staffan lowers his eyes. "We even considered looking for a different place to live so that Kerstin would have peace. Although we love our house. The two of us don't really need such a big house, but we would prefer not to move away."

"I guess we don't need to think about that anymore." Kerstin looks self-consciously at her husband, and they nod in mutual understanding.

"No, now we can stay living here," he says, but his expression turns uneasy. "Or should we be worried after what happened next door?"

Emma shakes her head. "I don't think so."

72.

The hours pass without anything happening. No news or any new information. Cornelia sits and stares at the wall in front of her, waiting for another attorney. What will everyone think of her? Astrid's teachers, the real estate agent, the neighbors? What are they thinking right now? Are they already speculating wildly that she was the one who lost it with the knife? That she'd had enough and killed her husband like a madwoman. Or are they standing up for her and feeling sorry for her? Do they realize she's innocent? Cornelia has no idea.

The flowers. She suddenly remembers that she promised the next-door neighbors she would water their flowers while they were in the Canary Islands. Cornelia fumbles for her cell phone before it occurs to her that it's not here. The habit of reaching for it is so deeply ingrained that her fingers are itching, a symptom of withdrawal.

When there is finally a knock on the door, Cornelia

guesses that it's time. She takes a deep breath, gets up, and makes an effort to straighten her hair with her fingers. She is prepared to leave and never come back. The disappointment when she sees the food cart outside is almost paralyzing. She stares at the beef croquettes and overcooked potatoes before reluctantly taking a plate, which she then sets on the small mounted surface that serves as a nightstand. During her stay in this cell, she hasn't had a bite of food, but she feels nothing even close to hunger. There is so much else occupying her awareness that her primary instincts have disappeared. She feels dizzy and lies down on the bed, but then her face ends up much too close to the beef croquettes and she feels nauseated.

During all the years she lived under constant threat, she always got up and fought on, firmly resolved to let her strong survival instinct overcome everything else. But in this restricted space, cut off from reality and with only a soiled picture of Astrid at hand, the energy is running out of her in record time. As time passes, she is getting more apathetic. The will to get justice is starting to weaken; she knows that nothing is going to be the same after this anyway. Her trust in other people is gone forever, and she'll never be able to erase the memory of what it's like to be treated like the dregs of society.

She can no longer even cry. Instead, Cornelia makes note of what she's learned: If you've made the mistake of ending up here, the right to make decisions about your own life is taken away from you. You don't even get a sporting chance to end it. That, of course, was why they took her belt and shoelaces; it took a full day before she made the connection. Her eyes fall on the silverware. Of course it's plastic, so that prisoners won't be able to injure themselves or a guard.

But Cornelia doesn't want to die. Now that her life was about to start over and she would finally be able to live in peace, she wants nothing other than to be with her child. Bake, decorate Easter eggs, draw, teach her to write, read bedtime stories, wipe her runny nose, bandage her knee when she falls and scrapes herself. She wants to experience all the joys of being a parent, instead of constantly being on guard.

Cornelia hopes Astrid's night terrors aren't something serious. She wants to be able to google it—to find out if they're dangerous and how you should handle them as a parent. What if they were caused by the sight of her father's mangled body? Perhaps just seconds of an impression would be enough. Cornelia wants to consult with a child psychologist, but as long as she's locked up she can't. She can do nothing other than wait and try not to give up, keeping her fingers crossed.

But it's infuriating that she can't even ask Josefin what happened last night. Cornelia gets up and kicks the wall hard. The subsequent wave of pain in her foot is liberating. She continues pounding with all her might and doesn't notice that guards have come into the cell until they force her down. Her head hits the floor so hard she sees stars.

"Get a grip," they warn in hard voices before leaving just as quickly as they arrived.

When she gets on her feet again, her whole body is shaking and her toes are throbbing. She is going to perish if she sits here one more night staring into the darkness, incapable of helping her daughter.

73.

SATURDAY, APRIL 5

I would give a lot to be able to hear what's being said inside the sparsely furnished two-story villa. It must be something serious, considering the sullen expressions I see. There must be triple-pane windows, because I don't hear a sound, not even when I put my ear against the glass. The woman seems worried about something. She stands by the lilies on the counter pretending to pick away withered leaves.

With a despondent look, she sits down at the kitchen table. He is there at once and catches her hand. But she frees herself and twists her head in my direction. Quickly, I pull back so as not to be discovered, but I see her tears and empathize with her, because I know what a pig he is.

I curl up between a couple of good-size bushes and wait for the right moment to start up my surveillance again. There's not a single person out except me, even though the sun is shining. The neighborhood is empty, for the simple reason that no one lives here yet. It's just one big construction site with only one house finished, ready for showing.

But I know what lies buried below the ground. What stood here from the beginning. What we fought to be able to keep. Then everything quickly went downhill, and not just one life was lost, but two.

Now not a trace of the tragedy is visible.

I take out my binoculars and focus on the woman's name tag. I zoom in and read: "Helena."

So beautiful, but melancholy. Of course he has hurt her. Sooner or later it will come out what an asshole he is. For some that will be a relief, for others a sorrow. It's not hard to guess which of the alternatives applies to Helena.

I aim the binoculars at his face and discover a new sort of expression. Something I have never seen on Benjamin before. It takes a while before I think of what it is.

For the first time, he looks uncertain.

Nothing could make me happier. Except one thing: to see him dead.

74.

Helena avoids eye contact, and Benjamin doesn't know what he fears most—that she is serious when she says it's over or that she intends to reveal everything to Monika. Why right now? Was the stress too much after the murder? Does she suspect him of something? Actually, he's had a feeling for a long time that something was going on, but he chose to ignore the problem until it became unavoidable.

Helena is far too clever to agree to unreasonable conditions such as getting together only when it suits him. Benjamin always knew that one day she would demand more than he was prepared to give, and he can hardly blame her for that.

In fifteen minutes curious prospective buyers will be streaming in to see what this newly constructed, solid and timeless house is all about. Far too expensive for what you get, but of course he'll keep that to himself. He doesn't remember exactly what Helena wrote in the marketing announcement, but he knows he hummed in agreement when he skimmed through it. She has a gift for language and knows better than to pour it on with too many adjectives, like he himself does until she gets at his words with her red editor's pen. *"Idyllic" and "picturesque" cancel each other out,* she'd say. *Pick one of them. People aren't stupid. Cut down on the number of exclamation points too. Otherwise, it seems desperate.*

Getting potential buyers to come all the way to a construction site in Beckomberga required cunning. Right now the area is completely dead and anything but attractive. Benjamin has promised a spectacular open house, but in reality he hasn't prepared anything beyond the norm. Hans Göransson, convinced by Benjamin to invest in the project, would be turning in his grave if he knew. Lucky he's dead so that Benjamin escapes the embarrassment. The project is doomed to fail if he can't conjure forth buyers. But he's no magician.

His stomach knots up when it strikes him that perhaps Helena is going to quit and go to another agency. That can't happen. She has all the qualities a good real estate agent needs, and he's the one who trained her. He can't stand the thought of her with another logo on her name tag, or in another man's arms. All the languishing looks people throw at her have not escaped him.

"Listen, Helena, can't we talk about this after the open house?" he says to her back, which is on its way out of the room. "I love you, baby."

Helena freezes in midmotion, and Benjamin holds his

breath. He doesn't care to analyze whether he exaggerated his feelings with his choice of words. When she turns around and looks at him, he has no idea what is going to come out of her mouth. But he wishes sincerely that she buys his declaration of love. A declaration he hasn't even said to Monika in recent years.

"It doesn't matter what you say anymore. You're not prepared to leave your wife for me, so we can't go on together."

Benjamin is about to spit out something about giving her a raise in salary, as if everything can be solved with money, but then he turns sensible. He concentrates on looking her deep in the eyes, trying to get her to soften a bit. A winning concept that has always worked before. Now, however, she is unreceptive and he is forced to capitulate, but he has to assure himself that what has happened stays between them.

Monika would kill him if she got wind that he has been unfaithful—again. One time she could overlook, but she made it clear that she would cut his dick off if it happened again. He remembers that only now, a little late perhaps. The mere thought that Monika would carry out her threat makes him search with his hands for the holy of holies. Helena looks at him with distaste, so he pretends to adjust his package and then crosses his arms.

"Please, don't say anything to Monika," he says.

Helena's gaze darkens. "What the hell. How could you even bring that up?"

"So I can rely on you?"

A movement outside the window puts them both off balance.

"Already?" Benjamin exclaims. "There's at least ten minutes until the scheduled time."

Benjamin is provoked by Helena's relieved expression.

He looks out the window, notes that the "Showing in Progress" sign is standing where it should beside an outdoor candle, and that Helena has set out the box of shoe protectors. All that's missing is for someone to show up in the middle of their quarrel.

"I'll go check that everything looks okay upstairs," she says, scampering away before he can stop her.

Deep in thought, Benjamin stands there and looks around. Somehow, in the middle of all this, he has to settle down and get into a work state of mind. Find his way back to his profession. Deliver. He adjusts his jacket, checks that the cuff links are sitting properly, and lights the candles on the windowsills. Strangely enough he doesn't see any signs of a prospective buyer, but he goes and feels the sturdy front door, which is unlocked. Good, then folks can freely stream in. He takes a deep breath, tries to focus, and then sees his pleasant, confidence-inspiring face in the hall mirror. Enjoys his even suntan. Above him he hears tapping from Helena's high heels, which he bought for her in London. Frightfully expensive.

A sound behind his back makes him turn around. At an arm's length stands a man in a cap. His penetrating gaze makes Benjamin nervous, and he wonders where the man came from. It takes a moment before he calms down and welcomes him.

The man doesn't answer and doesn't move a muscle. He

stands so quietly that Benjamin almost wonders whether it's a mannequin.

"Would you like a flyer?" he asks, lowering his shoulders. He has run into stranger types than this plenty of times. Prospective buyers come in all possible forms.

"That's not necessary," the man answers coldly.

He has heard that voice before. It reminds him of someone, but Benjamin can't place him. He searches frantically in the invisible archive of people he has met during his career. Not because he usually cares to remember anyone other than important people, but because a warning bell is ringing. He experiences a freezing sensation when it occurs to him who this might be.

75.

Actually, I'm not even offended that he doesn't know me. For Benjamin, I guess I'm just one of the many insignificant people he has run down over the years. Of course he wouldn't recognize me right away. Over a year has passed, after all. I see that he is in agony now, thinking feverishly.

It's obvious when his memory starts to clear somewhat. His eyes turn glassy, and I enjoy seeing the sweat seep out of his scalp.

I pretend to be interested in the furnishings, but I deliberately avoid touching anything, because I don't have gloves on yet. There must be no mistakes.

Benjamin is keeping a watchful eye on me. Perhaps he understands that I am here to get revenge but thinks I'm out to destroy something in the house.

If only it were that good.

Wonder if he'll manage to put two and two together

soon and understand the seriousness. I don't have such high expectations of his powers of deduction. There is not a chance in the world that he can connect everything, figure out why Hans had to die.

Benjamin's heart is surely beating fast now. There is no time to lose. At any moment, eager buyers could show up and then my chance will be gone. I walk decisively toward the stairs.

It works. Benjamin follows, and I nod, trying to look impressed, although it doesn't look particularly appealing. It's not at all as nice as the old house.

Helena looks out from one of the rooms with an ice-cold expression, but she cracks a smile when she sees that Benjamin has company. Suddenly, I have their full attention, and I count down the minutes. There isn't much time to play with.

I ask them to show me the master bedroom. Now is when it has to happen.

When Benjamin meets my eyes again, it shows that the pieces of the puzzle are falling into place. First, Hans. Then the alarm that went off in the middle of the night. And now, here we stand, face-to-face.

For the last time.

76.

The foundations for the houses under construction are close together, but that's just the way Maria-Therese wants it. Then it will be easy for the kids to run over to each other's houses to play without any major effort from the parents. Friends won't be an issue for a while, because Viggo is only three months old, but time goes fast. It's not hard to picture the future. Especially not in a neighborhood with such great potential. Maria-Therese adjusts the blanket that Viggo has kicked off and parks the stroller outside the entrance. Going to their first open house feels like a major much-anticipated step in life.

"We can let Viggo sleep a little longer, can't we?" Maria-Therese asks her wife.

Angelica looks at her. "I think so. We'll be able to see the stroller from the window."

Together they go toward the door of what may be the first home of their own. Their little two-room apartment in the city hardly counts; it's a temporary solution that they have to put up with until they've found their dream place.

The door to the house is ajar, and through the gap classical music is streaming out. Obediently they put on shoe protectors and step in. Instantly, Maria-Therese is struck by how open and clean it feels. The air is invigoratingly fresh; it smells new and unused, with the faint scent of candles burning. The candles flicker in the window facing the spanking-new teak balcony. Even though it's the middle of the day, nothing has been left to chance. The real estate agents never tamper with the cozy factor. Maria-Therese glimpses the kitchen, and the mere knowledge that no one can have flushed any dirt down the pipes or used the refrigerator or dishwasher makes her ecstatic. It's almost too good to be true. She has to pinch herself on the arm. The dream of being able to move into a new house with the woman she loves may be fulfilled soon. Maria-Therese believes this and sees that Angelica does too.

"Strange that there aren't any real estate agents here," Angelica says.

That hadn't occurred yet to Maria-Therese; she has been so occupied with taking in the atmosphere, looking for the karma of the house. She agrees that it's odd but thinks someone will probably show up at any moment. Until then, they can get a sense of coming home, without a salesperson analyzing every move they make. That might even be the reason behind this. Weber's is known for being able to deliver that little extra. She remembers there was something about that in the company's ad.

"What do you think?" she asks when they stop in front of the minimalistic designer kitchen.

"Maybe a little too sterile for my taste, if I'm going to be honest," Angelica says, looking out the window toward the stroller. "He seems to still be asleep."

"Nice."

Maria-Therese doesn't let herself be discouraged by Angelica's objection. But the house isn't exactly free, so it's probably good that she chose to have a child with a realist. They complement each other nicely.

Another pair of prospective buyers shows up, and the sense of exclusivity disappears as soon as the others start chatting about where they will put the piano the woman has evidently inherited from her childhood home. Maria-Therese says hello to the competitors politely and whispers to Angelica that she wants to take a look upstairs.

"Of course," she says, smiling. "Take all the time you need."

The butterflies in her stomach are riding a roller coaster when she leaves Angelica to go up to the bedrooms. She didn't think she would still be so much in love after two years. But Viggo has brought them even closer.

Maria-Therese stops in the spacious hall and wonders which room she should start in. She chooses to go right, to the two small bedrooms next to each other. One they could use as a combined guest room and office until Viggo has siblings. The oblong room facing the garden can be his room. She mentally furnishes it, placing the crib by the window and wondering where the changing table could go if there isn't room for it in the bathroom. The glider will have to be by the window. She leaves the room to peek into the bathroom, which she hopes doesn't have any awful borders in Mediterranean blue. With a sigh of relief, she notes that it is completely white with a gray-black slate floor. With floor heating installed, naturally, a shower, and a laundry chute.

They have to live here.

Only the master bedroom remains with its walk-in closet, which the listing promised to be "something beyond the ordinary." Her expectations are raised before even entering. But with its white wall-to-wall carpeting, it looks like any standard room, so she goes straight to the closet and pulls the sliding door to the side.

Her eyes fall on some newly ironed white shirts hanging in a row, but the stylist didn't fully succeed. Some dark stains appear at the bottom. A solitary high-heeled shoe right by the entrance reinforces the feeling that something is off. Weber's is known for its unique open houses, but a stray shoe is just plain odd. Not to mention that it doesn't smell all that nice in here.

Maria-Therese sees a pendant glistening on the floor. She leans down to pick it up but stops right before she touches it. Even if she understands what she's seeing farther inside the closet, she can't quite take it in. Someone is lying on the floor—a man in a chalk-stripe suit. She follows his body with her eyes.

The scream comes when she realizes that something is missing. The head.

77.

After what had been a quiet Saturday morning, suddenly everyone is rushing around the corridors at work, and Emma is trying to get a handle on what happened while she was in the restroom. For there is no doubt that this is something big. Lindberg walks quickly toward her with a tense expression. It appears he's on his way to the big meeting room.

"A quick briefing," he says in passing.

Emma follows the stream and barely has time to sit down before Lindberg begins.

"Only a few minutes ago, it came to my attention that two persons were found dead at a real estate open house in Beckomberga."

The room becomes dead silent as everyone waits for Lindberg to continue.

"Everything indicates that the victims are Benjamin Weber and Helena Sjöblom."

Emma feels her ears start to ring. Only a few days ago, they were in Benjamin's house on Drottningholm, when he and Helena gave each other alibis for the night of the murder. Now both of them are dead. She and Nyhlén must have missed something. She supports herself against the edge of the table so as not to collapse.

"Emma?" Nyhlén whispers, next to her. "Do you need something to drink?"

Automatically, she shakes her head although she needs something immediately if she's not going to faint. Nyhlén seems to read the situation and hands her a glass of water anyway. Grateful, she takes it. She sees the worry in his eyes. Soon it will be inexcusable not to explain what caused the sudden fall in her blood sugar.

"A prospective buyer made the discovery," Lindberg says. "The poor woman found them in the closet in the master bedroom."

"The cause of death?" someone asks.

"I was just getting to that," Lindberg replies. "Both of them were shot, according to the police at the scene."

"Any witnesses?" is the only thing Emma gets out while she struggles against dizziness.

Lindberg shakes his head. "This is a model home in a new housing development, where only one house is finished. The rest is one big construction site."

"Construction workers?" Nyhlén looks hopeful. "Could any of them have been there?"

"Not on a Saturday."

"Who reported the incident?" Emma asks.

"One of the prospective buyers, Angelica Heikkinen. Evidently, there wasn't much left of Benjamin's head."

The information is scanty, so Lindberg proposes that Emma and Nyhlén go to the crime scene immediately to form their own impressions.

En route, Emma tests several conceivable scenarios in her head. Could Benjamin's wife have caught him and Helena and murdered them in rage? Or did Helena have a jealous ex who wanted revenge? But what she keeps coming back to is that Benjamin knew Hans, and that both died in less than a week.

The twelve-minute trip out to Beckomberga is bumpy and intense. Emma manages it only because she has primed herself with strong antinausea tablets. By the time Nyhlén brakes outside the crime scene, adrenaline is pumping through her body. An empty stroller is parked on the newly laid lawn outside the house. A nameplate with "Viggo" on it decorates the chassis of the stroller.

"Up the stairs, the bedroom to the left," says the uniformed officer who meets them at the door.

"Where are the witnesses who reported this?"

"In the construction trailer next door. We got hold of the contractor, and they sent some personnel to help out. They let us into their office, because it'd be stupid to have a lot of running around in here."

"Good thinking."

They are allowed to walk only on the floor protector laid out in the bedroom while crime scene investigators work feverishly to secure evidence. Benjamin's body is closest to the entry of the closet, next to a black high-heeled shoe. Helena is lying in the corner, facing the wall. Emma tries to avoid looking toward Benjamin's face, but that's not possible. Her eyes make their way there anyway, and she swallows when all she sees are remnants of what must have been his head. Helena, in contrast, was shot in the chest. A pistol is lying on the ground beside Benjamin, as if it slipped out of his hand.

Emma inspects them awhile, trying to put together a conceivable string of events: Helena flees into the closet. Benjamin comes after her and shoots her. Then he brings the pistol to his mouth and fires. But why?

The technicians ask to continue their work, so Emma and her colleagues back out of there. On the way to compile their impressions, they exchange a few words with the medical examiner, who has had time to make only a preliminary assessment. It turns out to confirm Emma's theory.

"We've found gunpowder stains on the male victim's hand, which suggests that he first shot the woman before he shot himself. But we shouldn't draw any hasty conclusions before we know with certainty that the ammunition was fired from one and the same gun."

78.

What a mobilization. There's no sparing of resources here, let me tell you. There's an ambulance, paramedics, and police cars. Blue lights are revolving, and more people are showing up all the time. Soon the *batabatabata* of a helicopter will sound in the distance too, but I won't be here then.

In the meantime, the investigators have something to chew on. Or actually not—I've made it easy for them. There is no doubt about how the whole thing must have proceeded. Soon the news will leak out, and it won't take long before the case will be considered solved.

Then all the pieces will fall into place.

The barricade tape is still being set up when I leave the site and drive toward the hospital. The mission is finished, but the adrenaline kick has not settled down yet. I've done my part. I wish that I could communicate that to her in some way, but I know it won't be possible to reach her.

I'll have to be content with the knowledge that justice has been served and we can both move on.

Now all that remains is to say good-bye.

This time, Hillevi isn't sitting by the window humming. She's not even in the room, but it takes only a few minutes before she comes back.

"Hi," she says with a new sort of light in her eyes. "When did you get here?"

"Just now," I say, noticing that a man in a white lab coat lingers by the doorway. Her physician.

"Can I have a few words with you?" he asks me.

"Of course," I say, but I feel a creeping sense of dread about what he might want from me. Is she getting worse?

The doctor looks at Hillevi, who seems to be more or less as usual. She shrugs and sits down on the bed with a newspaper.

I follow the doctor down a long, narrow corridor. At the last door, he stops and shows me into his office.

"Sit down," he says amiably, looking sly behind his eyeglasses.

The doctor's expression puzzles me. While I sink down on the visitor's chair with a padded cushion, I give him an inquisitive look.

"I finally have some good news to tell you. She has started to remember certain things."

A shiver shoots along my spine. "Oh yeah?"

The doctor's smile cools at my guarded reaction, and I attempt to brighten up, so as not to arouse suspicion. If

I'm not careful, I could end up in a closed ward for long-term psychiatric illness myself.

My thoughts race away, and I no longer hear what the doctor is saying. Nothing before suggested that she could get healthy after such a long time, and the worry about what this might entail is gnawing me apart. I have to pull myself together in order to focus on the doctor's words.

"So now she needs all the support she can get to stay anchored in reality. Then she'll finally be declared healthy. I know how much you've struggled to help her over the years, so I'm keeping my fingers crossed that she really will be able to go home soon."

"Thanks," I squeeze out, but I feel a growing sense of panic.

This wasn't part of the plan. At least not anymore.

79.

Maria-Therese is still struggling to get her breathing to return to normal. It's not easy when Viggo is shrieking desperately. He wasn't wakened by his mother's first scream, which came out of her when she saw the dead man on the second floor. Evidently, she woke her son when she screamed a second time, when she discovered that a woman was also lying dead.

"Now, now," Angelica says, and Maria-Therese doesn't know if she's trying to console her or Viggo.

"It's fine. I'll take him now," says Maria-Therese. "I'll try to nurse so he'll calm down."

But Viggo must be picking up on her stress, because he writhes unhappily in her embrace instead of taking a firm hold on her breast like he usually does. She does her utmost to appear at ease, but it doesn't fool him.

When Angelica massages her shoulders, she realizes how tense her muscles are. The light pressure cuts like a knife.

She forces herself not to put up resistance, and after a while she has wound down enough that Viggo finally starts to eat.

Suddenly, a woman is standing in front of them saying that she is from the police, here to investigate the deaths. She says her name is Emma Sköld, and Angelica introduces all three of them.

"Is it okay to talk while you're nursing?" the police-woman asks.

Maria-Therese nods. "I assume you already know I was the one who found them."

"Yes. How are you doing?"

A male police officer approaches, but he looks self-conscious when he sees that Maria-Therese is exposing her breast.

"I'll just stand over here," he says, looking to the side, and the policewoman nods in response. She almost looks amused, but only for a fraction of a second. Then she regains her serious expression.

Maria-Therese can't say for sure how she is feeling, but the policewoman already seems to have forgotten her question, because she asks a new one before she gets a response. "Can you tell me how you discovered them?"

Maria-Therese takes a deep breath and gathers strength to force herself back to the incident.

"I went upstairs while Angelica stayed down here to keep an eye on Viggo, who was sleeping in the stroller outside. First, I went to the two smaller bedrooms, then I checked the bathroom, and finally only the master bedroom remained. Almost immediately, I was drawn to the walk-in closet—the description of it was so enticing in the listing. Before the open house I read through everything about the area and about the houses planned here. I was really looking forward to this day."

"I understand," the policewoman says. "What did you see first when you opened the closet?"

"The shirts. I noticed that they were stained. Then I noticed a necklace and a high-heeled shoe on the carpet. And that was when I saw him. And then the woman. Everything happened in a few seconds. I think I screamed until someone came here."

Angelica nods. "Yes, that's right."

"It must have been horrifying," the policewoman says, and she appears to mean it.

Maria-Therese nods and feels her eyes tearing up. Only now, when she is able to sit quietly, does the aftershock arrive. It was pointless to try to hold back the tears. The policewoman hands her a tissue, and Maria-Therese blows her nose. Viggo releases her breast and stares at the police-woman before he returns to his safe haven again.

"He's really cute," says the policewoman.

"Thanks," Maria-Therese says. "When can we leave?" She looks around in the construction trailer, where some-one has taped up a poster of a naked woman.

"Very soon. We still need to get your personal infor-mation, but I'm also wondering if you noticed anything different when you arrived."

"We were the first ones here, maybe a few minutes early. We were eager to see the house, because we've talked about this a lot," she says. Looking at Angelica, she feels the need to correct herself. "Or *I've* talked about it nonstop. Angelica was probably not quite as excited as I was. In any case, we thought it was a little strange that the door was ajar but no one else was around. The 'Showing in Progress' sign was in place, and the shoe protectors. The candles were lit, the music was on. There was just one thing missing—the real estate agent."

"But you went in anyway?"

"Yes. Wouldn't you have?"

The policewoman shrugs. "Maybe."

"I didn't think it was a big deal. We figured he, or she, was out on the balcony or upstairs, or had stepped into the bathroom before the crowd came. Then more prospective buyers came in, so we weren't alone anymore. Maybe I would have started wondering at that point, but I was totally preoccupied imagining what it would be like to live in the house. But that was then." Maria-Therese strokes Viggo's cheek.

"I'm sorry," the policewoman says, looking warmly at the little baby. "I'm sure you'll find something even better."

"It can't get much worse than this anyway," says Maria-Therese, getting a nod of agreement from her wife.

80.

"I really feel sorry for them," says Nyhlén as they drive back to the police station. "Their very first open house—can you imagine?"

"Like she said: it can't get much worse." But Emma isn't thinking about the crime; she's thinking about the sweet little baby. It was hard to tear her eyes off him. Soon she herself will be holding her own bundle of joy. The thought is dizzying.

She is interrupted by a call from Lindberg.

"The murder weapon was found in the gun registry," he says. "And you'll never guess who is registered as the owner."

"Who?" Emma says.

"Hans Göransson."

Nyhlén looks at Emma with surprise. "What the heck does that mean?" he says after Lindberg ends the call.

"Besides that there's now a connection between the murders?" Emma says. "Perhaps Benjamin murdered Hans and then thought we were on his trail. Helena may have suspected something that she was about to reveal to us. Then she confronted Benjamin at the open house. In desperation, he took her life."

"And saw shooting himself as his only way out," Nyhlén finishes.

"But when did he get hold of the gun?" Emma says, thinking out loud. "Do you remember any gun cabinet at the Göransson house?"

"I seem to recall it was in the basement. Benjamin had access several times during the open houses, so it may not have been difficult to steal a pistol."

"Or he took it with him the night he murdered Hans," says Emma. "Then only a motive remains."

"We probably won't have that served up to us," says Nyhlén. "I mean, it's hard to squeeze any juicy tidbits out of a corpse."

Emma can't help but smile a little at his macabre way of expressing himself. On the other hand, it's not funny that he's right. But perhaps Hans and Benjamin had some quarrel with each other that the police will still find out about.

Nyhlén parks and Emma gets out, but everything is going black before her eyes. As she crumples to the ground, she realizes she stood up too fast. Nyhlén comes around the car and helps her to her feet.

"How did that happen?" he asks. "You're completely pale."

It takes a while before Emma completely recovers her sight, and she shakes her head. "It's no big deal."

"So you mean randomly passing out is completely normal?"

She brushes aside his comment. "I didn't faint. It's been a while since I ate, I guess."

Thank goodness he lets it go and no more incidents happen on the way up to the rest of the squad.

Emma goes first to her office, but then decides to visit the restroom. As she passes Lindberg's office, she glimpses Nyhlén inside and hears them exchanging words in lowered voices. She suspects Nyhlén is talking with Lindberg about her, but instead of being moved by his concern she feels irritated. Since she bit the bullet at work during the worst part of the pregnancy, it would be terrible if she had to go on sick leave now. So as not to end up collapsing again, she picks up a banana in the break room. Then she stretches and goes into the meeting room and sits down.

Lindberg notes that today's events most likely solve the murder of Hans Göransson.

"We shouldn't assume anything, but there is much to suggest that the background motive was a showdown between Benjamin Weber and Hans Göransson. It has come to our knowledge that Göransson had invested in the development in Beckomberga, and it turned out to be a losing proposition. Reportedly, it was Weber who brought Göransson into the project, so they were business partners."

"But if they weren't getting along, why did Hans hire Benjamin Weber to sell his house?" Emma says, feeling energetic again. The banana did the trick.

"Presumably, Weber took no fee," Lindberg says. "I asked the agency to produce the contract, but there doesn't seem to be one. We don't know what other kind of hold Göransson may have had on Weber. And how pressed Weber actually was. It takes a lot for someone to decide to murder someone."

"What about the murder weapon?" Nyhlén says.

Lindberg nods. "According to the forensics team, there was an unlocked gun cabinet in Göransson's basement."

Emma is impressed by how much information her colleagues have managed to collect in such a short time. At the same time, she can't help wondering why none of this was discovered sooner.

She also wonders what she should say to Cornelia. The poor woman has been held in isolation for forty-eight hours. Time she could have spent with her daughter. On the other hand, she's about to be released, as soon as the prosecutor has a chance to study the new information.

When the meeting is over, Emma heads for the door, but she is stopped by Lindberg.

"I need to have a few words with you privately," he says.

"Sure," Emma replies. "What about?"

"Let's talk about it in my office."

There is something in his manner that makes Emma hesitant. His shoulders are hunched and he seems uncomfortable as they walk silently beside each other in the corridor. When he closes the door behind them, she realizes this must be a personal matter.

"The colleagues are asking about you all the time," he says. "They've noticed that something's going on."

"I'll tell them, but I'd prefer to wait until next week, when I'm past the riskiest phase. If anything happens, I don't want everyone to know."

Lindberg clears his throat. "Actually, that's not the problem."

"What do you mean?" Emma asks, feeling an oncoming sense of panic. "Just tell me."

"I've had several indications that perhaps you aren't able to do your job a hundred percent at the moment. So I'm proposing that you take some comp time until you feel better. You have a lot of unused leave."

Emma can't believe Nyhlén would tattle to Lindberg instead of talking with her first. "But—"

"No 'buts.' I've already decided. We can't take any risks by having personnel in place who aren't at their best. There is far too much at stake. We need everyone to give a hundred and ten percent. You, if anyone, know that."

Emma feels her frustration coming to a head. "So why did you present it as a request then and not as an order?"

"I only want the best for you and the investigation," Lindberg says. "And as it appears now, we're basically at the goal. Everything points to Benjamin Weber being behind the murders. I'll keep you informed."

When Emma gets up on unsteady legs, she feels worse again, in part because she knows Lindberg is right. Deep down, she knows she's not feeling well enough to do her job fully right now. But she can't admit it to him. Not yet. She's too disappointed. She leaves the room without a word. She's on the verge of tears, but she swallows them back when she sees Nyhlén waiting for her outside. She can tell he knows what the conversation was about.

"What was that about?" he asks anyway.

Emma glances at him. "I'm going to be off for a while."

"Why is that?"

"Because certain colleagues have gone behind my back and gossiped to my boss," she says.

Nyhlén looks hurt. "I only said to Lindberg that I was worried about you, because you fainted earlier. Excuse me for caring."

Just as Emma is about to apologize and explain her situation, a colleague looks curiously out from his office. Emma keeps quiet and tries to put on a smile when Nyhlén tells her to get well soon.

Back in her office, she looks around. She seldom reflects about the room's appearance—fairly messy, with binders and papers everywhere. A thorough cleaning is what's needed, but it's not going to happen today. Right now she just wants to get out of here as soon as possible. She probably won't miss the desk, but she'll definitely miss the pace, the pulse, and the feeling of driving an investigation in the right direction.

She's still not sure why her instincts were off with Benjamin Weber, dealing a blow to her self-confidence. Sure, he behaved strangely and she reacted to his sudden absence, the lie about the open house, the fact that he knew Hans personally, and his secret relationship with one of his employees, but she didn't think he could have murdered Hans. The usual warning signals and gut feeling were never there.

Lindberg suddenly stops outside. "I'm glad you're still here," he says. "Please say hello to your sister and thank her so much for facilitating our work."

Yet another sore point. It's her fault that Josefin's last few days have been turned upside down. But Emma nods and promises to convey the message.

While she adjusts the piles from the last few days of work, she thinks about Cornelia in jail. There she sits without having the faintest idea that she'll be able to go home to her daughter soon.

81.

When the lock clicks and the door opens, Cornelia has prepared herself mentally for another interrogation, so she doesn't know what to think when a police officer says she can go.

"The prosecutor has decided to release you. You are still a person of interest in the case, but you don't need to be deprived of liberty."

Does this mean she gets to go home to Astrid? To her new life without Hans? Naturally, she doesn't want to question the decision, but she can't quite believe it's true. She decides that the young man in front of her must be playing a joke, messing with her to test how much she can take, and she can't even bring herself to stand up.

"Do you intend to come with me, or do I have to drag you out?" the officer asks.

Her legs don't obey when Cornelia tries to get up. She lifts them heavily off the cot and sets her feet down on the floor, seeing her inscription on the wall beside it: "Astrid." It looks like a child wrote it. Not much remains of the nail on the middle finger of her right hand, but it calmed her to have a task to carry out, with a specific, achievable goal. The photo of Astrid is on the nightstand. She can't forget that.

"What I want most in the world is to go home to my daughter."

"Be my guest," the officer says, holding open the door for her, almost like a gentleman.

When she gets her things back, the police officers on duty are a bit more pleasant than last time. Or else it's pure imagination that they no longer seem as judgmental.

The confusion is total when Cornelia is suddenly standing on the street, free to do what she wants. The jewelry around her throat feels strange and the belt much too large, even though she tightened it to the third hole like she usually does. The sidewalk, the cars, the trees—everything seems different, more colorful but, at the same time, frightening. It's as if something has happened to the world during the two days she lost. Or else everything is exactly like before, and she's the one who has changed or sees things with new eyes.

Slowly she starts to walk toward the subway. The tears are streaming down her cheeks as she turns onto Bergsgatan. Her first instinct is to jump into a taxi to be able to see Astrid as soon as possible, but the knowledge that they will soon be able to embrace each other again is enough for Cornelia to stop herself. At this point, it will probably be faster to take public transportation, and she will also avoid feeling enclosed in the backseat of a car. Her claustrophobia has intensified during the days in jail. She doesn't think her pulse ever went into a resting state; she was constantly on alert. Being locked up, and having no power over your life, is something she wouldn't wish on her worst enemy. When Cornelia takes the escalator down into the underworld, she turns on her phone. Josefin is the first one she calls.

"Is that really you, Cornelia?" Josefin exclaims.

"Yes," she croaks out, clearing her throat to get her voice going, which she hasn't used properly for a long time.

"How are you doing?"

"Pretty well, I think."

"Where are you?"

"On my way home. They just let me go, with no explanation."

Josefin sounds surprised. "So no one told you why?"

"No, not really. A police officer I hadn't seen before told me I was free to go."

"Then you haven't heard the latest?"

"I just turned on my phone. I haven't had time to read my texts, let alone the news."

"There's been another murder. Just this morning. The police are keeping quiet, but it appears there's a clear connection to Hans's death."

"Have they released the name of the victim?" Cornelia asks.

"Victims. There were two, a woman and a man. That's all I know."

"And it happened while I was in jail. That explains why they released me." Cornelia is relieved and dismayed at the same time. "Has anyone been arrested?"

"I don't think so."

"What does your sister say about it?"

"I haven't got hold of her yet," Josefin says. "But she wouldn't tell me anything anyway. How was she to you? Actually, maybe I don't want to know."

Cornelia chooses not to comment. "Where is Astrid now?"

"She's here. Do you want to talk to her?"

Of course she does, but she knows that it's better for Astrid that they speak to each other in person so she understands it's for real. "I'm on my way now, and I'd rather wait."

"Maybe that's best. She's been pretty worried."

Cornelia swallows when she hears that, so as not to fall apart. "Josefin?"

"Yes?"

"Thanks for everything," Cornelia says.

"No problem. I was happy to help out."

Josefin has made a major contribution, taking care of Astrid even though she has her hands full with her own children. Cornelia is moved that there are such considerate people and that she has become friends with one of them.

When she gets down to the platform, there are only five minutes left until the next train but not a person is in sight, which Cornelia finds creepy. Soon a woman comes down the escalator, and Cornelia breathes out. She feels better knowing she's not alone.

The woman stops a short way from her with her eyes on her phone. Then she looks up. Although she turns her face away at once, Cornelia can see who it is.

82.

Emma can't believe her eyes. Only a few steps away from her stands Cornelia, of all the people in the world. She can't pretend she doesn't see her. Emma knows that Cornelia saw her, and there is nowhere to hide on a subway platform. Emma decides that this peculiar coincidence must mean something. It may not be by chance that their paths are crossing here and now, so she may as well go up and exchange a few words with Cornelia before the train arrives and the possibility is lost. She should be able to manage three minutes of conversation.

"Hello," Emma says, getting a stiff nod in response.

For understandable reasons, Cornelia is not particularly welcoming, and Emma stops at an appropriate distance, a few steps away. But it is not far enough to avoid Cornelia's musty odor. Her clothes are dirty, and it's apparent that she hasn't washed her hair for several days. It's both matted and greasy.

"How nice to see you out here," Emma begins before biting her tongue. What does she mean by that?

"It didn't sound like you wanted me out here yesterday." Cornelia's gaze is piercing and full of contempt.

"I was just doing my job," Emma says without sounding convincing. "In a murder investigation we can't take into consideration—"

"Save your poor excuses for the police officers who are going to investigate you," Cornelia says, cutting her off in midexplanation. "You and your associates deprived me of two days of my life, and I don't intend to let that go as if nothing happened."

Emma tries to look composed. "I understand that you're angry."

"Do you? So you can imagine what I've had to go through the past forty-eight hours," she says, her eyes flashing. "How it feels to lie there sleepless on a rock-hard foam mattress with a disgusting blanket, locked into a cell, without knowing how your child is doing. Without being able to say good night to her. So you know what that's like?"

Emma backs up a few steps and checks the sign for the train. The train is suddenly six minutes away, several minutes delayed. Not even public transportation is on her side today.

"No, I didn't think so," says Cornelia.

"I'm sorry you ended up in a jam," Emma says with her eyes on the departure times. "But we haven't done anything wrong."

She senses a shoulder shrug in the corner of her eye and realizes that the conversation is doomed to failure. Cautiously she moves away and is relieved when a group of noisy high school students comes down the escalator, breaking the silence.

Cheered on loudly by his friends, one of them kicks an information board. Someone applauds, another gives a shrill whistle, and a third person laughs. Several in the group follow his example and start kicking wildly. In broad daylight, as if they owned the world. Cornelia moves away from the group, looking scared, and ends up even farther from Emma. As a police officer, Emma ought to intervene and stop them, but it all happens so quickly. Right then, the train rolls in and the doors open. The young people disappear into different cars.

Emma changes trains at Fridhemsplan, and it's not long from there to Alvik. When she arrives, she sees that the topmost entry on the board with the Nockeby line's departure times is blinking, which means the train is about to leave. A short-haired woman runs ahead of her and manages to get on right before the doors close. Emma is left on the platform.

Perhaps it's just as well that she didn't end up on the same train as Cornelia. But the next departure isn't for thirteen minutes, which feels like an eternity. She calls Josefin but gets no answer. What if she isn't at home? Her spontaneous impulse to go out to see her sister subsides. Especially when she understands that she's not going to be the only guest. It's clear that Cornelia is on her way there too.

What was she thinking? It took her almost halfway to Vällingby to figure it out. The insight fatigues her, and she changes her mind about the trip. She takes the stairs down to go around to the other platform and go home. Rest is what she needs. She can see Josefin tomorrow. Or any day at all. Now that she is forced to take time off, her days will be completely empty.

The train toward Hagsätra comes at once, and she gets on. Reluctantly, she tests the thought that the leave will do her good, as tired and dizzy as she's been recently. She still won't admit that she fainted; Nyhlén has a tendency to exaggerate. But she's not angry at him anymore. She's going to miss him. It will be lonely at home and hard to enjoy the free time. Especially when it's not her own choice, but an order from the boss.

At least the case was cleared up before she left. What a surprise that the real estate agent went off the rails and shot both his lover and himself. And killed Hans Göransson. So brutally, besides. That Benjamin saw no other way out is deeply tragic. She wonders what the talk is among Kristoffer's colleagues. He probably has a lot of facts and rumors about Weber's. That will be interesting to hear, but it will have to be tomorrow, because he's out with the guys tonight.

When Emma finally comes up at Sankt Eriksplan, she hurries home. She turns onto her street but stops when she sees who is waiting outside the building. Or is it really him? It looks more like a worn-out copy.

Not now, she thinks, but just then, he catches sight of her and waves eagerly.

83.

"Emma," Hugo calls, unable to contain himself. He starts walking toward her.

She seems to hesitate but continues toward him anyway. Finally! He has been hoping so much to see her face-to-face and have a chance to tell her how much she means to him. Everything he wants to convey is twirling around in his head, and he feels that he is already losing his train of thought before they've even started talking. For some reason, he didn't expect her to look so cold. What has Kristoffer done with his fine Emma? He can barely recognize her.

"Hi," he says when she stops in front of him, just far enough away to avoid hugging. He doesn't get out another word.

"You have to stop following me," Emma replies curtly.

The longing to touch her is so great that he is almost dying—it is borderline unbearable—and he hardly hears what she says. In his mind, he has staged the meeting and rehearsed the dialogue many times. The setup is completely clear, and he isn't prepared for any deviations. It takes a while before he realizes that she's not following the script at all. In fact, she's moving the conversation in a completely different direction, with the wrong lines. Reluctantly, he lets her words sink in, wondering how he can get the conversation where he wants.

"What do you mean?" he asks sincerely, trying to give her that look she could never resist before.

"Everything. I mean everything. Give up, Hugo," she pleads. "There's no point. I've decided. It's not you and me anymore."

She's saying one thing but means another. That must be it.

"Sorry, that's too much to ask. I love you," he says, trying to catch her hand, but she manages to pull it back.

"I've moved on now. Accept it." Emma's gaze hardens in a way that causes him to back up.

"Never."

Her expression turns gloomy. "I'm serious."

"Me too."

"Kristoffer is getting tired of your pranks. They're not going to lead anywhere. You're just making problems for yourself."

Hugo laughs. "So now you're going to take my only hobby away from me too?"

"Stop now. It's not funny." Emma kicks away a stone on the ground.

When she makes a dismissive gesture with her arms, Hugo manages to get hold of her left hand. No trace is visible of the ring. It's as if it had never been there. A wave of happiness spreads anyway when they have physical contact, but the joy is brief. Quickly, she frees herself. She looks like she's about to say something, but at the last moment she stops herself. Closes her mouth, remains silent. She shifts her leg position but can't seem to find the right spot. At last she stops moving and puts her arms at her sides.

"There's something I have to tell you," she says, a note of anxiety in her tone of voice. "Actually, I wanted to wait, but there probably won't be a better opportunity."

Hugo feels ill at ease. He tries to figure out what she intends to reveal. That they've moved in together, or even worse—that they're going to get married? His body gets goose bumps, and his ears are ringing.

"Do I really want to hear it?" he asks.

"Definitely not," says Emma, and his pulse races, pounding intensely in his temples.

He has no idea what is coming, but she only needs to place her hand over her stomach for him to understand. Even so, he can't believe it's true. It just can't be. If she is expecting Kristoffer's child, all hope is gone. Anything else he could handle, but not that.

Emma doesn't look overjoyed, but perhaps it is out of respect for him that she doesn't smile.

"I'll soon be in the twelfth week."

His upper lip quivers in an attempt to smile, but he stops short. His face is just as distressed as after a root canal. He ought to say "congratulations" or "good luck," but the words stick in his throat. He can't let her see that there are tears in his eyes; that would be too much. It's humiliating enough to stand in front of the one he loves and have it made clear to him that she doesn't love him back. Hugo pretends to have some dust in his eye. He blinks a few times before he starts moving away. He is unable to meet her eyes.

"Say something," Emma asks.

"There's nothing more to say," he answers, leaving her.

His feet continue automatically, but something inside him just died. When he comes around the block, he sees a woman on the other side of the street checking him out. Instead of responding, he turns away. She is certainly good-looking, but it doesn't matter; she's not Emma.

His life with Emma marches past in his mind. He thinks about her family. Her dad, Evert, and her mother, Marianne, are going to have another grandchild. And Josefin will be an aunt for the first time. They must all be so happy about the news. His legs barely carry him as he pictures Kristoffer standing next to Emma during the delivery and breathing with her through the contractions. It's so wrong, so unjust. Together with Kristoffer, Emma is going to experience the greatest moment ever.

A car honks. Hugo comes to and realizes that he has walked right out into the street without looking. Pity he wasn't run over; it would have been just as well. There's nothing left to live for anyway.

84.

It's tempting to go home first to shower and change, but Cornelia can't wait to see her daughter. Besides, she hardly knows where her home is anymore. She glimpses her reflection in the glass of the train and is dismayed at what a wreck she is. Astrid will probably ignore her mother's appearance, and Josefin is going to understand. But still.

When Cornelia gets off at Smedslätten, she hopes she doesn't run into anyone she knows. She hurries her pace to get there as quickly as possible. When Josefin and Andreas's house emerges from behind a tree, she almost cheers. Even if she isn't completely cleared in the murder investigation yet, she will get to see her daughter. That means everything.

She approaches the stone stairs and the door with the lion's-head knocker instead of a doorbell. The sound of eager children's feet approaching at a rapid pace makes her heart stop for a moment. The lock rattles, the door flies open, and there her daughter stands. But is it really Astrid?

Her hair looks like it got stuck in a threshing machine. For a fraction of a second, they look shyly at each other before Astrid reaches out her arms. Cornelia picks her up, and Astrid's chubby legs coil around her waist. She is so warm and smooth.

"My wonderful, amazing girl! How I've missed you."

"Where have you been so long?" Astrid asks, burrowing her nose into Cornelia's neck.

"I had to go away for a while. But now I won't do that anymore. Not without you."

"Thanks." Astrid holds her hard.

"Have you been doing okay?"

"Really good."

"No nightmares?" she asks.

"Well."

Josefin appears behind them. "Welcome. You've been missed."

"Thanks," she says, and then the words get stuck in her throat. She doesn't know how to describe how happy she is for what Josefin has done for her.

"Astrid, perhaps you'd like to tell your mom about your hair," Josefin says. She must have understood Cornelia's perplexed look.

"I wanted to look like you, Mommy."

Cornelia strokes her girl on the cheek and kisses her carefully on the tip of her nose. "So you cut it yourself?"

"Sorry."

"Don't worry. It will grow out. We can wait for long hair together. Because now I want to be able to braid my hair."

"Me too," says Astrid, nodding happily. Then she jumps down and takes off for the TV. Like a whirlwind that blows away, the reunion is over in less than a minute.

"Where are the others?" Cornelia asks. "It's so quiet here."

"Andreas took the kids to the indoor play center in Upplands Väsby so that I would get a chance to rest."

"Upplands Väsby?"

"Yes, he has some good friends there."

"I hope it hasn't been too tough for you," Cornelia says.

"Now let's not talk about me." Josefin gives Cornelia a cautious hug and asks if she wants anything to eat. And out of nowhere, Cornelia's hunger comes back, like a well-aimed kick in the solar plexus.

"Yes, thanks. I'll have whatever."

Josefin gives her a crooked smile. "You look paler and thinner than ever."

"And dirtier and more disgusting," Cornelia adds.

"How awful has it been for you, really?"

Without hesitation, Cornelia answers that it was the worst thing she's ever experienced. Josefin shudders and gives her another hug, which Cornelia tries to wriggle out of.

As they go into the kitchen, Cornelia's eyes fasten on the fruit bowl. She is so hungry she has a desire to chow down an entire banana without peeling it first.

"There are pancakes left from earlier, if you want some."

"This place is heaven," Cornelia says, meaning every word. She almost dares to believe that everything will turn out fine after all. That her luck has changed and that now, at this moment, life will start again.

85.

Hugo goes into the nearest bar after his encounter with Emma. It's not even five o'clock, but he decides to knock back a double vodka anyway. Then one more. And another one. After that, the bartender looks doubtful, and Hugo thinks maybe it's best to leave. He's lost count of how many times he has sworn out loud to himself during the past hour, how many times he's been close to crying over his failure of a life. As soon as he stands up, he feels like he's about to pee his pants. The neon-pink sign for the restroom points down a stairway, and he staggers past the arrow. With every stair step, his head feels dizzier, but that doesn't relieve his despair.

The stench in the men's room strikes him with full force. It's not clean by the urinal, which has splashes all over the place. Can it be so fucking hard to hit the target, which is as big as a sink? He shivers with pleasure as the pressure lessens.

Suddenly, hope about Emma returns, and he wonders once again how he can get at Kristoffer. His efforts to spoil his open houses haven't paid any dividends yet, but he's convinced Kristoffer has a little secret buried somewhere.

Like a gift from above, a brilliant idea shows up: the allotment garden. He'll go out to Stora Mossen and destroy Kristoffer's silly cottage. That swine has gotten Hugo's woman pregnant. The humiliation is total, but it's not something he intends to accept. Emma belongs to Hugo and not a smarmy real estate agent. It's just a pity she doesn't understand that herself. Hugo clumsily buttons his fly and starts breathing normally again once he comes out of the john. Decisively, he heads for the subway and feels in his pocket. Suitably enough, he finds a lighter waiting there.

On his way down the escalator, reason starts to catch up, but Hugo quickly pushes it away. He has to have an outlet for his aggression; then perhaps he can move on with his life. Somehow he has to get Emma to realize that Kristoffer isn't the right man for her. He can absolutely not imagine Kristoffer holding a baby—his tailor-made suit might get stains.

Hugo laughs to himself. An elderly woman with crutches glances nervously in his direction and seems to be relieved when the train comes and he chooses a different car.

Emma must be blind or living in denial. What was she thinking when she chose a real estate agent? Kristoffer is always going to be overloaded with work, and his family will always have lower priority. He'll show up at home late in the evening when the baby has fallen asleep and go to the office before the rest of the family is up. And he'll be on the phone night and day with prospective buyers and sellers. The poor child is going to grow up practically fatherless. Hugo wants to tell Emma all this, but there's no point as long as she keeps telling herself that Kristoffer is the man in her life.

Hugo is so deeply absorbed in his musings that he forgets for a while where he's going. He doesn't get up when the brakes of the train screech at Stora Mossen, scrambling off only as the doors are closing. Alone, he goes toward the exit, firmly resolved to carry out his plan.

As he approaches the high school near the allotment gardens, his rage increases. What kind of guy digs around in the flower beds every chance he gets like a fucking old lady? It can't be more obvious that something about Kristoffer doesn't add up. He didn't acquire the lot to grow his own asparagus—that much is certain.

Hugo turns into the area with miniature houses lined up in a row and hurries toward Kristoffer's garden, which is a little farther off. It's starting to get dark, so he picks up his pace. He opens the gate and goes in search of something to ignite. Gasoline would have been just the thing, but he didn't think that far ahead. Suddenly, the lighter in his pocket seems ridiculous. There must be something else that can help set fire to this shit.

He pulls open the door to Kristoffer's shed and searches in the little space. To his great delight, he sees the shears in the bowl of paint thinner.

86.

Josefin waves good-bye to Cornelia and Astrid, and then the house is dead silent. The relief is indescribable. Even though she is exhausted, she wants to go out for a run. She knows herself well, and running is a good antidote for most everything. It will be a great way to recharge for dinner with her personal-trainer friends at Stureplan tonight at eight. They meet once a month, and Josefin wasn't intending to go this evening, but she changed her mind when Cornelia called. For the first time in days, she has some time to herself.

She feels liberated as she ties her new running shoes. The sun is going down, but it's not too cold, so she won't need a jacket. She goes out and then closes the door behind her. It's nice they have a code lock so she doesn't have to drag the house key along.

Spring is in the air, and she wonders if the first few April flowers have popped up along the shoulder of the road. The sight of yellow coltsfoot blooms always give her butterflies, a promising sign that lighter days are approaching. Josefin keeps an eye out but sees nothing colorful sticking up next to the gray asphalt. The spring in her step is sharper than last week, and she almost flies along.

As she does her usual run, she thinks about how fun it will be to see her friends. A glass of wine or two will be really good. There has been talk of starting a business together— sharing a workout space and agreeable coworkers to boot. At the same time, it would involve greater expense that she doesn't have the desire to take on now. Especially not if she becomes single. She tries to imagine herself in a cramped apartment with three boisterous children. The idea is anything but enticing, so she lets it go for the moment, trying to push aside the image of Andreas with another woman and enjoy the run.

She passes Olovlundsparken, where the children often ice-skate in the winter. In a few months, they'll be able to swim in the wading pool, to Anton's great delight. The girls, however, won't be especially entertained by water that doesn't even reach their knees. They'll be happier about the zip line, as long as they don't quarrel about whose turn it is.

As Josefin runs through the Stora Mossen allotment gardens, she enjoys watching the sky turn pink. There is no more beautiful time of day. And there is something special about this place. All the small cottages make her nostalgic every time. In the summer, it's wonderful to walk along the lovely flower beds filled with hollyhocks, sunflowers, and showy apple trees. During the Midsummer celebration, there's even more fairy-tale charm, with a parade, raffles, and dancing around the maypole.

But gardening season doesn't seem to have really started yet. Some of the gardeners move in when it gets warmer and stay until October, when the water is turned off. Before Emma started seeing Kristoffer, Josefin knew nothing about the garden association, but now she has a better understanding. Sadly enough, there have been break-ins in the area, so she usually takes a look at Kristoffer's cottage if she's nearby, like now.

All the garden plots are deserted, and most of the windows are boarded up. But not Kristoffer's place, which she glimpses to the right. Still, from the road it looks peaceful and quiet, as expected. She slows her pace, peers at it as best she can, and considers whether she should take a pass around the cottage—just to be on the safe side. A quick movement by the corner of the cottage makes her sharpen her gaze and stop. Was it a bird? Or was she imagining things?

She wants to be 100 percent certain that no one is there, so she opens the gate and steps in. The handle seizes, and she sees that the brackets are both rusty and loose. Gravel crunches under her feet before she reaches the grass. Without taking her eyes off the cottage, she continues toward the rounded stone steps by the front door.

A shadow flutters from the back of the cottage, and she holds her breath. Maybe it was an intruder but she scared him off. She realizes that Andreas doesn't know where she is, and her cell phone is at home. At any moment it will be dark out, and it's unlikely anyone saw her come here. She knows she shouldn't go closer, but curiosity gets the upper hand.

"Hello?" she tries carefully. The shadow sticking out in the gravel behind the cottage freezes. "Is anyone there?"

Now is when Josefin ought to turn and run for all she's worth. Yet she stands there, firmly resolved to find out what's going on.

"Hello?" she says again.

No answer. No new movement. But just as she is about to round the corner, something comes toward her at furious speed. She throws herself to the side and strikes her hip on the raised stone edge by the flower bed. Then she sees a deer jump onto the adjacent lot, and she can't help bursting into laughter. Here she thought she was about to make a heroic effort to stop a criminal, and it was just an animal. Her legs are shaking, and her pulse is still racing as the deer stops on the grass, staring at her and looking equally shaken. So much for the burglar.

Josefin shakes off her fear and brushes the dirt from her tights. She wonders what she should wear this evening. It's not that often she goes to a restaurant nowadays. In her mind, she goes through her closet and stops at a red dress that is discreet but good-looking. She doesn't need to be that dressed up.

She casts an eye at the cottage again to assure herself that everything is calm and then sees the door ajar. She notices a sweeping movement inside.

When she sees who it is, she can hardly believe it's true. What is *he* doing here?

87.

When their eyes meet, Hugo wonders if he's hallucinating. He can't really put it together. What in the world is Josefin doing at Kristoffer's garden? Then he realizes it's even stranger that *he's* here. What will she think of him? Especially considering that he drenched the place in paint thinner. The answer isn't long in coming, because Josefin storms into the cottage and snarls, "Now you've gone too far!"

Her angry look stops at the windowsill, which he had to force open to get in. He simply followed the earlier break marks, but she wouldn't know that.

"Good Lord, what are you up to?" she says, holding her nose.

"Josefin," he says, noticing that he is slurring, "let me take it easy and explain." The words don't come out in the right order, and his tongue feels dull and shapeless. Not even when reality strikes him like a cold shower is he able to pull himself together.

"I came into the yard because I thought there was a break-in," Josefin says. "Apparently, I was right. But I never would have guessed that it would be you, of all people."

The disappointment in her eyes is tangible. Hugo likes Josefin and doesn't want to hurt either her or Emma. Somehow he has to work this out.

"Sorry. Gimme a chance to explain myself," he pleads, even as he understands that nothing he can say can fix what he has done. It's all about sheer jealousy and an idiotic impulse. He looks down and sees a mattress on the floor; you might almost believe that someone slept there recently. Then he discovers the lighter in his hand, and he smuggles it down into his pocket, as if that could stop the cottage from reeking of paint thinner.

"You can go ahead and tell me whatever you want, but don't think you're going to get away with this."

Hugo has never seen Josefin so upset. Or so worn-out. The bags under her eyes are standing out. She doesn't really seem to be herself.

When he takes a step toward her, he almost stumbles, clumsy and drunk as he is.

"Not a centimeter closer," she warns, and he holds up his hand.

"Take it easy. It's just me," he says, but he can see that the sentence doesn't reach her in the right way. Especially not when a belch follows his words out of sheer momentum. "I think there's something that's not right with Kristoffer."

"What do you mean by that?"

"He's hiding something. I don't think he's the person he makes himself out to be."

Josefin shakes her head. "You're out of your mind. You're the one who's not right, damn it, but the sad thing is that you don't realize it. I know what you've been doing. Emma told me. You ought to be ashamed, spoiling Kristoffer's open houses. But you don't even seem to have enough sense to see that it's over with Emma. She's never going back to you."

Hugo tries not to let himself be provoked. "Thanks," he says. "That's enough. I don't want to hear any more."

"She thinks you're pathetic. Damned tragic, that's what you are. Get out of here now and don't ever come back," Josefin says, waving toward the door.

"You're lying. You know as well as I do that Emma loves me. It's all because I couldn't give her a child."

Josefin fixes her eyes on him. "But now there's someone who can."

His anger explodes, and he pushes Josefin aside. It just happens, and he is as surprised as she is. Suddenly, she is lying on the floor and he hardly understands what happened. She is completely still. Shards from a ceramic vase lie scattered by her head, and blood is seeping out, forming a pool. Hugo just stands there, staring at her with dismay. What got into him?

"Josefin?"

She doesn't move even when he pokes her arm. After another tentative attempt to get a reaction, Hugo gets scared and backs out of the cottage. He looks around and sees that no one else is in the vicinity. His only thought is that he has to get out of there, immediately. His instincts take over. He casts himself over the iron fence at the back of the garden and runs along the walking path for all he's worth. But when he's halfway to the subway, fatigue catches up with him. He is forced to stop to catch his breath, and that's when he realizes his mistake. What was he thinking? Even if it pains him to turn back, there is no alternative.

Hugo wanders around the residential area, but he can't find his way. After a forced march that feels like an eternity, he finds himself on Mossvägen. Totally the wrong way. He decides to turn right, and when he sees the high school he knows that finally he is going the right way.

Darkness has settled over the area, and he is drenched in sweat when he reaches the narrow road that leads to Kristoffer's garden. He looks carefully around to be sure no one notices as he goes through the gate, and then he hurries up to the door, which is still ajar.

88.

It's burning like an inferno, more intense than I would have imagined. Here I thought it wouldn't be that easy to set fire to the place. I was so wrong. Now I'm watching the thick cloud of smoke climbing toward the sky, spreading out over the allotment gardens. It's hard to make out the treacherous smoke in the darkness. But the smell is evidence that a fire has broken out and is well on its way to spreading. The adjacent forest suddenly feels dangerously close. I didn't think about that. On the other hand, there was no choice. This is the last thing I'll do; I have to promise myself that.

I jump when a windowpane explodes. It's probably only a matter of time before someone alerts the fire department. I'm already standing by the fence at the back side, ready to jump over and discreetly distance myself from the scene. This time I don't need to stick around. On the contrary.

I take one last look at the cottage, both fascinated and relieved. Soon all traces of it will be swept away, and no one will accuse me of anything.

When I've come a little ways from the area, I sense the smell of fire pursuing me. My clothes and hair reek of smoke, so I can just forget about the subway. If the incident leads to an investigation, it would be idiotic to have been riding around stinking like a firebomb. I'll have to walk back to the city instead.

While I head toward the Traneberg Bridge, I think about Josefin.

What a nasty fall—right on the vase. So unnecessary.

89.

The only person she wants to talk with is Josefin, but naturally she doesn't answer when for once Emma has all the time in the world. It's not often that Josefin isn't available. Maybe it's because Cornelia is still there or she doesn't hear the phone because of the kids. But if Emma knows her sister, she's gone out for a run. There can't have been much time for that the past few days, considering that she's been taking care of yet another child. Not everyone would have done something like that.

Emma feels warm inside until she realizes she's nowhere near as considerate herself. Outwardly, she would probably assert that she's like Josefin, but deep down she knows that it takes a lot for her to put everything aside for another person's sake. Not that anyone would ask her for such a favor; she doesn't have such a close relationship with her friends. Even Josefin has stopped asking her for help. The insights fall like bowling pins, making Emma melancholy.

Sofie Sarenbrant

She wants to mean something to others and be helpful, not just be there for her work. But even though her job in the homicide group means being neighbors with Death, it's her lifeline. Outside the police station, she is nothing.

Emma makes a halfhearted attempt to start Netflix but gets an error message saying there are problems with the connection. So she surfs between TV channels without finding anything interesting. She seldom has time for TV and doesn't follow the program listings. It would have been nice to have someone to talk with instead, but Kristoffer probably isn't coming home for a while yet and he doesn't answer when she calls.

There must be someone else she can call; the question is who. Does she need to look on Facebook to see what friends she has? If so, then it's bad. Her mom might well be a candidate, but Emma has no desire to talk with her. Not with her dad either, who in a way is like Emma in the respect that he calls only if he wants something in particular.

The image of Hugo sweeps past again, but he's the last person on earth she can call right now. Poor guy. He looked really desperate when he realized she's expecting Kristoffer's child. Emma sinks deeper down on the couch and taps restlessly on the remote control. Now that she's had the chance to rest up, she is overwhelmed by anxious thoughts. It's better to keep busy so she doesn't brood herself to death. Dwelling on things is the worst.

What if Hugo gets so unhappy he throws himself in front of a train?

Emma shudders. He looked skinny, and she didn't remember seeing the dark-red patches under his eyes before. Should she call him and check that everything is okay? Emma knows she can't take responsibility for Hugo's actions, but she still feels guilty that he's not doing well. She has a hard time believing he would intentionally take his own life. But he might do something stupid when he's drunk. She can imagine him sitting at the bar right now, drowning his sorrows. At least, alcohol is what he used to deaden his feelings before.

Starting to get sleepy, Emma sinks down with her head on the armrest, trying to find a good position. The best thing would be to sleep away the immediate future. Even better would be to wake up around week twenty-two, feeling the baby's first kicks. She doesn't want to miss that. She passes out at last, and when she wakes up, Kristoffer is sitting beside her on the couch. He is chewing noisily on a piece of flatbread, and his breath testifies that the evening has gone as planned.

"What time is it?" she asks in confusion, looking around.

"Nine thirty."

Emma sits up. "Typical of me to fall asleep. Aren't you still supposed to be at your bachelor party?"

"I forgot my wallet here," he says, unbuttoning his shirt. "And the next place we're going is in your neighborhood, so I thought I would take the opportunity to get some cash and freshen up."

"I see," says Emma, who had hoped that he'd come to stay.

Kristoffer strokes her cheek. "Now I understand why you didn't answer the phone. I was actually worried when I saw that you were looking for me and I couldn't reach you. Was there anything in particular, darling?"

"There are a few things I'd like to talk about, but we can do that tomorrow."

"That's good, because I have to leave again," he says, looking at the clock.

"Are you always going to be so preoccupied?" she asks, although she knows it's the completely wrong moment to bring it up. "Later, that is?"

Kristoffer looks perplexed. "What do you mean 'later'?"

Emma places her hand on her stomach. "When there are three of us."

"Please. We'll deal with that then."

"No, I think I want to know now, while it's still possible to end it," says Emma. She wonders what has gotten into her. There is nothing that would get her to deliberately terminate the pregnancy, this miracle that has finally happened.

"Why are you saying that?" Kristoffer finally appears to be listening.

"Because you're so distracted and hard to reach. It's not the way I pictured it when I imagined the father of my child."

Kristoffer shakes his head, laughs uncertainly, and suddenly turns serious. "Have you been talking with Hugo? I hardly recognize you."

Emma shakes her head.

Although they're in the middle of a dispute, Kristoffer gets up. "I really have to go. We'll have to talk about this more later."

"So when? Have you thought about that? Shall we schedule a meeting?"

"Stop it. What's going on with you?"

"Nothing," she says, instead of telling the truth—that she feels alone. "When do you think you'll be back?"

"It'll probably be late. Don't sit up and wait for me."

Anger takes the upper hand, and Emma glares at him. "Then you can sleep at your place tonight. I have no desire to wake up when you stomp in at four o'clock, drunk as a skunk."

"As you wish," Kristoffer says, leaving the room quicker than usual.

The door closes with a hard bang. Tears roll down her cheeks, and she swears quietly to herself. Why should he wake her up at all? She double-checks that her phone really is set on "Silent" before she settles down on the couch. There's nothing new from Hugo, which surprises her. But perhaps she finally got through to him. The baby was probably the turning point.

90.

The strange dream seems to go on and on. Josefin is blinded by a light so strong she has to close her eyes. Her eyelids feel heavy as lead. She is constantly drawn toward the light, but at the same time she struggles against it. When she is awake again, she lies unmoving. She has no idea where she is. Before she makes an attempt to move, she listens for signs of whether someone else is there. But it is silent as the grave, and the air feels heavy to breathe. It's also damp and stuffy. Her head is pounding so intensely it's hard to keep from moaning, but she fears that the slightest sound may put her in mortal danger if she's not alone. Slowly, she opens an eye. It doesn't matter. It's just as pitch-black as she imagined. Carefully, she moves her legs and arms to make sure they're still part of her.

Then she hears a scraping sound above her head.

At once, she is quiet again. She tries to rewind the scene in her mind to recall what happened, but she only remembers

Astrid's excited face when she got to see her mom again and the tears of joy that Cornelia discreetly wiped from the corners of her eyes. The pounding in Josefin's head increases, and she feels like she's about to pass out again. The lovely sleep is too hard to resist; she is rocked into the clear light and strives to reach forward, toward a liberating end.

A strong smell of smoke brings her back to reality. She pictures herself waving good-bye to Cornelia and Astrid, tying her running shoes, leaving the house, and starting to run. The sense of freedom, the fresh air, and the anticipation of meeting with her personal-trainer friends makes her fly along over the asphalt. She looks for signs of spring and sees no flowers along the way. But life feels lighter and she can breathe, now that Astrid has her mom back. She still has to figure out everything with Andreas, though, to make a decision about the future: should they go their separate ways or try to find their way back to each other? The gravel crunches under the soles of her shoes on the way into the allotment gardens.

Then her memory fails. Everything gets fuzzy.

She lightly touches her fingers to her head and feels that it's damp and dirty. She brings her hand to her nose and wrinkles it when she realizes there's blood. The intense stench of smoke increases, and she notices that she's drifting off again. A coughing attack that won't stop clears her head.

She sees a deer in her mind, a shadow in the house, and an unlocked door.

Hugo! Fucking lunatic.

The anger in his eyes and his hard shove come back to her. She can't even guess where he has taken her now, but it feels like an eternity since she stood face-to-face with him inside Kristoffer's cottage. So why isn't anyone searching for her?

The answer is simple. Andreas thinks she's out with friends, whose names he barely knows because he hasn't bothered to ask.

She sees her life pass before her eyes. Julia, Sofia, and Anton. From births to lost teeth, the first goal in the soccer match, and a perfect pirouette while figure skating. Memory has selected the good bits, because no unbearable visits to the ER flash by. Nor do sleepless nights and worry about dyslexia and bullying. Everything is like a lovely postcard.

Josefin knows that she has done her utmost for her family. That she and Andreas have created three amazing children—children she loves above everything else. She doesn't want to die and leave them. Her chest contracts, and she tries to brace herself to get on her feet. She scratches with her fingers and feels earth burrow in under her nails.

Now the fear hits her with full force. Where is she? What if no one finds her? She thinks she hears scattered voices from somewhere far away, but she isn't sure. Her only firm conviction is that she has to get out of here. Hugo can't get away with this.

91.

SUNDAY, APRIL 6

Emma tries to stay in the marvelous land of sleep, but something is demanding her attention. It's impossible to ignore the sound that is disturbing her, and reluctantly she forces her eyelids open, looks around, and realizes she isn't lying in her bed. Her backside aches, which makes sense because she has sunk down with her rump between two flattened sofa cushions. Weakly, she pulls herself up to a sitting position, wondering what time it is. As if that has any significance, now that she doesn't have a schedule to stick to. Besides, it's the weekend.

The darkness in the room is proof that it's not quite morning, yet the doorbell is ringing. She wonders if she could simply not answer. If it's Kristoffer who has lost his keys, she'll be really mad. Her irritation increases as she approaches the hall and sees that it's only twenty past five. But when she looks through the peephole, the desperate face of Andreas terrifies her. Various scenarios start swirling around in her head. All she can conclude is that something awful has happened to Josefin or the children.

"Josefin is missing," Andreas says as he squeezes past her into the hall and sinks down on a stool.

"What do you mean?" Emma isn't sure she heard right. "What makes you think that?"

"She never showed up at the gathering with her friends last night."

"Haven't you heard anything from her since then?" Emma has to support herself against the door.

Andreas shakes his head. "No."

"But why didn't you call earlier?" Emma says, feeling worry start to turn into agitation.

Andreas doesn't look provoked by her accusatory tone. "I called you a million times, but you didn't answer."

Her cell phone is on the coffee table, and Emma has several missed calls and new messages. She checks quickly, but none are from Josefin. They sit down on the messy couch, and Emma looks steadily at Andreas. "Take everything from the start."

"Josefin was planning to go out with her personal-trainer friends last night. I took the kids to the play center in Upplands Väsby while Josefin was waiting for Cornelia to come pick up Astrid. The last few days have been tough for Josefin, so I thought it would be best to go away with the kids and give her a chance to rest. Later in the evening, I sent a message to her to see when she was coming home, but I got no answer."

"Didn't you react then?"

"Not really," Andreas answers, seeming evasive.

"Why is that?"

He throws up his hands. "It's been pretty turbulent for us lately, and I know she's disappointed in me. I work too much, and she thinks she has to take all the responsibility for the kids."

No wonder Josefin has looked so worn-out. But the question is what Andreas means by "turbulent."

"But there's nothing else I should know about?" she asks.

"Nothing I want to go into. I assumed she was mad at me and chose to ignore me because of that."

Emma is baffled. It didn't sound like the Josefin she knows. "Does she do that often?"

"Only sometimes," Andreas admits. "Last night the kids were wound up and fussing more than usual. So I had my hands full getting them to bed and didn't have time to think much about Josefin. I've had a trying week too, and it ended with me falling asleep next to Anton. I woke up at midnight."

"What did you think then, when she still wasn't home?"

Andreas took a deep breath. "Same thing, that she deliberately wasn't answering me. It was only after three or four o'clock in the morning that I really got worried. Then I started tracking down her friends through Facebook and finally managed to get hold of the cell phone number of someone who said Josefin wasn't at the dinner. Then I called you. And when you didn't answer, I decided to come over."

"She's somewhere," says Emma, looking at him. "Just not at home."

387

"What should I do?" Andreas has never looked so piti-ful before. "Where do we search when I don't even know where we should start?"

"We'll find her. That's all there is to it. She'll be home again soon, period."

Andreas looks doubtful. "I hope so."

"So you think Cornelia is the one who saw her last?" Emma shudders at the thought of needing to have that conversation.

"It seems that way."

92.

When the phone rings, Cornelia considers simply ignoring it, but she reaches for it anyway to satisfy her curiosity. Blocked number. Who would want anything from her at five thirty on a Sunday morning? That she is awake at all is due to the fact that Astrid was spinning around in bed like an eggbeater the whole night. And if that weren't enough, she screamed and talked in her sleep at regular intervals. Cornelia managed to fall asleep a few times, but eventually she couldn't settle down again. And now someone else is disturbing her.

After her recent experience with the police, she has a feeling she's going to be anxious for the rest of her life when the doorbell or cell phone rings. And where blocked numbers are concerned, it's rarely anything positive. She observes the lit-up display and breathes out when the persistent person gives up. Yet she can't relax completely. If it's the police, it's probably only a matter of time before a uniformed officer is tugging on her door handle. The mere thought makes her tremble.

The phone rings again, and Cornelia wriggles herself loose from Astrid, who was sleeping with both arms around her mother's neck. Cornelia's own arm has fallen asleep, and it starts to tingle as soon as she releases it and the blood starts flowing. Astrid seems to be sleeping heavily, because she doesn't move a muscle, not even when Cornelia answers.

"Hello?"

"Hi. It's Emma Sköld."

Just hearing her voice makes Cornelia cold inside. "What do you want?"

She moves to the kitchen so as not to waken Astrid.

"It's about Josefin. She's gone. According to Andreas, you're the last one who saw her yesterday."

Can she have heard right? Cornelia has to sit down. "What are you saying? Is Josefin missing?"

"Yes, since yesterday—after you picked up Astrid."

When Cornelia tries to think of what Josefin said she was going to do yesterday, there is a complete blank. "What does Andreas say?"

"He only knows that she was going out with some friends in the evening, but it turns out she never showed up. Did Josefin say anything about her plans to you?"

"Hmm." Cornelia rewinds again, but she can't remember anything other than a ravenous hunger in combination with indescribable happiness at being able to hold Astrid again. "I'm sorry, but I can't think of anything."

"Didn't she say anything about what she was going to do?"

"Andreas had apparently gone off somewhere with the kids so that she could rest up."

"To the play center?"

"Exactly. In Upplands Väsby, of all places."

"Did she say what she was going to do before dinner with her friends?"

"I'm sorry, but I really don't remember." Cornelia feels worthless, not being able to come up with anything.

"Anything at all may be of use to us in the search. Keep thinking," Emma says.

Cornelia exerts herself further. She imagines Josefin in the kitchen and tries to picture what clothes she was wearing. How did she actually look? Cornelia digs into her memory and retrieves an image of a laughing Josefin who is pulling on something. A black cord at her waist. All at once, it's crystal clear what Josefin was going to do.

"She was in workout clothes."

Emma thanks her for the help. "Call if you think of anything else. Anything at all may be significant."

When they've hung up, Cornelia's thoughts are spinning wildly. Here she thought all the misery was over, but there seems to be no end to it. She doesn't know if she can handle anything else. When she interrogates herself about her recent conversations with Josefin, she realizes that almost everything has been about Hans, Hans, Hans. As usual. Cornelia has been so occupied by her own problems that she has no idea how Josefin has been doing behind her seemingly orderly facade.

And now she's missing.

93.

"Does Josefin usually go out with her friends in work-out clothes?" Emma glances at Andreas, who is still sitting on the couch at her place.

"They were going to Stureplan, so I'd have a hard time believing that."

"Then it seems like she was going to work out. We'll have to see if her running shoes are gone. Do you have any idea where she usually runs?"

"More or less, but I can't say for sure," Andreas says, throwing out his arms. "She's always finding new routes."

"Is there anyone who usually goes with her, or does she run alone?"

"Usually she's out with her clients. Otherwise, she goes by herself."

Emma reaches for her jacket on the coffee table, ready to go to Josefin's neighborhood. "Who's taking care of the kids?"

"I woke Julia and said I needed to stop by your place. She's supposed to call if there's anything."

Once Emma is in Andreas's car, she listens to her voice mail. All calls except three are from Andreas. Kristoffer is the other one who has been trying to reach her. Once at two o'clock in the morning. As if she would answer then. She turns on the ringer in case Josefin tries to call. Emma can't understand what happened; why would her sister disappear during one of her usual runs in her neighborhood? There's no logic to it, and worry about what might have happened increases.

Still gnawing at Emma is the fact that Josefin was involved in last week's tragedy with the Göransson family. And that Cornelia is the one who saw her last. Cornelia, who had just been held under suspicion of murder in the death of her husband. But the events can't have a connection, can they? They just can't.

Andreas stares hard at the road as he turns through a roundabout toward Bromma. His convulsive grip on the steering wheel makes Emma nervous; perhaps he shouldn't be driving in this state. It's best if she waits to inform him about her vague theories.

"Could the murder of Hans Göransson have anything to do with this?" Andreas asks suddenly, as if he could read her thoughts.

"I have a really hard time believing that," she answers.

"I have a feeling something awful has happened."

"Don't say that."

The drive continues in tense silence. When they are

finally at the house, Emma sees that the lights are on upstairs. Andreas turns into the driveway and gets out of the car without bothering to shut the door. Emma follows him and sees little Anton come toward them in the hall with moist eyes and swollen red cheeks.

"Daddy, where did you go?" he bursts out desperately with Julia in tow.

Andreas hugs his son and carries him to the couch. The TV comes on at highest volume and Anton's crying escalates before Andreas manages to lower the sound. Julia looks completely exhausted, but she goes over to her little brother, climbs up on the couch, and holds him until he calms down. When Andreas goes upstairs to check on Sofia, Emma counts at least four pairs of running shoes in the hall that must belong to Josefin. She shakes her head sadly when Andreas comes back.

"Sofia is asleep," he says.

"Good. How many pairs of workout shoes does Josefin actually have?"

Andreas's eyes sweep over the mess in the hall. "Her new ones—the turquoise ones—are gone."

"So you think Cornelia's information may be right?"

"It looks that way."

Emma isn't sure she can take in everything that's going on, that she can reason logically. She keeps coming back to the fact that Cornelia was the last one who saw Josefin, and it's much too unbelievable a circumstance to overlook. But what does it mean? The sound of a ringtone startles her. "Kristoffer" is blinking on the display.

"Hi," Emma says.

"I've been trying to reach you! Some bastard set fire to my cottage," he yells right off, and it's impossible to avoid hearing how drunk he is. "The board called and said that the fire department tried to save the place, but it's burned down to the ground. Nothing left."

"I'm sorry, Kristoffer. That's terrible, but I can't talk right now."

"You can't talk? What the hell can be more important than this?"

"Josefin is missing," she whispers, looking toward the living room. Anton and Julia are sitting on the couch with their eyes fixed on the TV screen, and she doesn't want them to hear.

"*Who* did you say?"

"Josefin, my sister. She's gone." Emma swallows when she hears what she's saying. Suddenly, it becomes so real. She forces herself not to think anything other than that Josefin must be safe and sound.

Kristoffer hiccups. "What're you talking about?"

"Exactly what you heard. I'm at her house with Andreas now. We'll be in touch later. I'm needed here."

"Sorry, I had no idea," he says meekly. "Is there anything I can do?"

Emma shakes her head, not remembering that he can't see her. "Not right now. Good-bye."

Dizziness sets in, and she has to take hold of Andreas so as not to lose her balance.

"What was that about?" he asks once she ends the call.

"Apparently, someone burned down the cottage at Kristoffer's allotment garden."

94.

The headache from hell makes Hugo regret opening his eyes. There is a flash of light, and he shuts his eyes again to gather energy. *What is that smell?* His own breath nauseates him. He looks around to assure himself that he is safely at home; the memory gaps make him uncertain about what really happened yesterday. Only then does it occur to him that he is lying in the stairwell. Quickly, he gets to his feet.

The hangover makes him unsteady, and in a moment of deficient concentration he sets his foot too far out on the step. He loses his balance and falls. His chin is the first thing to hit the stone, and his teeth crunch as his jaws collide. The taste of blood grows in his mouth, and he fumbles for support to get up again, all the time knowing that it may only be a matter of seconds before some neighbor appears. He can't stay here in a heap on the stairs.

"What's going on?"

Hugo hears that the voice comes from somewhere above his head, but he can't see anyone.

"Should I call for an ambulance?"

A woman with gray hair and friendly eyes appears, and he can't decide if he is dreaming or awake.

"No," he mumbles, spitting out something sharp, which appears to be a broken tooth. That's all he needs.

With unexpected force, she takes hold of his hand.

The events of yesterday come tumbling back, and he sees himself with the lighter in that allotment garden cottage. But what else? The memory gaps are getting denser, and he can't separate fantasy and reality. A blurry image emerges and becomes clearer: Josefin lying on the floor with a head wound. A pool of blood.

"I think we have to call for help," the woman says.

"Thanks, but I'll manage," he answers, staggering into his apartment.

"Are you sure?" the woman persists. He thinks she's the neighbor one flight up.

"Absolutely," he says without turning around.

"You forgot your tooth," she calls after him, but he pretends not to hear. What would he do with it anyway?

Once inside the door, he breathes out. He has to go and wash. Maybe a long shower will perk him up.

When the water is streaming down over him, Hugo admits to himself that there was too much alcohol yesterday. It's probably best to forget about what happened and move on. Everything is already tough enough as it is.

Hugo inspects himself in the mirror after the shower

and realizes that Emma is right. He has really gone to the dogs, and he has to pull himself together. It's time to move on and let go of her. He feels strengthened by the thought. It won't be easy, but it's necessary.

When he comes out of the bathroom, he sees that he has a missed call. From Emma. All thoughts of giving her up vanish completely, and he doesn't hesitate to call back.

"What were you doing last night?" is the first thing Emma says when she answers. "You weren't at Kristoffer's allotment garden, were you?"

Several images from yesterday show up without his being able to prevent them. He pictures how he presses down the handle to the white gate and steps in.

"What would I be doing there?"

Her voice is filled with contempt. "I wonder that too."

"Has something happened?" he asks cautiously.

"Someone set fire to his cottage last night."

Hugo takes hold of his head with his free hand. "Is that true?"

"So you're denying it?"

"I . . ."

"Listen, I have more important things to think about right now, so we'll have to talk about this later." Hugo hears how worried she sounds.

"Has something else happened?"

"It's Josefin. She's missing."

Hugo remains sitting with the phone against his ear a long time before he realizes that Emma has already hung up.

95.

Hugo can say what he wants, but the fact that the cottage happened to burn down the same day he found out that she is expecting a child with Kristoffer is much too great a coincidence. There are plenty of signs that he'd do just about anything to destroy Emma's new relationship. But she'll have to deal with that later. Now it's crucial to devote all her energy to Josefin. One possibility is that she is consciously staying away from home. Discussing this with Andreas is unavoidable, and Emma braces herself.

"Is there any reason why Josefin might be staying away deliberately?"

Andreas looks alarmed. "The thought has actually struck me."

Emma is surprised. It's obvious he's withholding something from her.

"Tell me the truth. I have to know everything. No matter how awkward it is."

Her encouragement is like turning on a faucet. Everything runs out of him. Emma listens, trying not to judge, even though it's hard to accept that he seems prepared to leave her sister for a coworker.

"But even if Josefin is feeling hurt, she would never take off without telling me. If nothing else, for the children's sake," he says with his gaze focused nowhere.

"I don't think so either," Emma says, staring at her phone. *Why doesn't she get in touch?*

There are still some other possibilities. In the best case, Josefin checked into a hotel to be alone and think everything through. The problem with that theory is that she never made it to dinner with her friends, which she'd been looking forward to.

"So what do we do?" Andreas asks.

"I think I'd better call my dad."

Emma keeps her fingers crossed that her mother doesn't answer. She can't bear to tell the story twice.

"Yes?" she hears her father's gruff voice say, as commanding and authoritarian as usual.

"Hi, it's Emma, and I have bad news. I'm in Smedslätten with Andreas, and he doesn't know where Josefin has gone. It doesn't need to mean the worst, but—"

"How long has she been gone?"

"Since last night."

"*Last night?* Why didn't you contact me sooner?" The agitation in his voice is unmistakable, and in the background she hears her mother asking worried questions without getting any answers.

"Because various circumstances meant that no one missed her until now. She was going out with some friends, but evidently she never showed up. None of them called to check, so Andreas wasn't worried until he discovered that she was still gone this morning."

"I'll get the top missing-persons investigators on it."

"Will you and Mom come here? I think that would be good."

"Of course we will," he says without hesitation. "We'll leave right away."

When the call is over, Emma notices that she's shaking. But for Andreas and the kids' sake she has to remain calm. She searches for something good to say, but everything feels like an empty promise.

"It'll work out," she says anyway. "I'm sure there's a good explanation for what has happened. A lot of reported disappearances turn out to be misunderstandings. We'll find her."

Andreas nods. "I truly hope so."

Only then does Emma see Julia standing in the doorway with eyes wide-open. That can only mean one thing: she heard everything.

96.

Groggy and aching, Josefin can barely move when she wakes up. Her body is frozen stiff all over. She has no sense of how long it has been since she ended up here; it may be a matter of hours, perhaps days. The smell of smoke is no longer as strong, and the thought of her children and sister gives her strength.

Now the main thing is to get out of here, however hard that may be.

Josefin manages to turn onto her side and get up on her knees. She reaches with her hands for a way out. She must have come in somewhere. After some futile scratching in what feels like earth, she is forced to rest to catch her breath. But it's important to keep struggling. Frantically, she calls for help. Her voice breaks and becomes hoarse. She is about to give up when she suddenly happens to place her hand on something hard and cold on the wall. She quickly realizes it's a ladder. The entry must be above her, not to the side as she first believed. She has to get there at any price, even if it's the last thing she does.

Being in as good of shape as she is, she thinks it should be possible to climb up even with an injury. But persistence and a positive attitude aren't always enough. She can't even make it to the next step before one of her legs prevents her from going farther. In certain positions, the pain is so sharp she loses her breath. Can Hugo really have thrown her down into this hole to let her die?

Josefin tells herself to focus and not give up. To stop feeling. She is going to get out—that's just how it is.

A strength that she hadn't felt before makes her haul herself upward, step by step, all the way until she bumps her head on the ceiling. She gropes with her free hand and feels an opening. It must be bolted from the outside, because it won't budge. Suddenly, she loses her hold and falls down from the ladder. Her wrist cracks when it strikes the ground.

Josefin's whole body is shaking from the exertion and the intensely pounding pain. She cries desperately.

Now all she can do is try to hold on and pray fervently that someone will find her.

97.

As soon as Emma sees her distraught parents, she becomes like a child again. She wants to get down on the floor and scream. Instead, she throws herself into her mother's arms and sobs uncontrollably. Lets everything come out, not caring what they think. As if anyone would judge her for that. They seem to be as shaken as she is. After a while, she feels a hand on her shoulder.

"We've called up all resources," her father says, nodding at Andreas. "The police should be here any minute."

Emma hardly recognizes her dad. She can't remember ever seeing him look so hopeless.

"We have to go out and search ourselves," Emma says, putting on her shoes in the hall. "I refuse to stay here and just wait."

Andreas nods. "Same here."

"I'm afraid you have to stay, Andreas," Emma's father says. "You're the only one who can give the police all the information about Josefin and where she usually goes in the area. That's the best way for you to help out."

Andreas's shoulders collapse, but he nods. "You're right."

"I'll take care of the kids, so you don't need to think about that," Emma's mother says, hugging Julia, who is now initiated into what's going on. Strangely enough, she seems calmer than Emma, but perhaps she is paralyzed with fear.

"Thanks, Marianne." Andreas takes a deep breath and nods toward the couch where Anton is sleeping. "Don't say anything about Josefin to him."

"Don't you think he's going to suspect something anyway when he sees the police?" Emma asks.

They are interrupted by a newly wakened Sofia coming down the stairs. "Hi, Grandma and Grandpa! What are you doing here?"

The comment speaks for itself, and the mood becomes heavier. Obviously, they don't come to visit that often. Sofia's shy hug reinforces the impression that they're not particularly involved with their grandchildren, and Emma feels even sadder. That's not the way she wants it for her child.

"Do you have a bicycle?" she asks Andreas, who nods. "I'd like to borrow it to go out and search."

He points to a bunch of bicycle keys on the wall. "The one farthest to the left is for the black racer in the driveway."

"Where does she usually run?"

"When I'm along, we either take the road along the water to Alvik, or the forest loop past the sledding hill.

Although usually she runs on Alviksvägen, turns at Park Bakery, and continues on Västerled all the way to the pizzeria at the crossing with Djupdalsvägen, and then down to Alviksvägen again."

It's hard for Emma to follow what he's saying, because she isn't completely familiar with the area. "Anything else?"

"Sometimes she also does the stretch through Abrahamsberg and runs home through the Stora Mossen allotment gardens."

Where Kristoffer's burned-down house is presumably smoldering.

"Okay, I have my phone if anything comes up."

Emma rides to Alviksvägen and continues down toward the water. Of the options given, she would choose to run on the path toward Alvik. For one thing, the surface is gentle; for another you avoid the traffic for most of the stretch, and it's beautiful, besides. She pedals as fast as she can but quickly runs into obstacles. In some places she has to jump off and guide the bike past stones and tree roots, but she figures she'll see more if she moves slowly. A thought occurs to her: if Josefin fell and hurt herself near the trail, someone ought to have discovered her. That means she probably isn't here and that Emma's search isn't going to lead anywhere. She should go into the forest. Or to the sledding hill. If Josefin injured herself up there, maybe she couldn't make it down to the road. Emma doesn't know how often anyone walks on the hill during the month of April, so it's worth a try. She rides back, turns onto the loop, and approaches the hill. Then she sets the bike down on the ground, walks toward the top, and calls Josefin's name. She listens intently, but the only thing she hears is her echo and an owl. Then it is silent.

When she reaches the highest point, drenched in sweat, she looks out over the area.

Not a person as far as the eye can see.

98.

A sound from above brings Josefin to life. She opens her eyes and struggles to stay awake. Perhaps she will have only a single chance, and it's now. Of course, it's possible she dreamed she heard someone coming. It sounded like voices, but maybe they were only in her head. Perhaps she is dead; she no longer knows. Suddenly, the sound is gone, and she strains to listen for more signs of life.

After a while, the voices return, and she decides to call for help, to go at it for all she's worth. She screams at a volume she has never produced before. It doesn't sound like her at all. But the last of her energy is unexpectedly strong, and combined with fear her voice turns shrill and desperate. She doesn't intend to stop until her lungs fail. She doesn't know how long she screams, but it feels like an eternity before she hears a faint rustling above her head and someone talking. It sounds like Kristoffer, but she doesn't dare believe it's true.

"Here," she croaks, and it's not long before the light strikes her. Her eyes shut automatically when she is blinded, and she blinks impatiently to be able to see.

"Who's there?" he asks, and then she can tell that it really is Kristoffer.

"Josefin," she sobs in response. "It's me." She wants to cry from relief, but no tears will come.

Now she glimpses his head up there. "Josefin? What happened?"

"I'm cold, and I'm in pain."

"Call an ambulance," Kristoffer shouts to someone. "Say it's urgent."

She hears a man answer him.

"I'm coming down to you, Josefin," Kristoffer says then, putting his foot on the ladder. "The ambulance is on its way, and everything's going to be all right."

The pain is so intense Josefin has a hard time keeping her eyes open. She is constantly on the verge of passing out, and she has to force herself not to lose consciousness. When she feels Kristoffer's warm hand on her forehead, she understands how cold she must be. She hears him calling to the man above ground that he should try to find blankets somewhere.

"We'll get you out of here soon," he says.

"Thanks." She wants to ask for water, but she is too tired.

"My cottage burned down yesterday, so I came here with a man from the garden association to see what's left. Otherwise, I never would have found you. How did you end up here?"

"I—" Josefin can't get anything else out.

"Josefin? Are you okay?"

The last of her energy ebbs out, but it doesn't matter. Everything is going to work out. She is being rescued from the hellhole.

99.

The call from Kristoffer comes when Emma is pedaling at full speed. She slows down and answers, but at first she doesn't hear what he's saying, because he is talking so fast. Then she makes out his words.

"I've found her. Josefin is here."

"What? Where?" she says instead of rejoicing. She can't believe it's true. How the heck can Josefin be with Kristoffer?

"At the allotment garden. I heard her cry for help when I came here to see how extensive the damage was."

The tension releases, but Emma still doesn't understand a thing. "What do you mean? Where did Josefin call from? The house burned down, didn't it?"

She turns around and starts walking with the bike toward Stora Mossen, while Kristoffer explains.

"She was down in the root cellar."

Emma pictures a small red hatch she had never seen

open during her visits to the cottage. She had no idea there was room for a person down there. The sound of sirens is heard in the distance, getting closer and closer, and Emma guesses that the ambulance must be on its way to Josefin.

"How's she doing?" Emma asks.

"She definitely injured, but it's hard for me to say how seriously. The ambulance is coming now. Are you far from here?"

"No, I'm on my way. Should be there within five minutes."

"Good," Kristoffer says, hanging up.

Emma calls Andreas immediately. "She's been found, alive, in the allotment gardens. I'm almost there."

"Thank God." She can hear how relieved he is. "I'll be there as soon as I can."

No questions about the circumstances, or who found her and why. It's just as well, because Emma can't really explain. She rides along Västerled and turns off at the roundabout. Blue lights are rotating in the distance, and Emma sees that the ambulance has squeezed into the narrow lane outside the burned-down cottage. She gets off the bike and hurries onto the lot. It smells of smoke, and only charred remnants remain. You can't even tell that it used to be red and white.

Kristoffer meets her with open arms. He has dark streaks of soot and dirt on his face. The dark-red spots on his hands must be blood, probably from Josefin. Emma feels pressure in her chest and wants to hug her sister as soon as possible. Behind Kristoffer, she catches a glimpse of the EMTs and an empty stretcher.

"They're having problems getting her up," he explains. "But everything's going to be fine."

"I have to go help them," she says, trying to free herself.

But Kristoffer stops her. "It's too cramped. I already had to step aside so I wouldn't be in the way. You can't do anything other than wait."

Emma kicks the gravel and tries to convince herself that she can trust the ambulance personnel to know their job. Before long, she sees them come up carrying a bloody, dirty woman—in workout clothes. They lay her carefully on the stretcher and secure her neck. Emma tells them she's Josefin's sister. Gently, she places her hand on Josefin's cheek.

"Can you hear me?" she asks, and the clump in her stomach grows when she sees how pale Josefin is.

When she gets no answer, she turns to the EMTs.

"We have to leave right away," one of them says, nodding to his associate to lift the stretcher.

"I'll go with her," Emma replies.

From the ambulance, she texts Andreas, telling him to go straight to Karolinska University Hospital.

100.

The next time Josefin wakes up, she is lying in a carefully made bed, with clean sheets and a yellow blanket. It's like coming to heaven compared with the hole under the ground. Her vision is blurry, and it takes a while before she notices that Emma is sitting beside her. Farther off in the room stand Mom and Dad, talking in lowered voices. The only ones missing are Andreas and the children.

"Are you awake?" Emma says with red-rimmed eyes. She doesn't appear to have slept for several days.

"What happened?" asks Josefin.

"Darling," their mother exclaims when she realizes Josefin has woken up. "How you frightened us."

Their father maintains a certain distance and observes her from afar. He's certainly relieved, but it's hard to decipher his controlled expression.

"Where are Andreas and the children?" she asks.

"They went to get something to eat a while ago, but

they'll be back soon," Emma says. "Or do you want me to go and get them?"

Even though Josefin is dying to see her children, she shakes her head. Mostly she wants to properly wake up before she sees Andreas together with all the others in the room.

"The police are standing outside the room. They want to talk with you, but we'll take one thing at a time," says their dad.

Josefin understands from all the tense looks that they are waiting for her to say something more. She does her best to collect herself, although she feels unusually slow on the uptake. They don't seem to have skimped on pain relievers, because her body is completely numb.

"If Kristoffer hadn't found me . . ."

Emma wipes a tear from her cheek. "But he did, thank goodness."

"Otherwise, I wouldn't have made it."

"I just don't understand how you ended up in the root cellar on his garden lot," Emma says. "Can you tell us?"

"Was that where I was? I only remember being in his cottage."

"It burned down yesterday," Emma says.

"That explains why I smelled smoke."

"Who did this, Josefin?" their father says.

"Dad," Emma says. "Let her talk at her own pace. The main thing is, Josefin is safe and sound."

Josefin looks at them, one at a time, then answers without hesitating.

"Hugo."

101.

At the mere sound of Hugo's name, Emma falls back on the chair. Feelings of guilt invade from all directions. It's impossible to deny that she was the one who brought him into their lives. *Ugh.*

It's hard to look at Josefin lying there in a white hospital gown, surrounded by hoses and bandages. Her head is barely visible, both legs are in casts, her arm is bandaged, and she has an intravenous drip. She was covered with dirt upon arrival, and the nursing staff have done their best to clean her up. But there are still traces from the hours spent below ground, dirt under her nails and soil highlighting the faint wrinkles on her face.

"It was Hugo who threw me down into the root cellar," Josefin says.

"Why?" their mother asks. "I don't understand."

"Because I found him in the cottage."

The atmosphere in the room is tense, and Emma struggles

with conflicting emotions. She texts Hugo to report that they've found Josefin. Perhaps he'll have such a guilty conscience that he'll admit what he's done. If not, the police will deal with him once they've talked with Josefin; the main thing is that she's been rescued. She looks weak and probably needs to rest. But there are far too many questions to sort out first.

"What exactly happened?" Emma asks. "Can you take it from the beginning?"

Josefin nods. Then she tells about her run, which wasn't along the forest loop at all, but instead toward Abrahamsberg.

"So I was frightened by the deer that suddenly jumped out. Then when I was about to leave, I happened to see him inside the house."

"Hugo? What was he doing there?" Emma asks, glancing at her phone. No answer yet.

Josefin grimaces. "It's itchy under the cast."

"Should I get someone?" their mother asks.

"It's okay. I can just press the button if I need help," Josefin says, meeting Emma's gaze. "Hugo was drunk, and babbling something about Kristoffer. He was in the cottage to burn it down. There was paint thinner all over the place. I lost my temper and yelled at him. Said that you thought he was pathetic. Tragic. It was stupid to say that, but I was really upset that he was going to ruin things for Kristoffer."

Emma shudders. She doesn't know if she wants to hear more. Hugo must have been beside himself with rage after he found out about the pregnancy. He was also drunk—a recipe for disaster.

Josefin reaches for a glass of water on the bedside table, but their mother is quickly there and gives it to her. It takes time for her to drink, and everyone waits for the rest of the story.

"It was when I was just about to leave that things got out of control. I don't know if he meant to, but he knocked me over, and because I was completely unprepared, I fell and hit my head. I don't remember much after that."

But somehow Josefin ended up in the root cellar, buried alive, and then Hugo set fire to the place. Emma thinks it sounds crazy, but nothing with Hugo nowadays is the way it used to be. He has to be reined in.

Josefin clears her throat. "Did I mention he had a lighter in his hand?"

Emma shakes her head, but the course of events is starting to become clear to her.

"Then I woke up down there, underground. I lost consciousness a few times, and when I finally came to I tried to get out. It was pitch-black, and I was hurting everywhere, so I thought it was the end."

"Frightful. It's not possible to imagine," their mother says, squeezing her husband's hand hard.

"I couldn't bear the thought that I wouldn't get to see my children grow up. And their children," Josefin says. "Well, I'm sure you understand how anxious I was."

Just then, Andreas and the children barrel into the room. Anton clambers up into the bed and looks big-eyed at Josefin, feeling carefully with his hand as if to check that it really is his mom. The girls stroke her cheek while Andreas waits his turn.

"Thank God you're okay," he says, hugging her tenderly.

Their parents exchange tearful glances with each other. And Emma tries to restrain the loathing she feels for Hugo.

102.

Ever since Josefin woke up, there has been nonstop commotion at the hospital. If it's not doctors, police officers, or nurses in the room, relatives or friends come and go as if it were an open house. Just now, Cornelia and Astrid show up.

Josefin just wants to ask all of them to leave. She doesn't have the energy to tell the story over and over. Especially when she hasn't managed to process it herself. But when there is a knock at the door for the umpteenth time and she sees Kristoffer with a bouquet of flowers, she can't refuse to let him in. After all, he's the one she has to thank that she's lying here and not six feet under, in a cellar meant for storing potatoes.

Kristoffer looks worn-out, standing by the door with the flowers in his hand. He probably expects an explanation for what she was doing at his allotment garden.

"Come in," she says, and he comes up to the bed.

"I didn't bring a vase with me," he says apologetically, and Josefin smiles at the spring bouquet.

"How nice," she answers, bracing herself. "You must be wondering what I was doing at your cottage."

"We can discuss that later. The most important thing is that you're okay."

But Josefin wants to explain. "I ran past and thought I saw someone there. So I just wanted to go over to assure myself that it wasn't a break-in."

"And it turned out to be even worse," Kristoffer says, shaking his head. "You don't need to explain now. Rest. I just wanted to see how you were doing."

Josefin looks at the others and knows they're all wondering.

"Hugo got in through a window," she says. "He intended to set fire to the place. I'm really sorry."

"Me too, but mostly for your sake," says Kristoffer. "Even if it was my grandmother's to start with, it was just a small cottage. It must have been awful to be down in that hole so long."

Josefin nods, and there is silence for a while as Kristoffer sets the flowers on the table, which is already full of newspapers and boxes of chocolate.

"I don't understand what the point was to burning down the cottage," Kristoffer says, seeking eye contact with Emma.

"He was extremely drunk when I found him," says Josefin.

Kristoffer looks confused. "But how did you end up in the root cellar?"

"I don't know. He shoved me, then I lost consciousness. I guess he must have dragged me there."

"So you don't remember."

Josefin shakes her head and looks at Kristoffer. "Thanks for finding me and for bringing flowers. You didn't have to do that."

"No problem," he says, tilting his head and smiling.

Then the door to the room opens, and suddenly Hugo is standing there. Everyone freezes, and Josefin is speechless.

She holds her breath, waiting for someone else to take the initiative and say something. It is Emma who breaks the silence.

"You have some nerve to come here!"

Josefin is convinced that her sister is only seconds away from slapping him.

"I'm happy to see that you're okay, Josefin," Hugo says in a trembling voice.

At first glance, you might think he had been thrown down into a root cellar too. Hugo's skin is grayish, he is unshaven, and his clothes have dark stains. As if that weren't enough, he is missing a tooth and has a swollen lip.

"You're totally nuts to show up here," Emma says, her eyes narrowing. "But it's good that the police standing right outside can take you straight to the station."

Hugo looks desperate. "It's not the way you think."

103.

Why am I subjecting myself to this? The kid stares at me coolly, inspecting me from head to toe. She refuses to take her eyes off me. Maybe she recognizes me, even if that's far-fetched. Her bedroom was dark, and I was standing in the doorway when she opened her eyes. She can't very well connect me with the man who was in her house that night, can she? She was so cute and irresistible I couldn't keep from grazing her cheek. But now she's making me nervous, with her hollow gaze and her awful haircut.

I try to make eye contact with her, but I don't get the slightest response. Instead, she pulls closer to her mother and hides between her legs. But so far, no one seems to have listened to the girl, so why should they now? I can probably be calm, with 99.9 percent certainty she isn't a threat.

And then he's standing there too, that bastard. I have to get out of here before I'm suffocated by his mere presence.

Being in the same room as him is asking too much. It's bad enough with Cornelia, Emma, Josefin, and Astrid, not to mention Emma's parents—people who in some way have suffered because of me. Who are involved simply because I was forced to kill Hans and Benjamin.

I never intended to injure Helena, but because she was with Benjamin all the time, there was no choice other than to kill her too.

Fate, I think.

Then I notice that Cornelia doesn't look at all distressed standing there beside the bed next to Josefin. And it's becoming clear to me that I've done her a favor. Every cloud has a silver lining; this time too. Hans was a terrible character with no empathy. Someone who thought only about himself. Because of him, a small child was killed. For that, he deserved to meet the same fate.

104.

When the police lead Hugo away, Emma feels more despondent than relieved. Sure, he deserves to be punished; Josefin could have been disabled for life, or even died. Presumably, he had no idea what he was doing and what the consequences would be. His account is pretty illogical. Why would he run away and then go back to help her? The police are hardly going to buy his story that Josefin wasn't there when he returned. And Emma still doesn't understand what Hugo intended to accomplish. This kind of action only proves he's lost his judgment. Kristoffer hasn't done Hugo any harm, other than replace him in her life.

Emma flushes the toilet in the restroom and washes her hands while Kristoffer waits in the corridor outside. Hand in hand, they walk out toward the parking lot and get in the car in silence. Both are wiped out by the day's events, and Emma feels so tired she doesn't know if she'll be able to keep her eyes open until they're home.

"Thanks for coming," she says. "With flowers and everything."

Kristoffer snorts and puts the car in reverse. "That was a no-brainer."

"What are you thinking about?" Emma asks when she notices his worried expression.

"That it was lucky the cottage burned down, however awful that is. Otherwise, I never would have gone there and found Josefin."

There are goose bumps on her arms when she thinks about it. "I know. Ugh."

"Listen, I'm sorry it's been so awkward between us lately. I understand that you were disappointed about that apartment."

"Apology accepted," she says, making sure the seat belt is buckled.

"But I've found another apartment that I think we should look at."

"Really? I didn't think you took me seriously when I said I wanted us to move in together." Emma is sincerely surprised.

Kristoffer meets her eyes. "I want us to live together too—don't you understand that? There's just been so much going on at work lately. It's been really stressful, to be honest. But I'm not going to take on any new properties before Easter. That means that I'll have some free time soon."

"Me too," Emma says. "It's been so crazy that I haven't had a chance to tell you I'm going on leave from my job for a while." She gets an idea. "Can't we go somewhere?

It's been a long time since I was out of the country. Imagine being able to go away awhile, just the two of us. That would be nice."

"Why not?" Kristoffer says happily. "Shall we aim for Easter week?"

"Let's do it."

A feeling of warmth spreads inside her. She imagines them sitting on a beach together, enjoying the sunset. It will be warm, beautiful, and worry-free. Far from homicides, disappearances, and crazy exes. A welcome departure from the everyday, with no cell phones. Just the two of them. It strikes her that they've never been on vacation together before.

"I can spend all day tomorrow searching for trips," she says. "Because I'm sure you have a reshowing to take care of?"

"You're right about that, of course," Kristoffer says with a sigh. "It's Monday, after all. But it will be over by seven o'clock if no one insists on staying a long time, and then I think we should go out and have dinner. If you think you can manage."

"That sounds like an excellent idea."

Feeling satisfied, Emma closes her eyes. A new sort of calm settles in. She continues to fantasize about Kristoffer walking barefoot with her along the water. The waves sweep in over their feet, which sink deeper down in the sand and leave clear tracks behind. She gets sleepier and sleepier, and after a while she notices that it's no longer possible to keep herself awake. Now that everything has been resolved with the open-house murders and with Josefin, she can finally relax completely.

105.

Hans and Benjamin have only themselves to blame. If they had just listened from the beginning and let the house in Beckomberga stay standing, not had such one-track minds. So insensitive. But they wanted to remove it immediately from their land in order to develop a whole new residential area in a uniform style. They blamed it on the idea that the house was run-down; they called it a "shack," saying it was a hazard to live in, when in reality it was all about money. During my entire career, I've done my utmost to avoid having to deal with swine, but at last I couldn't escape.

Hillevi did everything to try to keep the house, but they had already decided. When she got too troublesome, they threatened her. I tried in vain to help mediate, but I knew what ruthless characters they were. It was hardly the first time they used dirty tricks for their own benefit. Hans and Benjamin didn't care at all about breaking a person's heart.

Until the end, Hillevi refused to leave the house, which had been in her family for generations. But when the demolition started, the unthinkable happened.

She had gone there to beg and plead with them to let the house be, and during a few seconds of confusion she lost sight of her little daughter. That was long enough for the accident to happen.

I still remember the phone call today.

Hillevi screamed and cried by turns. When I figured out she was at the emergency room, I went to her. But not until I got there did I find out that Felicia had ended up under the excavator and that it was impossible to save her life. Even though she wasn't my own child, I grieved her like a real father would have.

It took several weeks before I saw how seriously ill Hillevi was. That she didn't want to acknowledge that Felicia was dead. And it never stopped. Soon enough it sank in that it wasn't just Felicia that I'd lost. My whole life collapsed— Benjamin and Hans drove me to ruin.

Instead of expressing sympathy, they made it clear that I would regret it if I ever let it be known that they were behind the tragedy. They had destroyed our lives, and I was supposed to keep quiet about it? When they sent a veiled threat to Hillevi at the hospital, it was the last straw. That was when I realized that there was no choice other than to put an end to this.

Now at least I can console myself that they have received their punishment.

It's too bad Josefin had to be involved, but it was necessary to hide her in the root cellar to put Hugo in prison. I was just so tired of his idiotic pranks.

When a board member from the garden association called me and said that he'd heard screams from my cottage, I was already nearby and went straight there. I saw Hugo running from the area, and right afterward I found Josefin on the floor. I just had time to close the hatch to the root cellar when Hugo suddenly came back. Alone, thank God, and after a while he disappeared again.

Because he had drenched the place with paint thinner, I understood what his plan had been before Josefin put a stop to it. And he would get what he wanted. Even if it pained me to see my grandmother's charming cottage go up in smoke, it was necessary to get Hugo behind bars.

Then I got to play the hero by finding Josefin.

I cast a glance to the side. It doesn't look comfortable where my new love is sitting in the passenger seat, sleeping with her mouth open. With delight mixed with terror, I glance furtively at her stomach. It looks a little swollen, but there is otherwise nothing that reveals her blessed condition.

That a police detective turned to me when she was selling her condo must have been fate. Without her, it would have been much harder to plan how to get rid of Hans and Benjamin without going to prison. I've gotten valuable information about police work, and could avoid the most common traps.

So I have a lot to thank Emma for. I had no intention of falling in love. Much less becoming a dad.

Like a miracle, I get back what I once lost, although in a new form. A little better, even, because this time the child is mine. Now I just hope that Hillevi's recovery doesn't create problems.

Right outside is a parking space, and I squeeze the car in.

"Darling, we're here now."

ACKNOWLEDGMENTS

I t all started when we were going to buy a house and I went to an open house in Bromma. As soon as I entered, I had a sense that something wasn't right. There were dents on doors and walls, and I could smell alcohol in the study. There were also fewer prospective buyers than normal for such a popular neighborhood. The real estate agent wasn't around when I left, so I never said good-bye. An absurd thought struck me: How would she know if everyone had really left? Anyone at all could slip in through the basement door and hide until the open house was over and the family came home. After that, I couldn't let go of the idea of what an exciting mystery plot that might make.

For their help on *Killer Deal*, I want to thank . . .

. . . first and foremost, my husband, Tommy Sarenbrant, and our wonderful children, Kharma and Kenza. Without your support, there would be no books.

. . . Detective Inspector Lars Bröms at the violent crimes section of the Stockholm County Detective Unit, for invaluable help with questions about police work and for subsequent fact-checking.

. . . real estate agent Cecilia Prööm Andersson, who agreed to be interviewed and read through the manuscript.

. . . everyone at my publisher who is involved with my books in one way or another, especially my editor, Erika Söderström.

. . . graphic designer Maria Sundberg, for the third attractive cover in the series.

. . . Philip Sane at the Lennart Sane Agency, who makes it possible for Emma Sköld to travel outside the boundaries of Sweden.

. . . all my writer colleagues and friends, who inspire and support me.

. . . my parents, Ann and Svante Sjöstedt, and my siblings and their partners: Tom Sjöstedt and Maria Lindqvist, Linn Sjöstedt Dahl and Patrik Dahl, and Tyra Sjöstedt.

Last but not least, I want to thank my marvelous readers in Sweden and abroad, just for being there! Without you, it would be hard to stay motivated to sit in front of a blank Word document to be filled with a hundred thousand words. I'm so happy and grateful for all of the positive feedback you send me via social media.

Sofie Sarenbrant
Bromma, October 2015